BROKEN MADONNA

Anna Lucia

Warm wishes, .

Anna Lucia

A CIP catalogue record for this book is available from the British Library.

ISBN (PB) 978-1-0687470-0-7

ISBN (E) 978-1-0687470-1-4

Cover design: Patrick Knowles

Typesetting: Coinlea Services

Printed and bound by CPI Group (UK) Ltd, Croydon, CR0 4YY

fluency publishing

Published by Fluency Publishing

www.fluencypublishing.com

For Nina & Cara

Dreams can come true

Broken Madonna

Anna Lucia

Prologue

22 June 1938

River Mollarino, Apennine Mountains, Italy

Forgive me, piccina mia, little one.

Icy water rises up and grabs at the woman's stretched, empty belly. In the makeshift sling her newborn baby wails, strong fists and feet against her mother's swollen breasts. The baby opens her pale blue eyes, eyes that belong to a much older soul, and looks up.

The woman presses her pockets, feeling the weight of the pebbles, and she lifts her hand towards her child's face. Her fingertips hesitate on the baby's soft skin, the dimple on her right cheek.

She can't do it.

Her hands plunge back into the water, and she tears at her pockets. The stones are too heavy.

The river pounds downstream, glistening in the moonlight, and swallows the wretched cries from the baby's tiny body.

As the woman tries to edge backwards, her feet struggle on the slippery riverbed.

'Almost safe, tesoro,' she lies, as the baby lets out a terrified cry.

A wave hits the woman's side.

All at once, they're sucked down, deep into the water.

No, no, per l'amore di Dio, no.

The sling is unravelling.

The woman kicks with all her strength, but the water pulls her this way and that. Her back strikes a boulder, hard. Suddenly her head breaks the surface of the water. She's gasping for breath, the sling clutched tight in her hand, but there is no weight to it.

'Elisabetta!'

Her scream echoes across the valley. The water is dragging her back into its cold embrace as she hears a voice.

A young man, crying out, thrashing in the water nearby.

Just before she disappears, she sees her child in his arms.

Part 1

1949

1

Atina, Apennine Mountains, Italy
Orfanotrofio Santa Scolastica

Adelina

I bit down on my chewed thumbnail and stared at a pockmark of crumbling plaster in our orphanage basement. The walls were bare, except for the wooden crucifix above Elisabetta's bed.

Hurry up, Elisabetta.

Her tired hairbrush lay waiting on the blanket. I ran a strand of her silky, chestnut hair between thumb and forefinger, all the way down its length. Surely, she would be back soon for our bedtime routine. Watching in the mirror, still and quiet, while I brushed her hair one hundred times, *come una principessa.*

If she didn't come back soon, I'd have to make up a story for the nun at bedtime inspection. I didn't want to be in trouble with Sister Beatrice again.

Outside the last birds had fallen silent. With my back to the mirror, I pulled my worn nightdress over my head while wriggling out of my smock and underwear beneath. Almost transparent in places, the thin white cotton now stopped well above my knees. It clung to the breasts I hated and skimmed the dark hair down below. As I fumbled with the chipped buttons, the tight seam ripped at the armpit.

My face hot with shame, I climbed into bed and covered myself quickly with the blanket. Nobody would know that I hadn't said my prayers. Santa Scolastica and the rest of the angels and saints could wait until tomorrow. Elisabetta would disapprove, but she didn't need to know.

My eyes struggled to stay open while I strained to listen out for her on the stone steps. Feeding and cleaning the new babies in the nursery was hard work. But when no-one was watching, I'd get to play peek-a-boo with them. I liked how they gurgled and smiled at me.

~

When the door of our room did creak open, it made me jump.

Elisabetta slipped in, silently pulling the door closed behind her.

'Where have you been?' I rubbed my eyes, reaching for the light, annoyed at her for disturbing my sleep.

She touched the cracked red cover of the book she was clutching. Slight in her bright white nightdress which flowed down to her bare feet, her hair hung loose in long dark waves across her back. A mischievous grin lit up her face.

'What have you done?' My eyes flicked from the book back towards the door. 'What if Sister Beatrice finds out?'

'*Così bambina!* Why are you always so scared?'

She traced the gold letters on the spine of the book with a careful fingertip, her pale blue eyes flashing. 'I'll have it back on her shelf before she's even noticed it's missing.'

'Really? Are you sure Sister Beatrice won't—'

'Don't worry.'

The iron bed sighed and she patted the space beside her. 'Come here. There's a picture I want to show you.' Elisabetta reached out her hand.

Her fingers curled round mine as I perched next to her, one eye still on the door. If Sister Beatrice discovered her most prized possession, *Il Grande Libro dei Santi*, gone under the cover of darkness, there would be no escaping her stick. She'd never believe that little Elisabetta could take her precious book about the saints. Any punishment would be mine.

Elisabetta opened the book with great solemnity, raised her hands heavenwards, and took a deep, slow breath in. She turned and scowled at me.

We couldn't hold in the giggles for long. Mimicking Padre Bosco was one of her many talents. Neither of us cared for the old priest with his stale garlic breath who made it clear that we disgraced children of the orphanage were not worthy of his attention.

As Elisabetta flicked through the pages of the book, my eyes skimmed over the words. They were a complicated puzzle I had no way of solving, so I took in the pictures. There were stern old men with pointy noses and shifty eyes.

'Look at this one.' I laughed, careful not to touch the yellowing paper with my finger.

A straggly beard fell on the saint's chest, giving him the air of a beggar rather than a holy man.

Elisabetta laughed too but moved quickly through the pages. I glanced up at the door, trying to ignore the nerves in my stomach and what Sister Beatrice might do if she found us huddled together with her book.

'Here she is,' announced Elisabetta with a flourish, pushing the book towards me.

A blurred photo of a young woman wearing a nun's habit lay in front of me. She was holding a wet piece of clothing and a flat wooden paddle.

'She's washing clothes with the other sisters,' said Elisabetta, her finger resting on the text beneath the picture. 'Communal laundry, 1895.'

I already knew who she was. Santa Teresa di Lisieux had always been Elisabetta's favourite. The young girl who wanted to become a saint. I remembered Sister Beatrice's stories about Santa Teresa, even though I had little interest in the teaching of the church.

'Look at her, Lina! That's why I took the book. I wanted you to feel the power of Santa Teresa and her smile.'

I examined the photo, not wanting to disappoint her. Santa Teresa had a pleasant smile, but it looked painted on, like a fancy lipstick. Her sad eyes drew me, not her smile. It was a look I recognised. The ability to appear happy, only for the eyes to tell another story. It was the same expression I'd seen in Elisabetta in the six years since she'd arrived at the orphanage, when she was five and I was nine, the tired old building already my home for a couple of years. We'd been together ever since.

'I hope Santa Teresa brings you some comfort,' said Elisabetta, squeezing my hand. 'I know how upset your Mamma's birthday makes you feel.'

We reached for one another, her thin little body against mine. Tears pricked my eyes. She held me tight, as I had her held so many times, especially when she woke from her nightmares, the sheets wet.

'Sometimes I can't remember her face,' I sniffed. 'I'm scared I'm forgetting her.'

Mamma had died from a fever, a couple of years after Papà had left for the war. I'd clutched at Mamma's legs as we watched the army trucks leave the piazza, the cries of the women, handkerchiefs being waved. After the telegram arrived, she wasn't the same again.

Papà's relatives had come from the north, an elderly silent woman, and her stooped husband. But they didn't take to me, looking down their noses when they stayed at our home, complaining that I cried continually for my mother. They left me in the orphanage, signing in a book for Sister Beatrice, looking away as they did so. I was seven years old.

Santa Teresa's eyes stared up at me. Elisabetta shushed me as if she were the older of the two of us, not the other way round. The way she acted and talked, she was always wise beyond her years, and it was easy to forget she was only eleven years old.

'I'll ask Sister Beatrice if we can light a candle to remember your Mamma at San Donato,' Elisabetta said in her soothing voice.

'You think she'll allow us to go?' I replied, brushing away a tear.

'If *I* ask her,' she pronounced.

I snuggled up to Elisabetta and put my head in her lap. Mamma used to stroke my hair or sing me a lullaby when I did that, and Elisabetta knew what to do.

~

'What's going on? Who said you could take my book?'

Sister Beatrice's shrill voice pierced my sleep, and I leapt up, my back pressed against the cold bars at the head of the bed.

Red with anger, Sister Beatrice's face fixed on me. She snatched at my hand to drag me from Elisabetta, whose body was curled into a ball beside me. Why was she pretending to still be asleep?

Sister Beatrice lashed out towards the book lying between us. The hard edge of her bony palm caught my face and I recoiled against the hard bars, my hand testing my stinging cheek. She leant forward to take the book, but it was wedged beneath Elisabetta's body. The battered cover came away with a few torn pages in her hand.

'I can explain.' Elisabetta raised herself to her knees, clutching the remaining body of the naked book. 'It was my fault—'

Sister Beatrice cut her short and turned back towards me. Her tight headdress was rising with her temper.

I gripped the metal bars of the bed, my eyes scrunched shut, ready for the next blow.

It never came.

Elisabetta fell backwards towards me, and I caught her limp body in my arms.

All at once, Elisabetta turned rigid. She shook and jerked. I'd never seen her like this before and I gripped her as firmly as I could. She was flailing, and it took all my strength to keep hold of her, struggling to stop her body hitting against the wall or the bars of the bed.

Sister Beatrice remained rooted to the spot, open-mouthed, the colour draining from her face.

Without thinking, I snatched the cover of the book of saints from Sister Beatrice and pushed it between Elisabetta's teeth so that she couldn't bite her tongue.

Her eyes rolled in their sockets and foam drooled from the side of her mouth.

'I'm here,' I repeated over and over again, shushing her, wiping her mouth with the corner of the bedsheet. My insides were churning but when I was little, I'd had a cousin who suffered from fits, and I'd

15

seen how Mamma had helped him.

Elisabetta gradually stilled. As she did, my heart started to slow but my hand in hers was still shaking.

On her knees beside the bed, Sister Beatrice watched in silence. Her knuckles were clasped so tight they had turned white.

When Elisabetta seemed to be finally sleeping, I loosened the cover of the book from her mouth. It was wet from her spit, with a clear semi-circle of teeth marks in the leather. I tried to wipe the cover clean, but the scratchy blanket only spread her saliva further.

Hesitating, I offered it up to Sister Beatrice. She accepted it, slipping the body of the book back between its covers.

'It can be mended.' She set it down on the chair and took Elisabetta's hand.

'Forgive me,' she whispered. 'I shouldn't have shouted like that.'

Elisabetta sighed, seeming to drift deeper into sleep.

Sister Beatrice must've seen my expression, that I was shocked that she was so tender towards Elisabetta. But she had started to recite a prayer.

I'd always known Elisabetta was her favourite child in the orphanage, singled out for special lessons in her study because she was bright and interested in her endless stories about the female saints. Normally she was strict, and she certainly never showed any affection towards the children.

When Elisabetta's breathing was calm and even, she stood up and turned to me.

'You did well, Adelina.'

Proud, I sat up straighter on the bed and smoothed Elisabetta's hair away from her face. It was the first time Sister Beatrice called me by my name or said anything nice to me.

'Look after her. If need be, I'll fetch for Dottor Visconti.'

'I'll take good care of her,' I replied, eager to please Sister Beatrice.

She nodded, allowing her eyes to rest on Elisabetta's fragile sleeping body before closing the door quietly behind her.

~

During the night, Elisabetta didn't stir. Eager to obey Sister Beatrice's instructions, I watched over her like a cat waiting on a bird. Her breathing was deep and even. There were none of her usual night-time terrors and the sheets remained dry. It was the reason we had our own room near the steaming cauldrons of the basement laundry. Upstairs the scrapping children were stacked twelve to a dorm.

Outside, the birds were singing, welcoming the day. The nuns' footsteps echoed on the stone steps as they brought clothes down to the laundry and then returned upstairs. Bright shafts of sunlight broke through the splintered shutters, warming the room, catching my cheek where I sat beside Elisabetta. With her chestnut hair falling onto the pillow and her pale complexion, she looked like a *bambola*, a beautiful doll. Like a big sister, I was relieved to be looking after her, keeping her safe.

When the chimes for seven o'clock rang out across the small town of Atina from the Church of San Donato, I startled awake. I must have fallen asleep briefly.

Elisabetta was sitting upright in bed, a broad smile lighting up her face.

'How are you feeling? I was so worried about you.' Yawning, I climbed onto the bed beside her. I twiddled a piece of her long hair around my index finger, something I always did after one of her nightmares.

'Something happened,' she said.

'Do you remember? Sister Beatrice… the book?'

Elisabetta shook her head. 'What are you talking about?'

'You don't remember?'

'Should I?' She shrugged and brushed an invisible fly from her face.

Elisabetta took both my hands in hers. She was excited and pulled herself onto her knees, so that we were facing each other on the bed.

'A beautiful, radiant woman came to me.'

Her voice was shaking with emotion, but her smile seemed to make her pale blue eyes shine brighter than usual.

'She was surrounded in golden light.' Elisabetta raised her arms above her head, drawing a circle with her hands.

An uncomfortable sense of dread took hold in my stomach, a bit like the feeling I got when our teacher, Signora Rossi, asked me a question. As in class, I stayed silent, too slow to make sense of what was happening.

'She was there just for me,' she said, pressing my hands.

I wasn't sure what she was saying, sleep and the heat in the room muddling my thoughts.

'I feel so special, like I am the only person who matters to her. It's like she wants me to know her.' Elisabetta rose to her feet, standing tall above me, her arms outstretched. 'She told me to come to her.'

'What?'

She continued, as if I hadn't spoken, the dimple in her right cheek widening her smile. 'I walked towards her embrace and joy entered my heart.' Elisabetta held her hands in a tight fist to her chest.

I was confused. Stupid, trying to understand, the girl who always made Signora Rossi cross when I didn't have the answer ready in lessons. Should I get up and join Elisabetta or ask her questions about what was happening?

She didn't give me the chance.

'River Mollarino is special to her. If we go there, with love in our hearts, I know she'll come back to me. She'll guide us.'

I'd never seen her like that before, so happy, so excited. What sort of friend was I if I didn't go along with what she wanted?

2

The next day, Elisabetta was insistent. 'It'll be an adventure, you'll see.'

'If Sister Beatrice finds out, she'll take it out on me, not you!'

'But she's not going to find out, is she?'

'How can you be so sure?'

'Everyone is fast asleep at that time, you know that. It'll be easy. We just slip through the window, and we'll be back before everyone is up for breakfast.'

It was true. We were often awake as the small dark hours of the night gave way to a flurry of competing bird calls, a gentle light easing away the fears that regularly awoke Elisabetta. It was always the same nightmare, that she was drowning and unable to breathe. If it was a good night and I'd calmed Elisabetta before she wet the bed, I would climb in with her and snuggle up close. We listened to the birds together, turning our favourites into one big happy family. Papà was a booming, determined bittern, whose voice I had off to a tee. Elisabetta copied the graceful Mamma. Their children squawked as they flitted from branch to branch.

'Maybe the birds will come with us!' said Elisabetta.

'How did you know I was thinking of them?'

'Because I know you better than you know yourself.'

Elisabetta went to poke me in the chest, but I pushed her away.

'Come on, don't be angry with me!' she said, turning on the whiny voice that always got her on the right side of Sister Beatrice. 'It'll be fine, *te lo prometto*.'

~

For the second night in a row, Elisabetta enjoyed the sleep of angels.

I tossed and turned, my worn sheet wrapping me in a tight straitjacket.

It must have been a dream, the beautiful woman who came to her. That's what I told myself. Something from her clever mind. One of the stories she made up, like the happy family of bitterns. Or how she exaggerated Sister Beatrice's tales about the female saints, adding in details as if she were Santa Teresa herself. Elisabetta always had such wonderful ideas, so said our teacher, Signora Rossi, who would clap at her 'brilliant imagination' and praise her 'vivid detail'.

All I could think of was what punishment Sister Beatrice would have in store for me if we got caught out. The thwack and sting of her cane on my knuckles, how she would remind me how stupid I was. I'd be the one to blame for leading Elisabetta astray.

~

Elisabetta woke a few minutes before daybreak, cheerful and excited.

'Are you ready?' she whispered, taking my reluctant hand.

She opened the window and then the wooden shutters, which creaked more loudly than I'd expected. Elisabetta put a finger to her lips. I clambered after her with some difficulty, my long legs getting in the way as I squeezed through the small gap.

We hurried into the breaking light, me close behind Elisabetta, through knee-high tufts of grass dotted with the first poppies, towards the pine woods. Above us, a pair of egrets sailed past. The booming calls of the bitterns grew louder.

'I told you they'd come!' cried Elisabetta. As she turned to me, two little bitterns landed on the ground between us.

Before I could reply, they'd taken off above Elisabetta, heading towards River Mollarino. We ran after them.

Elisabetta's plaits bounced on her back, and she laughed as she looked over her shoulder towards me. My cheeks tingled in the morning air. I ran my fingers through the feathery grass, plucking out a poppy which I tucked behind my ear. The trees were alive with birdsong, which seemed to stretch up and away into the mountains all around us. Flecks of dust danced in the rising sun as it peeked through the canopy of trees.

Elisabetta disappeared into the woods.

'Wait for me!'

I knew she wouldn't be able to hear me over the growing sound of water over pebbles and it didn't matter. The birds were singing; the sun was on my face.

When I caught up with her, Elisabetta was sitting at the river's edge, dwarfed by the tall, dark trees and the noise of the river as it rushed downstream. She was facing the wide stretch of turquoise water, her knees drawn towards her chest.

I walked slowly up to her.

Even with the crunch of my footsteps on the pebbles, Elisabetta didn't stir or turn towards me. As I sat down a few paces away from her, I realised her eyes were closed.

The air was light, tinged with the scent of damp moss. I took a deep breath in. With the flat of my palm, I smoothed my nightdress towards my knees.

She turned to me, her eyes flickering open.

'She was here. I saw her again.'

'I don't understand. What do you mean?'

Looking older than her eleven years, she addressed me in the schoolteacher manner of Signora Rossi.

'We're to come back. She wants me to know her.'

The order in Elisabetta's voice was clear. It didn't matter what I did or didn't think or understand.

~

Each daybreak for a week, we crept out of our dark basement, towards the magic of the river. In my excitement to follow Elisabetta, I barely slept.

'You look like a fish with your mouth open like that,' barked Signora Rossi, exasperated by my constant yawning in class. The other children took to following me, pretending to swim with pouting mouths. For once, their taunting didn't sting. After being called dumb for my many embarrassing mistakes, and *giraffa*, on account of my never-ending legs and long neck, *'pesce'* seemed mild.

'Ignore them,' said Elisabetta, linking her arm in mine. They soon shied away when Elisabetta was around, not knowing how to be around the little girl with her otherworldly air, beloved of Sister Beatrice, and Signora Rossi's star pupil. She was the only person ever with me.

The beautiful woman was our special secret. Those early mornings at the river were my escape from the routine of prayers, lessons, and meagre meals of polenta and minestra. I'd already been kept longer at the orphanage than most, probably on account of not passing my leaving certificate at school, but it was never explained why I was still there. I never asked, fearful of life without Elisabetta.

That morning, Elisabetta skipped ahead of me towards the river. I let her go. She was happier than I'd ever seen her and hadn't had a nightmare or wet the bed in a week. The air carried the delicate scent of the violet *giaggiolo* which had appeared, and I brushed my fingertip across their little beards of downy white hair. Swinging my boots by their laces, I jumped in and out of the icy water of little streams and dropped twigs into the water, watching as they floated away.

When I approached Elisabetta, she was in her usual spot, eyes closed.

'You can sit with me,' she said, pointing to the pebbles on her left.

'You looked like you wanted to be quiet.'

'I'm making sure…'

'Making sure of what?'

'Where she wants me to be.'

'Who?'

I looked around, as if someone might emerge from the trees on either side of the bank. Nearby leaves fluttered, rustling on a light breeze.

'She comes to me when I'm sleeping. And she comes to me here.

22

She's telling me I've found the right place.'

'What are you talking about?' I was building a small tower of pebbles beside me, but the last dark grey one was too heavy, and my wobbly construction collapsed.

'Oh, Lina, she's so graceful, with long, dark hair. You can only see some of it because she has her head covered. It's like she's in a pool of light.' Elisabetta circled her hands around her face.

I squinted at her, the sun shimmering on the river, but there was nothing there, except for a grey heron that had captured its prize and was taking off.

'Her eyes are so blue, so gentle. When she looks at me, I feel like I'm the only person who matters to her. She was here with me, just now.'

Elisabetta turned to her right, smiling, and held out her hand as if she were placing it into another.

Beside her was only an empty stretch of pebbles sloping down to the river.

'Why can't I see her?' My voice had the same spiteful tone that the bullies at the orphanage so often turned on me.

'It's me she wants to be with...'

With her downcast eyes, Elisabetta gave me a look that reminded me of the photo of Santa Teresa in the book of saints. She reached out to me, but I shrugged her off.

'I don't know what's happening, but since your fit, you're not yourself. You're imagining things.'

'Please, Lina. Don't be jealous. I need you with me.'

'What for?' I scuffed the pebbles with the toe of my boot, startling the little grebes who shook their red necks and glided away.

Elisabetta turned to me, her face paler than usual.

'When she's with me, I feel so special, like she wants me to know all about her. But I feel sad too, like it's not going to last.'

I turned away from her. 'It's time to go back,' I said, sweeping the pebble dust off my nightdress.

The pebbles under my feet were slippery with moss but I hurried away in the direction of the orphanage. I wasn't going to let her see how she'd upset me.

'Please, don't be angry with me!' Elisabetta cried.

I pretended I hadn't heard her.

'Her name is Maria,' Elisabetta called out, her voice shaky.

A shiver ran though my body, stopping me in my tracks.

Alone, her arms holding her knees to her chest, Elisabetta looked tiny against the river and the mountains with their snowy white caps. She was crying, but I stayed where I was.

But then her body started to jerk. I rushed towards her, turning my ankle on the greasy pebbles as I went.

'Elisabetta! No!'

I knelt and gathered her writhing body into my arms.

'I'm sorry, I'm sorry,' I cried as she flailed and struggled. Her elbow caught me on the chin but my hold on her was firm. My heart was pounding fast.

Her head resting in my lap, I stroked her hair, lifting loose strands from her damp forehead. With the hem of my nightdress, I wiped the froth and drool from the corners of her mouth. Gradually she grew quiet.

Although my ankle had swollen, I was able to lift her up, she was light and barely weighed anything at all. Holding her close to my body, I hobbled as quickly as I could back towards the orphanage, stopping once every so often to rest, my ankle throbbing.

As we got closer, the sound of children chatting and playing on their way to school reached me. I swallowed hard. Our absence would have been reported to Sister Beatrice by now.

The orphanage loomed into sight. Elisabetta's limp arm dangled in front of us, pointing at the ground.

Sister Beatrice was standing at the open window to our room, her arms folded across her chest. As she caught sight of us, she ran to meet us, one hand trying to keep her bouncing coif in place, the other hitching up her long skirt.

'What happened?' She took sleeping Elisabetta by the shoulders, while I held the lower part of her body. 'Same as last time?'

I nodded, eyes on my feet, stomach lurching.

~

Tucked into her bed, Elisabetta had the air of a sleeping angel. Sister Beatrice looked at her with the expression of a concerned mother. But as she turned towards me, her face was cold, eyebrows raised.

'Are you going to tell me why you weren't in your room?'

I breathed in, trying to push down the panic rising in my body.

Sister Beatrice waited, hands on hips.

An image of Il Duce, Mussolini, flashed through my mind. Mamma had always told me he was a brave man. In playful homage, I used to copy his gestures. Legs apart, back straight, chin up and jutting forward.

I raised myself up and remembered how to be Mussolini.

Sister Beatrice shifted in response and her stare seemed to soften.

'You want to know why we were out... where we had gone?'

I took my time, remembering how Mussolini always delivered his speeches with long, dramatic pauses. First, I looked to the ground for inspiration. Then upwards, to the crucifix above Elisabetta's bed.

'Continue.' Sister Beatrice's voice had lost its hard edge.

I held the silence for as long as I could.

'Elisabetta wanted to tell you herself.'

'Tell me what?' Sister Beatrice's body arched towards me.

'I'm not sure it's my place to say.'

'I think you'd better tell me what you mean, since Elisabetta's clearly not in a position to tell me herself.'

'She wanted to be sure before she came to you.'

Elisabetta and I had never talked of sharing our secret of the beautiful lady with Sister Beatrice.

'That time, after the book of saints and the first fit...' I stuttered.

Sister Beatrice was growing impatient. 'What are you talking about?'

'I knew she was different. Before she even told me...'

'What do you mean? How was she different? What did she tell you?'

Each question came faster than the last.

Caught in the tangle of my thoughts, I capitulated. Just like Mussolini.

'She sees the Madonna. She comes to her at River Mollarino.'

Sister Beatrice gasped. Her eyes were wide. She looked over at the peaceful, sleeping figure of Elisabetta in her bed and rushed to her, taking the rickety seat beside her. The corner of her mouth lifted into a gentle smile as she placed Elisabetta's hand in her own.

My palms were sweating. Why did I say the Madonna? Maria, I should have said Maria, like Elisabetta did. She'd be cross with me, I was sure of it, she'd never said about telling Sister Beatrice.

I felt sick and couldn't bring myself to look at Elisabetta or Sister Beatrice. I hung my head. At my feet, a busy column of ants was marching towards a crack between the floor and the crumbling wall. My heart was thudding.

Eventually Sister Beatrice turned towards me.

'You've seen nothing at all?' Her voice was softer than usual, and I had to raise my head to catch her words.

'It's only Elisabetta, not me,' I replied, relieved to be telling the truth.

'Anything unusual?' asked Sister Beatrice. 'A change in the air?'

'No,' I replied obediently. 'I went with Elisabetta to River Mollarino because she asked me to go with her.'

Sister Beatrice nodded and seemed satisfied with my answer.

'I always knew Elisabetta was a special child.'

The jealously lodged in the pit of my stomach stirred, but Sister Beatrice continued:

'I never imagined... Santa Scolastica... the Contessa...'

Her voice trailed off as she looked out of the window in the direction of the river. She dropped to her knees beside Elisabetta's bed.

'*Ave Maria, gratia plena.*'

The words of the Hail Mary poured from Sister Beatrice. With her flushed cheeks, she looked happier than I'd ever seen.

I mumbled along with the words, grateful that Sister Beatrice seemed to have forgotten I was there.

'*Ora pro nobis peccatoribus, nunc et in hora mortis nostrae. Amen.*'

Pray for us sinners now and at the hour of our death. Amen.

3

Elisabetta opened her eyes.

Startled to see Sister Beatrice, she urgently scanned our room, looking for me. I hung back. Sister Beatrice gently shushed her and gave her a glass of water.

'How are you feeling?' she asked. Elisabetta gulped down the water and handed back the empty glass without speaking.

'There's nothing to worry about. You were at the river, but Adelina brought you back safely.'

Elisabetta's skin had taken on a clammy, grey hue, which Sister Beatrice also seemed to have noticed. Fumbling, she reached into the pocket of her habit, and produced a sweet in a shiny wrapper, and offered it to Elisabetta.

Her eyes lit up. Sweets were a rare treat, Easter and Christmas only. She untwisted the wrapper and sucked noisily. My stomach gurgled as I imagined the sugar dissolving in my mouth, knowing that another sweet would not appear for me. Elisabetta felt for it with her tongue as it became smaller and smaller.

On my bed, I sank against the wall in the corner, trying to ignore the fruity smell, which was making my mouth water.

Once the sweet was no more, Elisabetta pulled herself up in bed. She had regained her colour. Sister Beatrice placed Elisabetta's hand in hers and looked towards the window, as if the words she was searching for might be found on the path to the river. The silence was uncomfortable. When Elisabetta turned to me, her expression searching for an explanation, I couldn't bear the tension any longer.

'I told Sister Beatrice… about why we've been going to the river.'

The words caught in my throat. I was expecting Elisabetta to be cross with me, to say something about it being our secret. But as if I wasn't even there, she addressed herself to Sister Beatrice.

'At first, I didn't know what was happening, when she came to me.'

Sister Beatrice nodded. 'Go on,' she whispered.

Elisabetta leant forward in the bed towards Sister Beatrice, as if the two of them were the only ones who should hear her words.

'Maria is so radiant. She told me she wants me to be at River Mollarino.'

'She told you her name?'

'Yes.'

Elisabetta settled back on her pillow.

'And only you see her, not Adelina?'

'Of course, she only wants to speak with me! Adelina doesn't see her. I only got her to come with me because…'

Her brow furrowed as if she was searching for the reason. Neither of them looked my way.

'There's something Maria wants me to understand. I'm to keep going to the river, so that I might know her better.'

Elisabetta withdrew her hands from Sister Beatrice and paused.

'There's something special about River Mollarino. I can't put it into words, but when I'm there quietly, I feel Maria is watching over me.'

Sister Beatrice took a deep breath and brought her hands together, as if to pray.

'I think it's time I told you the story of how our Benedictine order came to own this orphanage.'

Sister Beatrice drew Elisabetta towards her, who nestled in like a baby chick.

I turned away. Mamma came to mind, how she used to hold me close. The familiar ache of nerves and sickness returned, sharper than I'd known in a long while. I watched the two of them from the corner of my eye.

'Tell me.' Elisabetta's voice irritated me, sucking up to Sister Beatrice, as ever. 'Is it a secret?'

'As you know, Santa Scolastica lived in this area, *molte lune fa*. That's why the orphanage is named after her,' replied Sister Beatrice, taking a breath. 'But there's more to her story.'

I leant forward in my dark corner to hear better.

'Really?' Elisabetta released herself from Sister Beatrice and looked up at her, eager to hear more. 'You know how much I like to learn about the female saints!'

I wanted Elisabetta to look at me, to include me, but she didn't even glance my way. I was there, but of no interest.

Santa Scolastica, Sister Beatrice reminded Elisabetta, was the devoted sister of San Benedetto who'd established his monastery at nearby Monte Cassino. With the same rules of poverty and chastity, Santa Scolastica had set up a community of women, the first Benedictine order of nuns, which now looked after the children in the orphanage.

I'd heard the story so many times before. Every year on Santa Scolastica's feast day, February 10th, we had to listen to it again at a long mass said in her honour. How she was the patron saint of nuns and children, that we should always keep a special place for her in our prayers.

'But not all the women who followed Santa Scolastica became nuns,' continued Sister Beatrice, her voice dropping to a whisper.

'What do you mean?' Elisabetta sat up on her haunches. I shuffled forward on my bed.

'Some women baptised others.'

'Women priests!' Elisabetta clasped her hands to her mouth, her eyes shining.

Sister Beatrice nodded.

'Their messages were simple. To love one another, to look after the poor and the oppressed. They became very popular and well respected.'

'But what happened to them?'

'The men of the church were more interested in themselves and fine buildings than the lives of ordinary people. They did everything they could to discredit the women, calling them by all sorts of names.' Sister Beatrice blushed. 'Their worship went underground, and they continued to meet in secret.'

'Here at River Mollarino?'

It wasn't really a question. Elisabetta had her knowing, top-of-the-class air.

'Yes, yes,' said Sister Beatrice, delighted by Elisabetta's understanding. 'These women would urge others to follow the mother of Christ, of a life of service and devotion. Until the day they disappeared without a trace. That was when the Madonna started to appear.'

Elisabetta sat back on her pillow, looking pleased with herself.

From my dark corner, I wanted to ask what any of it had to do with Elisabetta, but it was already too late. I slumped back against the cold wall.

'Contessa Monti, who left her home to our order, what is now the orphanage, saw the Madonna herself as a child at River Mollarino.'

'What happened to her?' asked Elisabetta with a look of concern.

'The only person who believed her was the Mother Superior at the time. She had aunts and great-aunts who were members of our order. Progressive women who believed in education for girls and the wisdom of the local women.'

Sister Beatrice smiled as she spoke.

'They kept diaries and records of the lives of local women and the stories of their mothers and grandmothers. Mother Superior knew that women going back many years had worshipped the Madonna with the female priests at River Mollarino and many had witnessed her.'

'Did Mother Superior help Contessa Monti when she was a little girl?'

'Yes, she did. That's why the Contessa left her house to the order, upsetting all her family. Some of her grandchildren still believe the house should be theirs.'

Elisabetta sidled closer to Sister Beatrice.

'The church always dismissed the apparitions because they didn't want the stories of the women priests to be told.'

Elisabetta rested her head in Sister Beatrice's lap. She looked tired

31

again and Sister Beatrice brushed her cheek.

'Perhaps it's a little too much to take in, all at once.'

'You believe me, about Maria?' said Elisabetta.

'I believe you,' Sister Beatrice replied without hesitation.

Elisabetta settled into Sister Beatrice's lap like an exhausted kitten. She glanced at me briefly before closing her eyes. There was a hint of a smile on her face.

Sister Beatrice stroked Elisabetta's hair as she drifted off to sleep.

Neither of them noticed me slip out of the room.

~

The corridors of the orphanage were empty. A trail of crumbs along the long wooden tables and benches of the refectory was all that remained, the children gone to their classes.

My stomach rumbled for the missed breakfast. Still in my nightdress, I wandered through the orphanage, past the scruffy dorms and the simple chapel. The knot inside me grew as I thought of how Sister Beatrice had held Elisabetta, like Mamma used to hold me.

The stories of apparitions and Santa Scolastica were nonsense, I told myself, pushing down the jealousy that had hold of me. I'd never had time for a God who'd taken away Mamma. At the orphanage, I'd had to go along with it all, the never-ending prayers. Water being turned into wine and bread into fishes. Eating the body of Christ and drinking his blood when we went to mass. In my mind, they were just stories. Nothing more, I reminded myself, pinching at the skin of my wrist.

Outside, the sun was harsher in the sky. It seared through my thin nightdress. The seams under my arms chafed at my skin. I entered the cover of the woods quickly.

I breathed in the cooler air and the comforting smell of lichen and ferns, only to be startled by a sudden movement. Five or so metres away, the eyes of a young deer were staring straight at me. I wasn't sure who was more frightened, her or me. My swollen ankle was hurting. Elisabetta wouldn't be scared, I told myself. I waited and stood quietly. The deer turned, her lithe form gliding away, deeper into the woods.

Emboldened by my encounter, I walked through the woods to the riverside. Close to the willow tree, I took the place where Elisabetta had sat earlier.

Here the river lapped gently, forming an arc alongside a broad stretch of pebbles. Ahead was the natural bathing pool, a favourite of the younger orphanage children during the summer months after school. Behind the pool rose a dark stretch of velvet trees up the mountainside. The gentlest of breezes tousled the branches. Tits chirruped and chattered as they flitted around.

The river was a place I'd known all my life. But it wasn't until that week that I saw its perfection.

One of our bitterns called from the reeds ahead of me, deep and clear. It flew across my eyeline, away from the river, towards a natural clearing in the trees. Where it landed stood a crag of exposed rock. Its base was dark green, covered in delicate mosses.

I walked over and crouched down by the natural spring. My hand slid over the pebbles, and I picked out some that I liked. There were smooth and flat ones, others rounder or jagged edged, in shades from chalky white to ash grey. With great care, I pieced them together. A semi-circle of pebbles in a wall around the spring.

4

'It's so beautiful, isn't it?' Elisabetta's delicate fingers lifted the lace collar of a pure white dress, which glinted in our bare wardrobe.

'Why has Sister Beatrice given you a first communion dress?' I said, unable to push down the bitterness in my voice. 'You made your first communion years ago.'

The fine material shimmered. I longed to feel its smoothness beneath my fingertips.

'Sister Beatrice said it was a present, that she understands how I've been feeling,' she replied brightly. She undid the belt at her waist and stepped out of her drab smock.

'What are you going to do with a dress like this?' My tone was even sharper than I'd intended, but Elisabetta wasn't listening.

She stood in her greying vest and knickers in front of me, clutching her arms across her chest as if she was cold, and cocked her head towards me.

Like a reluctant servant, I took the dress from its hanger. I bent to the ground in front of her, holding the dress open for her to step into. Looking down on me, she pointed a dainty ballerina foot and then hopped into the dress, giggling.

The satin glided over her skinny frame as I pulled it upwards, over the ridges of the bones in her back.

'Hurry, do the zip!' she ordered, smoothing the silky fabric over her flat stomach. 'I want to see how well it fits.'

I jerked the zip upwards.

'Ow!' she screamed, gathering her hair over her shoulder. 'You caught my hair, be more careful!'

Without waiting, I pulled the zip all the way up, half hoping it might catch more strands. It didn't, and Elisabetta turned round with a flourish.

34

'How do I look?' She twirled so that the lower part of the dress rustled and swished.

'*Come una principessa.*' It was the truth, even if I didn't want to admit it.

'I'm to go to Sister Beatrice. She wants to see me when I've got the dress on,' said Elisabetta, not stopping to notice that I wasn't sharing her excitement. She was swaying on the spot, as if dancing with an imaginary prince.

'Why? What for?' I was back on my bed, picking at the tired fabric of my smock, trying to ignore how Elisabetta was glowing in that dress.

'Sister Beatrice says you're to come too.'

'What does she want with me?'

'You're not in trouble, don't worry.' Elisabetta gave me a smile of encouragement and swirled past me. 'Come on!' she said, heading out of the room.

'But you haven't got any shoes on!' I called after her.

I hurried after Elisabetta. Whatever Sister Beatrice had in mind, she'd thought to include me. She'd noticed me, called me by my name, trusted me to look after Elisabetta. Maybe I wasn't as stupid as Signora Rossi kept reminding everyone in class.

~

Sister Beatrice was waiting outside her study door, fiddling with the beads of her rosary. But rather than tell Elisabetta off for running down the corridor towards her, she gasped and raised her hands to her mouth. When Elisabetta reached the nun, she threw her arms around her. Sister Beatrice returned her embrace and pulled a handkerchief from her habit, dabbing the corners of her eyes. '*Bellisima!*' she exclaimed, smoothing the fabric along Elisabetta's arm with pride. I moved closer to Elisabetta, but Sister Beatrice didn't even look my way.

Elisabetta had on her smug, favourite child of the orphanage smile. I hung back sulkily. There was something different about Sister

Beatrice. When she looked over her shoulder, I noticed she was wearing powder on her face, a little rouge that made her cheeks look fuller. It was odd, but it seemed to match her mood.

'Oh, I almost forgot,' said Sister Beatrice, turning back towards her study. 'Wait here!'

'What's happening?' I hissed into Elisabetta's ear, 'What's going on?'

'Sister Beatrice has given me a special privilege. I'm to lead the rosary in honour of the Madonna at her new prayer group.'

My heart sank. Not more prayers and being on my best behaviour, with no way out.

'Why didn't you tell me before?'

'Because if I told you, you wouldn't come with me,' she said, turning us away from the approaching Sister Beatrice. 'Please do this for me.'

'Why? What difference will it make if I'm there or not?'

Elisabetta looked tiny in her too big dress. I caught my reflection in her pale eyes, the tall adolescent who ought to know better than to be jealous of a sickly, younger girl.

'*Va bene*,' I replied, a little chastened. 'I'll come, just in case you need me. But you know how much I hate going to church.'

~

A small red velvet box lay in Sister Beatrice's hand.

'For you,' she said, offering it up to Elisabetta.

Elisabetta squealed as Sister Beatrice brought out onto her palm a gold medallion and chain. She handled it with great care, brushing away flecks of dust from the serene Madonna and child.

The necklace Mamma used to wear came to mind. Hers too was gold and a Madonna, her only precious possession. Mamma's Madonna used to rest on the smooth cleft between her breasts. She'd run the flat length of the chain between thumb and forefinger, stopping to fiddle with the medallion as she spoke. But Mamma's Madonna della Pietà held her crucified, dying son in her arms. She'd promised it would be mine one day, but I never saw it again after she died.

Sister Beatrice was fumbling with the clasp of the necklace, her hands shaking while Elisabetta held her long hair to one side.

'Forgive me, these clumsy fingers of mine.' Sister Beatrice tried again, but the colour was rising in her face to match the rouge.

Still thinking of Mamma, I stepped forward and took the chain from Sister Beatrice. I brushed loose strands of Elisabetta's hair away and with a swift movement, secured the clasp. Elisabetta touched the medallion on her chest and gave me a smile.

Trailing some way behind Elisabetta and Sister Beatrice down the stone steps, Mamma was still on my mind. When was it going to start hurting less?

Outside a few of the kids were playing jacks with stones in the dirt. At the sight of Sister Beatrice leading out a radiant Elisabetta, the game stopped abruptly, and they fell silent, gazing open-mouthed.

One of the cheekier lads, Enzo, caught my eye, and stepped up, trying to block my path. I pushed him away to follow the unlikely couple. But when I looked, they had not turned right towards the church of San Donato. Instead, the barefoot Elisabetta was stepping on the pebbled path towards the river, as if walking without shoes came naturally to her. She was chatting with Sister Beatrice and, although I couldn't hear what they were saying, I recognised Elisabetta's tone. It was that annoying voice she affected for Sister Beatrice, the one that set her above and apart from me and all the other children in the orphanage.

I trudged along, allowing the gap between us to grow bigger.

I was still thinking about Mamma. She'd always taught me to say my prayers, to be a good girl, kind and caring to others. I'd tried to carry on as she would have wanted. At the orphanage, the constant praying with the nuns was too much. I didn't want to be part of saying the rosary with Sister Beatrice and Elisabetta. But I didn't want to be left out either. What if Elisabetta had one of her fits again? She needed me by her side. Mamma would want me to be there to help her.

The two of them were almost out of sight, entering the woods. I ran to catch up.

My mouth fell open.

At the same spot where I'd piled my chosen pebbles around the spring in a semi-circle, rose a statue.

Sheltered by a rock boulder, it was the discarded Madonna who had once stood at the entrance of the orphanage.

One of the boys had clipped off her right arm with a misplaced shot at goal, sending her toppling to the ground. That was Enzo too, I remembered. He was given forty lashes for his sin and didn't make a sound. But when his beloved football was confiscated for good, he howled for so long that everyone in the orphanage understood his pain.

The broken Madonna had been given a touch of paint, her cloak a fresh sky blue, her face chalky white. But beneath the surface of colour, she looked fragile. Her arm was still missing, leaving her unbalanced, as if with a slight push, she might be toppled once more. At her feet, bright flowers had been arranged in two neat vases, one on either side, providing her with a frame of support.

Behind the little pebble wall I'd built, sat half a dozen nuns from the orphanage, plus some of the most devoted parishioners of San Donato, each on their own blanket, as if gathered for a parish picnic. They were the old crones who sat in the front pews of San Donato every Sunday when the children from the orphanage were dragged to mass. A band of war widows who shushed us and tutted loudly whenever we made the slightest sound. Their icy stares always frightened us into quiet submission.

Each of the women held a rosary before her.

The person I was surprised to see was Signora Visconti, sitting at a slight distance from the others, turning her diamond earring between thumb and forefinger. The younger wife of the ageing doctor, her refined clothes and upright posture set her apart as someone not born into the life of our small valley.

At the sight of Elisabetta, resplendent in her white dress, there was an audible intake of breath. The women looked at one another and smiled. A queasy feeling rose up from my stomach.

Elisabetta bowed her head and genuflected in front of the amputated statue. A silence fell among the gathered women. They too bowed their heads.

Sister Beatrice gestured for Elisabetta to take one of the two seats placed nearby.

I hesitated at the edge of the group, my unease growing. One of the older women tapped me on the leg and pointed to the space on her blanket.

From her throne, Elisabetta indicated with a slight nod that I should take my place. As usual, I obeyed and sat down, cross-legged, directly opposite her.

When all was completely still, with just the sound of the river gurgling over the pebbles, Sister Beatrice raised her head from her prayers and began to speak.

'Sisters, we come together for the first time in this sacred place, with joy in our hearts!' Her voice was trembling.

The women nodded as one, some allowing the briefest glimpse of excitement to escape their serious features. Sister Beatrice took in a deep breath of the pine-scented mountain air and stood taller. I was chewing my nails.

'We have known, through the centuries – as handed down from mother to daughter, from grandmother to granddaughter, from aunt to niece – that this river of ours is a source of healing waters. That many girls and young women have witnessed the Madonna here, like our kind benefactor, Contessa Monti.'

At this, there was a flurry of eager recognition among the women. They looked at one another, and towards the river, and one raised her voice in exclamation.

'Yes, it is as our mothers always said!'

The other women joined in to form a chorus. I looked at Elisabetta, panic growing in me, but her gaze went beyond me, as if she was interested in something other than the group of women.

Sister Beatrice motioned with her hands for calm and the women fell quiet.

'And now we have confirmation of the ancient beliefs.'

An excited murmur swept through the group.

Sister Beatrice hushed the women.

'The Madonna has made herself known to Elisabetta.'

There was a collective gasp, followed by high pitched excitement. Some women remained silent, some covered themselves with the sign of the cross and others chattered feverishly. Even Signora Visconti's normal reserve was replaced with a broad smile. A couple of the nuns raised their arms towards the sky.

All eyes turned to Elisabetta. Her head was bowed.

Sister Beatrice was speaking again.

'I have asked you here today, those of us who have whispered our secret knowledge to one another. We women of faith know how Santa Scolastica and the Madonna want us to follow their way, to love one another, to help the poor and the oppressed.'

I wanted to get up, to tell Sister Beatrice to stop, and to take Elisabetta away. I didn't want to hear her stories. But I was rooted to the blanket, fidgeting as the pebbles dug into my buttocks.

'Stay still,' the woman beside me hissed, firing a line of saliva into my face.

Sister Beatrice reeled off incantations to the collective wisdom of our female ancestors, who knew the value of worship and dedication. The time had come, she said, for women to make their voices heard. Elisabetta was proof that we should once again listen, that the Madonna was making herself known through this shy and innocent girl.

I bristled at the description of my friend. I expected to see her beaming at the attention, but her head remained bowed, her eyes on her neatly folded hands. For a moment I felt sorry for her. Maybe she too was worried that Sister Beatrice was getting carried away?

Sister Beatrice asked Elisabetta to lead the group on the first chapter of the rosary. Elisabetta dutifully obliged. I mumbled along, holding my hands in my lap in a way that could be concealing the rosary beads I didn't have. As the female voices grew in strength, Elisabetta looked around at the assembled women. Her eyes sparkled as bright as the river as she raised herself upright.

5

After the prayer group, the nuns gathered around Elisabetta outside the orphanage, their voices full of excitement.

It made me think of the fussing mothers in the piazza after a first communion mass, showing off their offspring for all to behold. Mamma was still alive when I made my first communion. Although my little white outfit of dress, veil and gloves was much simpler, I remembered the weight of her proud hand on my shoulder as she greeted friends and neighbours outside San Donato.

Above the chatter, I could hear Elisabetta.

'It was so wonderful!' She was running her palms along the fine material of her dress, as if committing it to memory.

'We could bring together our little prayer group regularly. And if you were to lead us in the rosary, you could wear your special dress each time.' Sister Beatrice smiled. The nuns alongside her nodded in enthusiastic agreement.

'Really?' replied Elisabetta, stroking the fabric with her fingertips, turning towards me with a gleeful look. 'But what about Adelina? Can she come too?' Her whiny voice made me want to tell her to shut up.

They turned round, embarrassed they'd forgotten me.

'Yes, she can come too,' said Sister Beatrice, a little flustered. 'If the two of you come together, it'll give me the opportunity to make sure all is in order at the *santuario* beforehand.'

At the word '*santuario*', the dread that had been growing in my stomach during the prayer group rose to my throat. It wasn't a shrine. I'd only arranged the stones around the spring to make it look pretty.

It was my stupid fault. I was the one who'd built the pebble wall, who'd told Sister Beatrice that Elisabetta saw the Madonna. Why hadn't I kept my mouth shut? I didn't know what Elisabetta was seeing, but whatever was happening, it needed to stop.

'Sister Beatrice...' I ventured.

But Sister Beatrice had gone already, Elisabetta alongside her.

~

When she was back in our room, Elisabetta stood expectantly, her back to me.

'Help me out of the dress!'

Had she turned round, she would have seen me sitting on the edge of my bed, pulling at the ragged edge of a nail with my teeth.

'I don't want to take it off, but at least I'll get to wear it again soon,' she said, a gloating note in her voice.

I got up without enthusiasm.

'Come on, Lina. And hang it up properly so that it doesn't get creased.'

Elisabetta chattered while I unzipped her. About how wonderful the *santuario* looked and had I noticed it was the same Madonna who used to greet visitors to the orphanage. And wasn't it incredible to hear Sister Beatrice's story about the women priests at River Mollarino and how they baptised believers.

The pious Elisabetta had become an over-excited chatterbox. She didn't notice that I hadn't replied. I hung the dress as instructed.

Eventually, she turned to me. 'What's wrong with you?'

'Nothing.'

How could I tell her that I wished I'd never gone with her to the river or told Sister Beatrice that she saw the Madonna. That I wasn't sure what she was seeing, but it didn't feel right?

'You don't want to see me happy, do you?' said Elisabetta. 'You're jealous that I'm wearing the special dress. That it's me leading the prayer group.'

'Why would I be a jealous of a prayer group?' I replied, not meeting her eye. 'You know I just go along with it all, the masses, the prayers. Just like the nuns want us to.'

'But don't you see? This is different.' Elisabetta was serious and looked older than her eleven years. 'This is about us sisters, together.'

'Listen to yourself,' I said, getting angry. 'You're just repeating what Sister Beatrice said. She's getting carried away.'

'It might be Sister Beatrice doing the talking. *I'm* the one who has seen Maria. *She* wants me to go to the river.'

An image of Elisabetta in my arms after her fit came to mind. Small. Vulnerable.

'You were ill,' I said with genuine sympathy. 'You weren't yourself. Maybe you got a bit confused.' I didn't go as far as to say that I thought she might have imagined it all, even though it was what I was starting to think.

'I've been ill, yes. But Sister Beatrice believes me,' said Elisabetta. 'Maybe you're the one who's not right in the head. You cry at night sometimes too.'

Her words landed like a punch to the stomach. Sometimes, I couldn't help it, when I thought of Mamma, my sobs burying into my cold pillow.

'Please,' I replied, winded. 'It's not too late. Tell Sister Beatrice that you got carried away with your imagination.'

'I've seen Maria many times. I know her,' Elisabetta sniffed. 'She wants me to keep going to the river.'

'You've swallowed all of Sister Beatrice's stories. You'll do anything to please her!'

'At least she believes me! You're too stupid to understand!'

I grabbed her by the shoulders. With a force I didn't know I had, I shoved her backwards onto her bed.

Elisabetta's body jerked as she slid into the first stages of another fit.

~

For the next month I helped Elisabetta into her dress and fussed around her, ashamed but grateful that she couldn't remember how I'd pushed her towards her last fit. I plaited her hair either side of her angelic face and kept her dress spotlessly clean.

'Hurry, Lina! You know everyone is waiting for me!' Elisabetta said, gathering the flowers ready to lay at the foot of the Madonna.

The bunches of white campanulas had been my suggestion. Sister Beatrice had been reluctant at first. But when she saw the reaction among the women at the sight of little Elisabetta placing the flowers so reverentially, it soon became part of Sister Beatrice's ceremony. It was my job to pick and prepare the flowers. I enjoyed the freedom of going out on my own, in the early morning mist of the river, accompanied by my favourite birds. Careful to pick only the stems of bells at their best, I discarded those with even the slightest discolouration. Only the best would do. By now, Elisabetta had become known as The Barefoot Flower Girl of Atina.

What started with a few of Sister Beatrice's friends from the front pews at San Donato and the nuns from the orphanage, had quickly grown over that month. Once it was known that Signora Visconti was always in attendance, more of the educated gentle women of Atina joined in too. To her face, everyone treated Signora Visconti with the same courtesy she greeted her husband's patients when they took a seat in the smart waiting room of her home. With her neat bun and slender figure in a stylish dress and cardigan, she seemed a little out of place among the women in their rough headscarves and baggy skirts. When I caught wind of the other women gossiping about her, saying how much makeup she wore and how it was easy to keep your figure when you hadn't gone through pregnancy and childbirth, I felt a little sorry for her.

Sister Beatrice led the ceremony each time, which lasted an hour or so. Although I was still unsure about what Elisabetta was seeing, as her special friend, I was treated kindly, even with a certain amount of respect. I liked being part of this grown-up community of women, with their gossip about the old priest, Padre Bosco, and the goings-on in Atina. When I grew uncomfortable at what was happening and couldn't remember the sequence of the rosary, I reminded myself that Mamma would be proud of me, looking after my friend, trying my best with the prayers.

Each time, Sister Beatrice started with a variation of the same story, about female wisdom and how Santa Scolastica had encouraged the women priests, and how they had baptised believers in the river. They brought the sick into the healing waters here, where so many were cured, with the knowledge of the herbs and plants of our mountainside.

'Our sisters were not afraid! The men of the church then, just as today, wanted to keep us quiet! But we will not be silenced!'

After her rousing speeches, Sister Beatrice invited Elisabetta to lead the rosary. At first, Elisabetta's voice had been quiet, sometimes a little shaky, which seemed to endear her to the women. Now her initial nerves had melted away, and she'd grown in confidence. She seemed to captivate the women in equal measure to Sister Beatrice.

My habit was to sit behind Elisabetta, slightly to one side. I told myself it was important I was there. With all the fervour, Elisabetta might have another fit. She would need me to be close at hand to help her. I was the only who knew what to do, even if I had been the one who'd pushed her towards her last fit.

During that month, Elisabetta was healthy and well. She stopped waking at night and did not wet her bed. Each morning she awoke bright and lively, but she no longer climbed into bed with me. I missed having her beside me.

She was full of how Maria came to her in her dreams, with special messages only for her.

'Sister Beatrice will want me to tell her all about it!' she exclaimed. Yet when I asked her what Maria had said, the words were all so ordinary and without any meaning, that I couldn't even recall them.

'What's does she sound like?' I asked.

Her answer surprised me.

'She speaks like us, in our dialect,' Elisabetta replied, as if the thought had never occurred to her.

'Why would she speak in our rough language, not proper Italian?'

Elisabetta's forehead crumpled at the question, but she shot back, quick as a flash.

'Sister Beatrice warned me about people who don't believe.'

'I'm your friend…'

'You've never believed me, have you? You think I'm making it all up, don't you?'

Elisabetta shot me an angry look and didn't wait for a reply.

'I'm going to see Sister Beatrice. I don't have to listen to you.'

She slammed the door behind her. On my bed, I curled into a tight ball and hugged my knees, trying to convince myself that I wasn't alone in the world.

6

Alongside the prayer group, Sister Beatrice taught Elisabetta about the women of the church. Half an hour a day was set aside after school lessons, when the other children were playing outside and the babies in the nursery were having their afternoon nap. Despite our last argument, Elisabetta still expected me to accompany her, even though I was tired from spending more time looking after the babies with the younger nuns.

In the month since the prayer group had started, Sister Beatrice had given permission for me to be called out of school lessons when an extra pair of hands was needed in the nursery. This happened frequently, and I was only too happy to leave behind the writing exercises and sums that I never grasped and was grateful to Sister Beatrice.

'*Lina!* Stop your dreaming!' Elisabetta prodded me as I lay on my bed, resting after the busy morning. 'It's time for my lesson.'

I followed her, too exhausted to object. It wouldn't have made any difference if I had.

Elisabetta knocked gently at the door to Sister Beatrice's study, and we walked in. Whatever the weather outside, it was always cold and gloomy in that room. All but one shutter, which looked out onto the entrance of the orphanage, were kept firmly shut.

As usual, Sister Beatrice was hunched over the book on her desk. She peered at the many columns of numbers through a pair of spectacles, the bridge tied with a knot of fraying string. Concentrating on that book, she always looked much older. She took off her spectacles and lay them carefully on top of the ledger. Elbows on the desk, she leant forward, kneading her forehead with her fingertips.

'Whichever way I add it up, it's never enough.' She sighed, pushing the ledger away.

Elisabetta coughed weakly and Sister Beatrice turned, startled.

'I didn't hear you…' she said, a little flustered, closing the ledger. 'How are you today, Elisabetta?'

'I'm well, thank you,' Elisabetta replied, all sweetness and light.

'No more dizzy spells?'

'None.'

'*Bene, bene,*' replied Sister Beatrice, regaining her composure. She indicated for Elisabetta to take up her usual place beside the desk and gave a nod in my direction, where I sat on a wobbly three-legged stool in the corner.

I heard little of what was said next, staring up at the curled, stained remains of a rosebud print, which had once covered the walls. Ever since Sister Beatrice had told us about how the orphanage came to be in the possession of the nuns, I spent the time during Elisabetta's dull lessons trying to imagine the orphanage as the home of the Contessa, enjoying a life of parties and fine food. It was hard to conjure up luxuries I had no experience of. I couldn't get past the faded, peeling wallpaper.

From time to time, I caught a few of Sister Beatrice's words as she read. Full of enthusiasm, she told of determined women from volumes which she handled with great reverence. Sometimes she returned to the bible, and the story of Ruth, about a woman who stayed with her mother-in-law when her husband had died, and eventually became the grandmother of King David. I liked this story of loyalty and its happy ending of love. Ruth was a true friend, Sister Beatrice stressed, like the very meaning of her name. One who showed devotion to other women. When Elisabetta annoyed me, I told myself, I could try being more like Ruth.

All the while, Elisabetta listened attentively. She'd developed a new habit, repeating back to Sister Beatrice what she'd said, with just a few different words. Although this irritated me, Sister Beatrice was delighted, and she would continue her lesson with even more gusto.

If Sister Beatrice got too carried away, Elisabetta would ask her a question.

'Why do you think she chose to do that?' was one of her favourites.

The words sounded odd to me, but for Sister Beatrice it only seemed to add to her joy at teaching Elisabetta. She gave long, rambling answers. At any pause, Elisabetta nodded in response. As she did so, she looked down slightly, a hint of a smile on her lips.

~

One day, the books remained on the shelf and Sister Beatrice opened the drawer of her desk. She indicated that I too could approach, pushing aside the ledger and a pile of bills. Together we looked at the centre pages of a newspaper.

'Women can influence much,' Sister Beatrice announced. 'I know the female saints of the past may be hard to relate to,' she continued, her eyes briefly meeting mine, 'but you know of Santa Maria Goretti, who has recently been canonised.' Elisabetta nodded with a pious smile, while I looked away, guiltily.

In front of us, Sister Beatrice pointed to a photo of a packed square, full of the faithful, holding banners and photos of a young woman. Alongside was another photo of the same young woman in a coffin.

'See all these people at the Vatican. She is an inspiration to us all, particularly to a younger generation of women. It falls to us to follow her example.'

The woman in the photo had the look of so many in Atina. A careworn face, neither attractive nor unattractive. Unremarkable.

Sister Beatrice told us about Santa Maria Goretti, a woman violated by a man who instead of seeking justice, had forgiven her persecutor. She preached of love, even for sinners. All the time I kept looking at the photo for something, anything that might mark her out as special. But as Sister Beatrice continued, all I saw was an ordinary woman, perhaps in her thirties. The reason so many were drawn to Santa Maria Goretti, according to Sister Beatrice, was that she had suffered pain that so many women could understand. Elisabetta leaned across the desk, her finger moving quickly under the lines of close-printed text of the newspaper, eager to understand the story for herself.

So engrossed were we in the newspaper that none of us heard the knock at the door. But we all jumped, even Sister Beatrice, at the sound of the voice that we all instantly recognised.

'What is this? Private catechism?' exclaimed Padre Bosco. A short, wiry man with a full head of generous white hair, he was a little stiffened by age but carried the authority of a man respected and feared by his community for the last half a century.

Sister Beatrice hastily retrieved the newspaper, pushing it back into the drawer while bowing in deference to the priest.

'I was giving Elisabetta a grounding in the saints,' she stuttered.

'Elisabetta?' he repeated, as if fresh lemon juice had hit his tongue. 'The Barefoot Flower Girl of Atina?'

Elisabetta smiled, ready to receive the same deferential treatment she was growing accustomed to from Sister Beatrice and the other nuns and women at the prayer group. She hadn't picked up the sarcastic edge to Padre Bosco's voice.

'You're causing quite a stir, I understand, at River Mollarino,' he said, his expression turning sour, while Sister Beatrice looked on, pained.

'What makes you think you're so special?' he said, raising his voice. He jabbed an angry finger towards her. Elisabetta recoiled but the priest had turned away from her, towards me. Heat rose in my cheeks.

'You don't claim any apparitions, do you, young lady?'

'No, Father,' I replied, the tang of his stale breath reaching me as I concentrated on my feet.

'Sensible young lady.'

My shoulders dropped in relief, but he turned back to Elisabetta, who looked so young and powerless beside the priest. Sister Beatrice made to step forward and fill the space between her and Padre Bosco but thought better of it.

'So why aren't you like your friend?' he shouted at Elisabetta. 'She sees nothing, so why should you?'

The old priest started to wheeze. He leant on the desk, trying to catch his breath. Sister Beatrice rushed forward to help him into a chair. Agitated, she waved us away.

'You're nothing but a born troublemaker!' he hissed at Elisabetta, spitting at her as the words flew from his mouth.

Elisabetta ran out of the room, snivelling. I followed her, but slowly enough to hear Padre Bosco's words to Sister Beatrice.

'I told you, that child is a fantasist, Beatrice. Yet you've gone against my advice. Again. This has to stop right now!'

~

The heavy door of the Church of San Donato groaned shut behind me, making me even more nervous. I reached for the font and dipped my finger in the holy water and made the sign of the cross. Ahead of me, the church was dark and quiet, save for some candles burning at the altar. Beside the confession box, two elderly women were on their knees, waiting.

I hesitated in the side aisle, looking up at a marble carving of Christ in his agony. I'd never liked going to confession and avoided it as much as I possibly could. The sins you had to invent and list, the prayers I could never remember. The confession box made me think of a prison cell, the grille separating priest from sinner.

I was about to turn on my heel when a warm voice reached me, accompanied by the sound of a walking stick thumping against the tiled floor.

'When I didn't know what to say, I used to find sitting in the Chapel of Our Lady and closing my eyes would help.'

I'd seen Giulio many times serving at mass, but I'd never spoken to him before. Everyone in Atina knew Giulio, with his wounded leg and the facial injuries he'd suffered in the war. I'd watched him so many times from where the orphanage children took their place at mass. He'd always seemed distant, sad.

Beside me, he was different, gentler. I realised he was much younger than his injuries had led me to believe.

He accompanied me to his favoured pew, his stick marking his slow rhythm. I fell into step with him, aware of his breathing, and mine.

'It's never as bad as you imagine,' he whispered with a smile, and with his outstretched hand, he guided me ahead of him into the pew.

As he left, I was still holding my breath and followed his return to the altar, my eyes on his broad shoulders.

The second of the two elderly women had returned from the confession box and was kneeling to pray. I looked up to the altar where Giulio was laying out the cloth. He smiled at me and nodded, sending an unfamiliar sensation through my body.

Smiling at the kneeler by my feet, colour rose in my cheeks. When I got up, I approached the confessional with a timid knock.

'Enter,' Padre Bosco intoned. Through the grille, I could see he was setting back the stole, which he had been in the process of taking off.

I shifted on the wooden bench, still thinking of Giulio's kindness.

'Bless me Father for I have sinned…' Padre Bosco recited the words slowly, allowing me to repeat after him.

'Tell me in your own words what brings you here,' he said. There was none of the usual sarcasm he saved for parishioners he judged wanting.

I raised my head, searching through the pattern of the grille for the courage to continue. I knew what I had to do, but I was so scared. He nodded and waited.

'I'm worried about Elisabetta,' I whispered eventually. 'When you came to the orphanage yesterday…'

'Go on,' he said, his voice even and calm.

'She's not herself. I think she's ill.'

'In her body or in her mind?'

'Both. She's been having fits and sometimes it's after these that she says she has her visions.'

'And what do you think about what she says?'

'I'm not sure what's happening to her. But the other day, I provoked one of her fits, saying that I didn't believe her.'

'I see.'

Tears ran down my cheeks. 'She's my best friend. My only friend. Without her...'

Padre Bosco produced a pressed white handkerchief and slipped it under the grille. I took it and blew my nose.

'It's natural you should be concerned for your friend.'

'But I've done a bad thing, haven't I, Father?'

'Sometimes we act in a way to protect those we love the most,' he sighed, taking his time over the words.

'I haven't been able to say this to anyone, but when you came to Sister Beatrice's study, it made me think that what's happening isn't right. Sister Beatrice accepts everything Elisabetta says, but I'm not so sure.'

'You did well to come to me,' replied Padre Bosco. 'You are motivated by love for your friend.'

Padre Bosco was breathing heavily. Panicked, I wondered how many Our Fathers and Hail Marys he was about to give me for my penance. The silence was awkward, and I was getting frightened, thinking my sin so great that Padre Bosco was weighing up a big number of prayers.

When he still said nothing, I became even more worried. And guilty I'd told a priest I didn't believe Elisabetta. But that's why I'd gone to confession, so that only Padre Bosco and God need ever know.

'What's my penance, Father?' I asked, tentatively.

Padre Bosco stirred. 'Um... no penance, my child... No penance.'

My shoulders dropped and I leant forward, hardly believing my luck. I got up to leave, bowing to the grille.

'Just come and speak to me whenever you want about the situation with Sister Beatrice and Elisabetta,' came his voice.

The command was clear.

7

Giulio

Giulio's stick struggled to gain purchase among the pebbles. Dripping with sweat and cursing his leg, he finally made it to the willow tree. He lowered himself with some difficulty, pushing down on his stick, onto the fallen log beneath the leaves that had become his seat. There was still time before the prayer group was due to start.

As a wounded soldier, then prisoner of war, he'd held the memory of River Mollarino as tight as a clenched fist. When he thought he couldn't go on, he imagined the clear mountain water, the sound as it rushed downstream, how he might fish there again. All through those years, he'd kept a smooth grey pebble from its banks in his breast pocket, close to his heart.

Hidden behind his willow curtain, he'd been watching the prayer group for weeks. The number of women had been growing steadily. He knew them all. Some he greeted as he went about his routine as sacristan to Padre Bosco at San Donato. They swept the aisles of the church with a battered broom and polished the chalice, monstrance, and candlesticks with vigour. You could set the clock of the town hall by them, dedicated as they were to their duties.

Others, when they looked at him, he didn't know what to do. These were the mothers, their faces haunted by grief, whose sons hadn't returned. His friends in the local unit. Unable to bear the pity and envy of these women, he kept to himself.

Familiarity had drawn him back to San Donato after those lost years of the war. His belief in God had long since shrivelled away. Padre Bosco hadn't questioned him about his experiences or how he came to suffer his injuries and he treated Giulio as if he'd never been away. They never talked of faith. He wasn't to know that Giulio had wished himself dead, many, many times.

With his one good eye, Giulio watched as the women arrived. Some engaged in hushed chatter, others were quiet and prayerful. Anticipation crackled through the gathering. Signora Visconti, the doctor's wife, was smiling broadly, looking far less pinched and serious than her reputation.

The women started to sing, in perfect harmony. Their heartfelt 'Ave Maria' was lifted by a gentle breeze up into the cathedral of trees.

Giulio relaxed, comforted by the simple beauty of the melody. He hadn't expected to experience the solace of the prayer group. It'd been years since he'd genuinely prayed, although he went through the motions at San Donato. After his friends had died, there didn't seem to be any point.

Yet here he was.

Despite the effort of dragging his useless leg and body to this spot, he kept returning. Cocooned in his own contemplation, he was safe behind the willow curtain.

It was the girl, Elisabetta. When she was there, his jagged mind stilled. He experienced a deep peace that he longed for. The awful memories of the war and the voices in his head receded.

~

As the singing ended, Elisabetta made her entrance.

Slight, with long, dark hair in plaits, her bare feet seemed to glide over the pebbles. Perhaps she was eight or nine years old, but Giulio knew little about children.

The older girl was always close behind her. He knew her name was Adelina, after Sister Beatrice called out to her to arrange a cushion for Elisabetta. There was care and concern in how Adelina watched Elisabetta's step. He was surprised when Adelina had appeared at San Donato the previous evening for confession, and found himself wanting to speak to her, make her feel comfortable. He couldn't help but notice that Adelina wasn't really a girl, more a young woman. She had almond eyes, and a self-conscious way of trying to disguise her height.

Elisabetta was holding a small bunch of white flowers ahead of her. Although tied with a piece of rough string, she carried them as if they were a fine bridal bouquet. She walked towards the statue of the Madonna. Making the sign of the cross, she knelt in front of the Madonna and placed the flowers at her feet. Alongside was an arrangement of painted pebbles, the latest additions to the shrine.

Over the weeks, Giulio had witnessed the changes to the *santuario*. The Madonna with the missing arm and chips of plaster in her cloak was now surrounded by ribbons and lace hanging from the lower branches of the trees, either in the blue of her cloak or in pure white. They fluttered in the breeze as Elisabetta prayed. Behind his willow screen, Giulio put his hands together in prayer.

Elisabetta rose to her feet, and she greeted the assembled women with a gentle nod. Adelina followed close behind. The women pulled out rosaries from folded handkerchiefs or from between their breasts and waited for Elisabetta to take her place at the head of the group.

The little girl stood as still as the statue of the Madonna. A heavy silence fell on the group.

She was staring straight at the willow tree.

Behind the curtain of leaves, Giulio flinched. He could feel heat rising up his neck into his face. She could see him, surely.

Elisabetta stood quietly, her eyes fixed in his direction.

One by one, the women turned their gazes across the pebbles towards the tree.

Nerves seized Giulio's body. His heart was pounding.

Slowly, Elisabetta lifted outstretched arms towards him.

She was drawing him to her. Like a magnet, a pull he couldn't resist.

He took a deep breath in. With the aid of his stick, he pulled himself up and pushed back the curtain of green leaves.

A gasp went up among the women.

Elisabetta looked at Giulio as if they were the only people present, a delicate smile on her face. He looked into her pale blue eyes, transfixed. He stood quite still. A wisp of a memory passed through his body. For the briefest moment he remembered the young man he'd been before his injuries, how different it had been to live without burdened movement, without scars, being able to see through both eyes. Without carrying the overwhelming guilt.

Leaning on his stick, he took a laborious step towards Elisabetta's outstretched arms, concentrating on her eyes.

The group looked at one another for answers. Sister Beatrice put a finger to her lips before anyone tried to speak.

Elisabetta took a few steps towards Giulio, her arms still outstretched. Adelina quietly stayed a few paces behind her, slightly to one side.

At each of the steps Elisabetta took towards him, Giulio's body experienced a lightness. He was becoming the young version of himself again. The grinding despair and the grenade which had shattered his body were falling away.

As she approached, Giulio raised his head. A wave moved through his body, with the contorted vertebrae of his spine unclenching, like a line of dominoes falling against one another. He rolled his neck from side to side, which gave a couple of soothing clicks. A surge of energy coursed through his body, and he straightened up, adjusting himself into a new but familiar posture. He caught the look on Adelina's face as he did so. Her hand was raised to her mouth, her eyes shining.

Elisabetta was a few steps away from him.

'Don't be afraid.' She reached out her hand towards Giulio and he stepped towards her.

His stick clattered to the pebbles. There was a sharp intake of breath among the women, which they held as he took his second, and then his third step unaided towards Elisabetta. She nodded, encouraging him, and took his hand.

'You're safe,' Elisabetta said, her voice quiet and calm. A tear rolled down his cheek from his good eye.

She led him slowly towards the group of women, a little like a proud father walking his daughter down the aisle. Giulio's steps were slow but steady. He didn't falter. Adelina clapped with joy as they passed her. A wave of excitement rippled through the group.

By the time Giulio reached them, he'd grown 20 centimetres taller, his hunched posture no more. His face softened, and the unblemished right side lifted into a smile, a glimpse of the innocent eighteen-year-old soldier who had left Atina nine years before.

Elisabetta stepped aside, leaving Giulio at the centre of the throng of women. Some were hesitant, others rushed towards him. They looked him closely up and down, reaching out a guiding hand to Sister Beatrice's chair. She was standing beside it, urging him to take her place.

'Praise be to the Madonna of the *santuario*!' cried Sister Beatrice as Giulio lowered himself onto the dusty woven seat, feeling his legs with his hands.

'And praise be to Elisabetta, our own flower girl. Behold this second virgin who brings miracles to this sacred place, known to women through the ages!'

Giulio and the women turned as one towards Elisabetta, a tiny, slight figure being swallowed by the crowd of women pressing in on her.

Elisabetta lowered her eyes and seemed to brush away a tear.

The words 'It is she who is to be praised. I am…' were barely audible before Elisabetta's head lolled onto her shoulder. She fell backwards into Adelina's waiting arms.

The women pushed forward, calling to the Madonna, God, Santa Scolastica and all the angels and saints.

Adelina raised her voice above the commotion. 'I know what to do. I just need to get her back.'

Giulio stepped forward, scooping up Elisabetta in his arms as if his injuries and walking stick belonged to the distant past. Dark hair from her loosened plaits brushed against his hands.

'Show me the way.'

Adelina blushed. He drew Elisabetta closer to his chest while Sister Beatrice and the women crowded in, but he parted them and followed Adelina.

8

Adelina

An out-of-breath Dottor Visconti arrived in our room, his wife, Signora Visconti, two paces behind him, her cheeks unusually pink.

'I came as quickly as I could. Mafalda told me…'

Sister Beatrice rose to her feet from where she had been perched on the side of Elisabetta's bed and greeted the old doctor with a slight bow of deference.

'She's a little better now but…'

He placed a reassuring hand on her arm.

'And Giulio? Where is he?'

'Taking some air in the garden.'

'I'd like to examine him after I've seen Elisabetta.'

'Of course.'

~

Placing his battered leather case on the chair between our beds, Dottor Visconti nodded towards me and turned to address his patient.

'What have we got here?' he said in a friendly voice. 'Good to see you sitting up, young lady!'

Elisabetta was pale and, although still weak, she managed a faint smile for the doctor.

'And you've been taking good care of our patient?' he said, turning back towards me as he pulled his stethoscope from his bag.

'It's happened a few times recently, the fits and fainting,' I offered, flustered at being asked a question. 'I help her until she calms. I hold on to her to make sure she doesn't hurt herself. Mamma taught me… I had a cousin…'

'A fine nurse,' said Dottor Visconti, looking at his wife, who inclined her head.

'And…' I raised my hand towards my forehead and tapped it lightly, hoping Dottor Visconti might pick up on my meaning. I couldn't understand how Giulio came to be walking freely but I wanted him to know there was more to Elisabetta's illness.

Sister Beatrice rushed forward, filling the space between me and the doctor, but from his frown, I knew he'd registered my gesture.

He peered round the imposing Sister Beatrice and smiled. 'You're a loyal friend.'

While her husband took Elisabetta's pulse and listened to her heart, Signora Visconti sat down on Elisabetta's bed and took her hand.

'How are you?'

'A little weak, tired,' replied Elisabetta. She looked over towards me with wide, frightened eyes but I looked down at my feet, guiltily.

'Anything else?'

'I still feel faint,' she hesitated. 'And my head hurts.'

'Do you remember what happened?'

'Giulio walked towards me, and I had the strangest feeling that I know him.'

'Of course, you know Giulio!' Dottor Visconti replied sharply before remembering his child-friendly intonation. 'Everyone in Atina knows Giulio. His is hardly a face you forget!'

'Go on,' said Signora Visconti to Elisabetta, placing a calming hand on her husband's arm.

'I can't explain it, just that we know one another somehow,' she replied.

'And after that?'

'Nothing. Sister Beatrice told me I fainted again. And that it was Giulio who carried me back here.' Her voice was calm, the words delivered as indisputable facts.

'How do you explain that young lady, given that Giulio is an invalid?' Dottor Visconti's lip curled upward with a hint of a sneer.

Elisabetta looked towards Sister Beatrice, then to me.

'I've no explanation,' she said, her features showing no emotion.

Dottor Visconti remained silent, but he turned to his wife.

'As a man of science, you always look for the facts,' she said, laying her hand on her stomach, 'but sometimes science does not offer the answers.' Signora Visconti shot a look across to Sister Beatrice.

'And as a man of science,' he huffed, 'I will need an analysis of the patient's urine and blood. I will also get a second opinion.'

'But you have an opinion?' asked Sister Beatrice.

'Low blood sugar may be causing the fits and fainting. As for the rest of it,' he said, rummaging in his black leather bag, 'a different kind of analysis is needed. I'll send to Roma for a specialist to come and examine her.'

'Perhaps your wife is right, Dottor Visconti, that there is no medical explanation?' ventured Sister Beatrice. 'What happened with Giulio…'

'You women with your fanciful thoughts!' He laughed. 'Will you have me believe, like Mafalda, that this child of ours is the product of a miracle? Even you know, dear Sister, that's not how babies are made!' Dottor Visconti was smirking as he patted his wife's slightly rounded stomach. He winked at the nun.

'You're pregnant?' exclaimed Sister Beatrice. She looked towards Elisabetta, who received the news with no reaction.

Signora Visconti nodded and stroked her stomach. 'I'd given up any hope, after all these years. But the Madonna has seen fit to finally give me the gift of a child.'

She glanced at her husband, who turned away. 'Forty-five isn't really the time to have a first child, but Alfredo assures me I am in good health and, provided I look after myself, there is no reason all should not be well.'

Sister Beatrice stood quite still, her mouth hanging slightly open. She turned to Dottor Visconti.

'Your own wife pregnant after years of childlessness! Giulio walking properly after his injuries! What evidence do you need?'

63

Signora Visconti added her voice to Sister Beatrice's, but Dottor Visconti turned a deaf ear to them and ushered his wife towards the chair beside Elisabetta's bed.

'*Amore*, don't go raising your blood pressure. You know it's not good for you in your condition.'

Sister Beatrice glanced over at Elisabetta, quiet and still in her bed. 'And our patient? In the meantime?'

'Some medication, plus small, regular meals. Certain foods are to be avoided. I shall write out a list. A diary must be kept of what she eats to see how she reacts. Perhaps Adelina can do this?'

At the sound of my name, I nodded meekly. The news of Signora Visconti's pregnancy was a surprise, and I was wondering what Dottor Visconti had meant by the specialist from Roma.

'We'll make sure Elisabetta's well looked after,' replied Sister Beatrice, 'and I'm sure Adelina can record what Elisabetta eats. Can't you, Adelina?'

When I realised what I was being asked to do, a wave of panic swept over me. How was I supposed to write a list when the letters always jump around the page and turn themselves inside out? But it was too late to refuse. Dottor Visconti was already saying goodbye to Elisabetta.

'You're to stay here until you are fully recovered, young lady.'

'I'm not allowed to go to the *santuario*?' said Elisabetta, tears rising in her eyes.

'Not for now, it's for your own good,' he replied, not looking at her.

'But Maria wants me to keep going there.'

Signora Visconti took Elisabetta's hand, but she had started to cry. 'All in good time, Elisabetta,' she said, shushing her gently.

As the clasp of the doctor's bag clapped shut, he turned towards Sister Beatrice. 'A word if I may, before I see Giulio? *In private*.'

'Of course.'

Dottor Visconti left the room, with a flustered Sister Beatrice in his wake. 'Adelina,' she gestured hurriedly, 'find Giulio in the garden.

Tell him Dottor Visconti will come by to see him soon.'

I got down obediently from my bed, although my mind was still racing at the thought of having to write a list. Might Elisabetta help me? She was bound to be cross that I was checking up on her and would probably leave me to try and piece together the words on my own. Signora Visconti leant forward to comfort Elisabetta, and I slipped out of the room, unnoticed.

Rather than go directly to the garden, I went to the toilet first. I tidied my hair in the mirror and tried smiling to calm myself, thinking of Giulio. All I could see were nervous eyes, a wide mouth and a big row of teeth.

As I walked along the corridor towards the garden, the sound of raised voices reached me from Sister Beatrice's study. When I heard Dottor Visconti say Giulio's name, I couldn't help myself. I paused by the door, still as a statue.

'Giulio suffered in the war. We all know that. All I'm saying is don't go getting carried away with these thoughts of miracles.'

'But Giulio's walking properly again. Many people witnessed what happened. It wasn't just me who saw what Elisabetta did.' Sister Beatrice's voice was higher than usual.

'What did Elisabetta do *exactly*?' asked Dottor Visconti, sarcasm dripping from his voice. 'All she did was walk towards him. Giulio chose that moment to walk properly again.'

'*Chose?*' Sister Beatrice sounded upset.

'Come now,' said Dottor Visconti, 'Giulio has always been one who does how he pleases.'

'But his injuries, everyone can see.'

'His face, yes, his eye, of course, and no small measure of distress. But as his doctor, I can tell you I've always doubted there's anything wrong with his left leg.'

Sister Beatrice didn't reply. I leaned in closer, wanting to hear more about Giulio from Dottor Visconti. Giulio wasn't a liar, I was sure of it, but I couldn't understand what had happened, how he was walking properly again, carrying Elisabetta back to the orphanage.

'It's quite common for young men coming back. They've had their lives taken away, they make the most of their injuries. Anger can take many forms.'

'But why would he *choose* to start walking again at *my* prayer group?' asked Sister Beatrice, her indignation clear.

'Why indeed,' replied Dottor Visconti. 'With all the things that are said at your prayer group… do you think anyone in the church hierarchy is going to take this seriously as a miracle, given the other claims you make? Women priests, baptising believers?'

'But your own wife, having a baby after all these years. At her age!'

'Nothing but coincidence. Surely a clever young woman like you can see? A damaged soldier and an older woman who is pregnant. That's all.'

Dottor Visconti's chair scraped across the tiled floor. Startled and not wanting to get caught eavesdropping, I hurried down the corridor towards the garden.

9

Giulio was taking slow, deliberate steps along the uneven path, glancing down at his legs. His fingers glanced the top of a bush with small thin leaves, and he plucked a sprig and brought it to his nose. From where I was standing, I could only see the good side of his face. Tight dark curly hair, an even nose, thin lips. But as he turned towards the bench, the scars and rippled skin on the left side of his face and his sealed eyelid became visible. A man with two faces, I found myself thinking. But I couldn't stop myself wondering what the molten skin of his face might feel like beneath my fingertips.

'Sorry, I didn't mean to stare…' My cheeks warmed as Giulio spotted me from the bench where he'd sat down. 'Sister Beatrice sent me. Dottor Visconti will be coming to see you soon.'

'I'll wait here,' he said. 'Please,' he said, indicating the space on the bench beside him. 'Come and tell me how Elisabetta is.'

I sat down as gracefully as I could beside him, but my hand accidentally caught his arm, sending a ripple through my body. Giulio smiled and shifted to create a space between us. I folded my hands across my chest to hide where the buttons of my dress were straining.

'She's weak, but she's sitting up in bed now,' I replied, looking at the weedy earth, tucking my dirty, shoddy boots to one side, away from Giulio.

'I'm pleased she's recovering,' he replied, casting his eyes across the garden. 'What does Dottor Visconti say?'

'He's given her some medicine and is going to send for another doctor.' That much was true, and I found myself pushing away the conversation between Dottor Visconti and Sister Beatrice which I shouldn't have been listening to.

'Dottor Visconti…' Giulio frowned but didn't finish his thought. 'This garden is so beautiful. I had no idea it was here.'

I looked around at the clumps of tangled bushes and shrugged my shoulders. 'Sister Beatrice doesn't let us out here without supervision, says it's too dangerous, what with the overgrown pond and the walls falling down.'

A silence fell between us as Giulio surveyed the garden with his good eye.

'How's your leg? How are you feeling?' I asked, not daring to look at him.

'I've never felt better,' he said, touching his leg, his voice bright.

'You look well.'

We both laughed, a little nervously, knowing our words were feeble in the light of what had happened.

A gentle breeze delivered confetti from a nearby tree. Pure white petals fell onto my head. Shaking them off, I gathered loose strands of hair back into my bun.

'You missed one,' said Giulio, picking a last piece of blossom from my shoulder, presenting me with the delicate petal as if it were a fine jewel.

I slipped it into my pocket without meeting his eye, my heart beating fast at his gesture.

'Perhaps you can show me the garden?' said Giulio as I stroked the silky petal with my fingertip in the hidden crevice of my pocket. He got up without difficulty. 'You can tell me more about Elisabetta.'

We walked slowly in step with one another, side by side. The gap between us seemed no wider than the blades of grass growing in the path.

Conversation came easily. As I spoke, he leaned slightly towards me, as if my every word was precious. Soon I had told him about *Il Grande Libro dei Santi*, and how the visions had started. I described Elisabetta's nightmares and now her fits, how I knew how to look after her because of how Mamma had looked after my cousin who'd also suffered from seizures.

'I could always tell how kind and caring you are,' said Giulio, looking at me in a way that made me blush.

'What do you mean?'

It was Giulio's turn to turn red from the neck upwards.

'I've been watching the prayer group for the last few weeks… from behind the willow tree.'

'Why didn't you make yourself known?'

He looked away. 'I was too embarrassed to join in, with it only being women. But there was something about Elisabetta that kept drawing me back…'

We came to a right angle of the path where a cherry tree was bursting with ripe fruit. Giulio stopped in front of the tree. He searched through the branches and clumps of swollen red fruits to pick out the two best bunches of cherries. He handed one to me.

The flesh was sweet and juicy, the delicious nectar oozing from the corners of my mouth. Giulio produced a handkerchief from a trouser pocket, watching as I dabbed at my lips. The cherries were the finest I'd ever tasted.

'There you are!' cried Dottor Visconti, leaning heavily on the gatepost to the walled garden. 'I've been looking for you everywhere, Giulio!'

We sprang back from one another like guilty thieves, and I swallowed the rest of the cherry with its stone. It happened so quickly, and I was relieved when it slipped easily down my throat. Giulio cast his stone into the weeds and walked confidently towards Dottor Visconti.

'I wanted to see how you are,' said Dottor Visconti, panting as he approached us, 'but I can see you're moving well.'

'I believe I am cured,' replied Giulio.

'Would you come inside, so that I can examine you?' said Dottor Visconti. By the time he reached us, he was puffing loudly with a hand on his chest.

'I don't think it's me that needs the examination,' said Giulio, indicating the bench with his head.

The elderly doctor eased himself down onto the seat, using the arm of the bench for support. 'It's nothing, just the heat and old age,' he said, catching his breath between words as he mopped sweat from his brow.

'Shall I fetch Signora Visconti?' I asked.

'No, no, that won't be needed,' he replied. 'I don't want her worrying, not in her condition.' He nodded at us to ensure that we understood that what we were seeing was to go no further.

'Some water?' I offered.

'Yes, please, my child.'

Giulio's eyes followed me, but Dottor Visconti held him back with a stern look.

'Let her go, while we talk alone.'

10

Giulio

He hesitated at the door of Sister Beatrice's study, nervous and still angry at the old doctor. Dottor Visconti had arched his eyebrows and shook his head at Giulio's replies. What did the man expect? Giulio had never been good with words and how was he supposed to explain what he himself couldn't grasp? All he'd been able to say was that he had been healed by Elisabetta and couldn't the doctor see that for himself.

When Sister Beatrice opened the door, she greeted him with a smile and a gentle touch on his forearm that let him know that he didn't need to explain himself to her. Giulio's shoulders dropped with relief. A simple painting of the Madonna clutching the Christ child to her breast on the wall ahead of him caught his eye. The Madonna's features were serene, accepting. Pale light peeked through the shuttered window.

'You'll stay here, at the orphanage,' Sister Beatrice said, ushering Giulio to the seat by her desk. 'The chance to recuperate, some peace and quiet.'

With those few words, Sister Beatrice wrapped Giulio in a blanket of comfort and kindness he hadn't known since the warmth of his formidable Nonna, who he'd always looked up to when he was growing up.

This was a blessed chance, he knew it, offered by a woman he admired. She'd set up the prayer group, supported Elisabetta, ran the orphanage with so many children. He was happy but wasn't sure what to say, still a little in awe of her.

'At the piazza they'll pester you about how you're feeling the whole time. Endless enquiries about Elisabetta, the Madonna, at every turn.'

Giulio nodded. She was right about what the reaction would be, the gossip and idle chatter. He had no desire to be the centre of attention, having hidden himself in the cold confines of San Donato for so long.

His hand was resting on his left leg. Beneath his fingers, it was tingling, tiny electric sparks where there had only been dull numbness for so long.

He thought of how he'd been lifted from his body as he'd approached Elisabetta. He'd looked down on himself, the shattered body and soul who'd lived through the blast that had killed every one of his friends in his unit.

'Giulio?'

'Sorry… Yes,' he replied, rolling his shoulders. He found they were loose, freed of the guilty weight he'd borne as the only survivor.

Sister Beatrice sat back in her chair and smiled. 'The old brick shed in the garden. With a bed and a stove there, you'll be comfortable.'

Giulio's mind jumped back to his walk through the overgrown Eden with Adelina and found he was smiling. The uneven paths, the crumbling walls, shrubs choked with weeds, trees reaching unevenly for the sky. Like him, they were all waiting to be remade. Released from years of neglect.

'I'll work for my keep, clear the garden for you.'

He was thinking how he'd take a scythe to the main beds, find their original shape. What might grow best there when the sun was at its highest.

'That would make me very happy,' replied Sister Beatrice.

She was speaking again, telling Giulio about a herb garden she'd tried to start and plants for medicines. His mind was racing ahead.

'It's become so overgrown. There's always so much to do here, and funds, well…'

Sister Beatrice looked across her desk to the open ledger and sighed.

Giulio could already feel the handle of a pickaxe, breaking up the walls, carving up the space. He'd create a paradise of calm and escape for Sister Beatrice. The garden would heal Elisabetta. She could come with Adelina. He would do it for them too.

The garden was his chance at life. He wasn't going to let slip away. He owed it to the memory of his friends.

~

Giulio was true to his promise.

Each morning he made a start at daybreak, leaving the shed that had become his home. In the mornings he mixed mortar. Brick by brick, he slowly built up the walls. In the late afternoons, after a siesta, when the heat of the day had passed, he worked methodically through the beds. Digging out the weeds took all his energy, but he persevered. What he gave the garden in toil and effort, he was well rewarded. Not only was he rejuvenated, but the garden was responding to his careful touch. Order and symmetry were starting to emerge.

Lunch was the best part of the day. Coarse bread, sharp provolone cheese, and a flask of strong red wine. Sometimes even a tasty small salami, which he cut into thick slices with his penknife. He looked forward to seeing Elisabetta and Adelina and was pleased Sister Beatrice had agreed to his suggestion that some fresh air each day would do Elisabetta good and help build up her strength again. They were given the errand of delivering Giulio's lunch, accompanied by a watchful nun chaperone, and were allowed to stay to eat with him. The nun soon complained of the heat and left Elisabetta and Adelina alone with Giulio, satisfied with the arrangement.

Under a shaded shelter, which Giulio had fashioned from felled trees, the three of them shared their food away from the glare of the midday sun. Elisabetta never seemed to manage more than a small crust of bread, and, although weak, she was happy in Giulio's company, as he was in theirs.

Adelina was shy around him, but he liked her too. At first, he was drawn to Adelina's kindness and care towards Elisabetta, but soon he realised that he liked how she asked him about his life before the war, how she listened. That she was interested in who he'd been before his injuries.

'What was your family like?' she asked one day, as she tore off a hunk of bread from the loaf and offered it to him, glancing at him beneath her long eyelashes. Elisabetta swept the breadcrumbs into her lap of her smock to feed the birds, a pair of sparrows who waited expectantly at her feet and always seem to know when it was lunchtime.

'My parents worked the land for the *padrone,* his fields of maize and tomatoes at the edge of Atina. They grazed his cows, milked them, sold the milk for him. We didn't have much, but we didn't go hungry either. Nonno and Nonna, my mother's parents, lived with us too, all in two rooms above the cow shed.'

'It must have been stinky, sleeping above the cows,' giggled Elisabetta, pinching her nose.

'We didn't know any different, though the other kids at school used to tell us we smelt of cowpats!' Giulio laughed. 'But they stopped when Carlo took them on. He had a temper and a good right hook!'

'Is Carlo your brother?' ventured Adelina, catching a change in Giulio's voice.

Giulio looked to the ground. 'Was. My twin. The first born, as he always liked to remind everyone.' He moved in his seat. 'Carlo was killed in a motorbike accident. We were seventeen. The year before I joined the army.'

Adelina looked at him, her wide almond eyes troubled.

'I'm sorry. I shouldn't have pried.'

Elisabetta walked over to Giulio, the breadcrumbs leaving a trail behind her, to the delight of the pecking birds, and leant her head on his shoulder.

'You weren't to know, please don't be upset,' said Giulio, quick to reassure Adelina. She blushed. 'In a way, it's good to say his name again. With the rest of my family gone, I never get to talk about him.'

Adelina chewed her bottom lip, watching a caterpillar wriggle along a leaf into the dense bush beside her.

'Carlo, my twin brother,' Giulio repeated, following Adelina's eyes to glimpse the last slither of the mottled green creature. 'I haven't said his name to anyone in so long.'

Elisabetta pulled away from Giulio, and peered into the bushes, trying to find what they'd been looking at, and when she couldn't see anything, asked, 'What was he like?'

Giulio hesitated, looking past Elisabetta towards Adelina.

'He was a bit wayward, always getting into fights. But he had a good heart underneath. He used to say it was up to him to take care of me, since I was so soft, and people were always taking advantage of me.'

'I'd like a big brother like Carlo,' continued Elisabetta. 'Someone to take care of me,' she said, looking up at Giulio. 'But it doesn't sound like he was a good altar boy like you!'

The corners of Giulio's mouth lifted into a faint smile.

'Carlo would never have helped Padre Bosco. He hated him, said he took money from the poor when he should have been helping them.'

'I'm not the only one who doesn't like Padre Bosco,' said Elisabetta, looking over to Adelina for approval, but Adelina didn't respond.

'Carlo thought I spent too much time at San Donato, but it pleased Mamma and Nonna, and I always liked the peace and serenity of the church,' replied Giulio, watching Adelina, who was rolling a fat breadcrumb back and forth on the table.

Adelina flung the crumb towards the birds who hopped around one another, picking at its edges.

'It's time we were on our way.'

Adelina got up suddenly and beckoned to Elisabetta. Giulio wanted to ask Adelina what was wrong, but he'd hesitated and Elisabetta was already following her out of the garden, waving Giulio goodbye.

~

Over the next few weeks, the girls helped Giulio with the herb garden, his surprise he'd been planning for Sister Beatrice. When she was feeling weak, Elisabetta sat under the shaded shelter and watched as Giulio walked Adelina around the plot he had carefully dug over, showing her how he'd created its shape, where he'd lifted out the larger stones, mixed in shovels full of chicken manure, raked the soil to a fine tilth.

'When you sow the parsley and basil, be sure to scatter the seeds well,' he said, smiling as he bent forward to show her how much distance to leave between them and how to cover them with a fine layer of rich soil. Her eyes concentrated on his fingers.

'Like this?' Adelina followed his instructions attentively, copying his movements.

'Perfect,' he replied, wiping the sweat from his brow as Adelina smiled.

When she was feeling better, Elisabetta helped thin out the growing seedlings to produce strong plants, taking Giulio's hand to help her back up to stand. As he dug up and divided rampant clumps of fragrant thyme and oregano and replanted them, he would tell the girls how by the end of the war, all of his family had passed away while he was in the camp for prisoners of war. He'd returned to Atina with only the pebble from River Mollarino in his pocket, to no family.

'We're all the same,' said Giulio, handing Elisabetta a watering can to fill at the nearby standpipe. 'Orphans. On our own. That's why we understand one another so well.'

Adelina nodded. Her eyes lingered on Giulio, but he had followed Elisabetta to help her open the tap.

11

Adelina

The doctor from Roma was a tall, thin man who made me think of a pencil. He had a severe expression and a full moustache, carefully curled upwards at the ends. Dottor Visconti and Sister Beatrice accompanied him, but they hung back as he took in our shabby room, one side of his moustache twitching in disapproval. When he saw Elisabetta, small and frightened in her bed, there were none of Dottor Visconti's kind words.

'Elisabetta de Angelis?' His tone was cold, the words clipped.

Elisabetta responded with a cowed nod.

He turned to Sister Beatrice, his eyes skimming past me.

'That will be all,' he said, dismissing the three of us with a sharp wave.

Elisabetta's face was etched with fear. I went to hold her hand before leaving, but the doctor's look stopped me in my tracks. I willed Dottor Visconti to say something that might put her at her ease, but he shuffled out of the room without a backward glance.

The doctor from Roma slammed the door behind us.

'What will he do?' I asked Sister Beatrice, but she was fiddling with the rosary beads in the pocket of her long black habit. She didn't reply.

~

In less than fifteen minutes, I was allowed to return to our room. A serious Dottor Visconti, talking to the doctor from Roma, moved aside to let me pass in the corridor. He didn't look at me, and the other doctor paused as I approached, the word 'deluded' hanging in mid-air as the two doctors continued towards Sister Beatrice's study. I wasn't sure what the word meant, but I could tell from the frown on Dottor Visconti's face that it wasn't good news for Elisabetta. I hurried back as quickly as I could.

Elisabetta was sobbing and I sat beside her on the bed and took her hand. She gulped for air, and I held her hand tighter, waiting until she calmed, while my own heart beat fast.

'What happened?' I asked, when her breathing had evened a little.

'He was so mean, Lina,' she sniffed. 'He asked me so many questions, one after the other, so fast.'

'That's his job, isn't it?' I replied. 'He's here to understand what's happening, to help you get better.' Although it hurt to see Elisabetta so upset, I was starting to think that maybe this doctor had the measure of Elisabetta. He'd sort the fits and fainting; we'd be able to get back to how things had been before.

'You don't understand, do you?' said Elisabetta, looking at me in the way I hated. Poor dumb Adelina, always slow on the uptake. 'Whatever I said,' she snivelled, 'he had the answers he wanted already.'

Maybe she hadn't meant to be mean to me. It stung, as it always did, but this time, I couldn't help myself.

'Stop crying! He's here to help you. You've got Sister Beatrice and all the nuns running round after you. Everyone is talking about you, the wonderful little Flower Girl of Atina! Stop feeling so sorry for yourself.'

Elisabetta was shaken and she looked up at me, her eyes pleading.

'What if you're right, Lina? Maybe I was confused... about Maria...'

Elisabetta's voice stumbled over the words. She was frightened but I was still angry.

'You had the chance to stop all this before it got out of hand. I tried to tell you. But you wouldn't listen to me...'

'I don't know what to think. Since what happened with Giulio, Maria hasn't come back to me.' Elisabetta was crying again. 'Perhaps I've made Maria upset. Maybe she thinks I'm drawing attention to myself.'

She pulled her sheet up towards her face to wipe her tears. 'I'm sorry, Lina. I'm tired, all my energy seems to have gone. I don't know what to do.'

I felt bad at having made her more upset. I got up and sat beside her, and she fell into my arms, sobbing. My fingers could feel the edges of her ribs, she'd become so thin.

'I'm sorry. I shouldn't have snapped at you like that,' I said, winding her hair around my index finger as she leant into my shoulder.

Eventually she sat up, still crying, and glanced out of the window towards the river. 'What if the doctor from Roma agrees with Padre Bosco... what will happen to us?'

Us? I looked down at my chewed nails, hoping for an answer to a question that hadn't even occurred to me.

~

She was still crying when Sister Beatrice entered the room.

'What have you done to upset Elisabetta?' Sister Beatrice's sharp words shot in my direction.

Neither of us replied. My eyes were fixed on the ground.

'Another wrong step from you, Adelina, and I'll have you moved from this room and send you to the big dorm with the other girls. You wouldn't want that, would you?'

'No, please don't, Sister Beatrice!'

'I give you the responsibility to look after Elisabetta and this is how you repay my good nature and treat your friend!' she said, waving a piece of paper at me. I recognised it straight away. It was the record of what Elisabetta had eaten which Sister Beatrice had asked me to keep, as Dottor Visconti had instructed.

'What is this?' she shouted. My stomach clenched tight. 'These are the marks of a five-year-old,' she said, pointing at the letters I had tried to form into words.

'I knew you weren't the smartest, but I had no idea you were this stupid! No wonder the doctor from Roma came to the conclusion he did. He didn't give Elisabetta a chance and you certainly didn't help!'

Her words were like a blow to the ribs.

'Be gone with you,' she said, dismissing me with a wave of her hand. 'I want to speak to Elisabetta alone.'

I hovered in the corridor, hot with shame. I wanted to hide away and cry. Again, I'd been found out as stupid and caused more trouble without meaning to. But Elisabetta was saying that she wasn't sure what she was seeing.

Giulio would listen. I was sure of it. Perhaps he could make sense of it all. It hurt that Sister Beatrice had told me off and she'd found out just how poor my writing was. Elisabetta was having doubts, then there was I'd heard Dottor Visconti say to Sister Beatrice, about Giulio's leg. What was I meant to believe? Giulio couldn't have pretended to have a bad leg, surely? Giulio was a good man, I was convinced of it, always so kind and understanding.

Before I left the building, I glimpsed myself in the glass of the door. I tidied my hair and smoothed my dress over my breasts.

It was a hot day and I searched for Giulio, in and out of the vegetable beds, among the flowers, by the herb garden. The door to his shed was shut, there were none of his tools lying around. Sweaty and tired, I sat on the bench, hoping Giulio might return, but he didn't. Thoughts of Elisabetta and Giulio tangled in my mind, like an old ball of string. That's when I remembered what Padre Bosco had said when I'd been to confession. I was to go back and see him whenever I was worried about Elisabetta.

I got up and made my way to the Church of San Donato. At least Padre Bosco didn't treat me as if I was stupid.

12

Giulio

There was a whirl of anticipation in the pews of San Donato, not unlike midnight mass on Christmas Eve, but without the tang of alcohol hanging in the air. Gossip about the famous doctor from Roma and his impressive black car had leapt from the market to the bar and to every home and farm. They all knew he'd been to examine the Flower Girl of Atina at the orphanage. Soon after, Dottor Visconti had been sighted, a folder tucked under his arm, creeping under cover of darkness to see his old friend Luigi, Padre Bosco, at the presbytery.

The church was packed, families squashed together in their Sunday best, people pressed up against one another in the pews. They'd all turned out to hear what Padre Bosco had to say about their brave little flower girl. Hushed chatter had replaced respectful prayer.

Heads turned as Giulio walked tall and resolute down the main aisle. Everyone gawped at him, nudging one another to get a better view, to see whether the miracle had held. Giulio looked straight ahead, ignoring the nods and smiles of encouragement from the congregation, the flurry of whispers. He'd not been back to San Donato since he'd been healed by Elisabetta and hadn't been seen in the piazza either. Rumour had it that he'd not resumed his sacristan duties because Padre Bosco had continued to denounce the girl as a fantasist. There was nothing Atina liked more than a front row view of a difference in opinion. Especially if it involved Padre Bosco, who people respected and loathed in equal measure, on account of his status as the priest and his liking for a backhander.

Giulio reached the front pews where Sister Beatrice had installed herself earlier, at the head of her community of nuns. The children of the orphanage were all in attendance, bar Elisabetta, who was understood to be recovering. Behind them sat the women of the prayer group, who having given up their customary seats at the front, had also arrived early. Together they formed a tight protective wall. They were calm, even the youngest children who normally fidgeted and yawned their way through mass. It was a contrast to the rest of the church, which could barely sit still.

Giulio genuflected without any sign of discomfort, all eyes on him, and took the place which Sister Beatrice had kept free between herself and Adelina, on the other side from Signora Visconti, hand on her pronounced bump. She was alone. Dottor Visconti had stayed at home, claiming a migraine.

'*Tutto bene?*' whispered Giulio as he took his seat. Sister Beatrice smiled as she glanced across at the nuns, children and women from the prayer group.

'And you?'

Giulio nodded, bolstered by the presence of the women.

When he turned to greet Adelina, she was biting her nails and looked away. He wanted to ask her what was wrong but the bell announcing the start of mass rang through the church.

The procession of Padre Bosco and his servers appeared, and the congregation rose to its feet, pews and elderly knees creaking as the first hymn began. Giulio looked again to Adelina, but she was staring straight ahead at the altar. The voices of Sister Beatrice, Signora Visconti and all the nuns joined in harmony with the rest of the congregation.

As the procession filed its way past their group, the young lads dressed up as altar servers couldn't help themselves and each one of them snatched a glance or turned towards Giulio to get a good look. The ragged line provoked a loud tutting from Padre Bosco who resolutely ignored Giulio, Sister Beatrice and the group of nuns and children.

Padre Bosco scythed through the opening prayers in quick succession, barely allowing the congregation time for their responses, leaving them a little giddy and confused. Children, including those from the orphanage, started to fidget and cry, the first to sense something was amiss. Agitated parents tried to placate them, hauling them onto their knees, popping dummies into reluctant mouths. The nuns shushed their charges. They knew to bide their time.

When Padre Bosco came to his homily, his face was red from making himself heard over the commotion and racing through the prayers. He still hadn't looked in the direction of Giulio and Sister Beatrice.

From his lectern, above his parishioners, he slowly held up an official-looking document, held together with black ribbon. He made a silent semi-circle with his eyes around his congregation and when he reached Giulio and Sister Beatrice, he thrust the document towards them. Everyone flinched and gasps rose from the body of the church.

Giulio pulled himself up straighter. Sister Beatrice mirrored him, and Signora Visconti reached out her hand towards Sister Beatrice and she gripped it. The wall of nuns and women from the prayer group drew themselves tight. Adelina stared at her feet.

'I have it here, the report from the doctor from Roma, the eminent *psychiatrist*,' sneered Padre Bosco, letting his fury rest on his last word. His face had turned as red as a ripe tomato, and a vein in his neck throbbed beneath his wrinkled skin. 'The girl is a fraud.'

He spat out the words towards Sister Beatrice and Giulio among disbelieving cries from the congregation.

'Epileptic episodes brought on by diabetes, resulting in periods of mania,' he continued in a slow, deliberate voice. 'Mania,' he repeated. 'Mad!' he shouted, to make himself completely clear. 'The girl is mad. That's what the doctor says.'

All around, people were shaking their heads, some in pity, others in disbelief, exclaiming about what had happened. It was only the group around Giulio and Sister Beatrice who sat completely still, unmoved.

Padre Bosco's diatribe continued, decrying the weak for easily falling prey to the so-called visions of a mad child. Some people shrugged their shoulders, older men nodded their agreement vigorously.

'The devil is among us, here in our small community, masquerading as a child, fed by those with their own motives!' His voice grew louder and angrier as he warmed to his theme.

Giulio had agreed with Sister Beatrice that silence would be the best response to Padre Bosco. Signora Visconti had warned them that her husband had given the report to him, and they'd been prepared for him to decry Elisabetta. But as Giulio sat there, his leg was throbbing. Rage was rising up through his body, a boiling hot anger he couldn't control. He'd felt it before when his brother died. When he'd been a prisoner of war, far from home. Learning that he'd lost his family. That time at the river, because of that same self-satisfied, manipulative man. Padre Bosco.

'Those who visit the so-called shrine are to be under no illusion! They will not be welcome in this church. The girl is a fraud and those who talk of female prophets commit crimes of blasphemy against the very foundations of our most sacred church!'

Padre Bosco was in his stride, and from the glint in his eyes, Giulio knew he was enjoying lording it over the people of Atina. Worst of all, he was condemning an innocent child. Elisabetta, a child he loved.

Giulio, the quiet, undemanding twin, couldn't take a single word more. He stood up with fire in his belly and conviction in his heart.

'You,' he said, pointing an angry finger at Padre Bosco. 'You can't ignore me. I can walk again.'

The old priest recoiled behind his lectern, his eyes glistening with anger, as a shocked collective intake of breath was heard across the church. People looked to one another, unsure how to react.

'Look at me!' said Giulio, his arms raised as he walked out into the aisle of the church and walked up and down for all to see.

'Look at me,' he cried, anguished. 'Elisabetta is no fraud.'

He swung round to face the altar. 'You!' he said, pointing to Padre Bosco. 'You should be ashamed of yourself. Call yourself a man of God? She's an innocent child! You're the one who doesn't recognise the Madonna.'

Under his breath, Giulio muttered a swear word he'd never used in his life but which everyone instantly understood.

Head held high, he marched out of the church. The women from the prayer group rose as one to follow him down the aisle. Next came the nuns and children. United, Sister Beatrice and Signora Visconti brought up the rear, with Adelina dragging her feet behind them. The only sound in the church was of women gathering their bags and children to follow them.

At the altar, Padre Bosco was left standing like a jilted bride.

13

Adelina

The white communion dress hung loosely on Elisabetta, swamping her. She looked in the mirror, her arms poking out from the folds of material like sharp sticks. She turned away. All the pleasure of having worn the dress before had disappeared.

'I'll ask Sister Beatrice if she has some lace or ribbon,' I said, pinching the excess satin between my fingers, 'I can tie a bow around your waist. It'll look better, you'll see.'

Elisabetta nodded without conviction. 'You'll stay close to me, won't you? You and Giulio, like you both promised?'

'Of course, we will.' I took both her hands in mine. They were clammy, and Elisabetta withdrew hers quickly.

'Perhaps Sister Beatrice is right,' said Elisabetta. 'If I go back to the shrine… I might see her again…'

I didn't reply. The beautiful, quiet time at the river, just the two of us, the excitement of doing something we shouldn't, was a faded memory. Now the talk was only of pilgrims, the next miracle or Padre Bosco's fury at San Donato. But I couldn't speak of this with Elisabetta. She was growing weaker each day, and I was trying my best to protect her.

'Do you think there'll be lots of people?' she asked.

I shrugged my shoulders, not wanting to frighten her. Sister Beatrice had received several telephone calls from journalists in Roma and even Milano. It was rumoured *La Stampa* and *Oggi* were coming. They were interested that a priest had denounced a little girl as insane and wanted to see The Barefoot Flower Girl of Atina for themselves. Large crowds were anticipated.

It was Giulio who'd told me, after I'd feigned to Elisabetta that I was checking on how the herb garden was coming along. I'd barely seen him for days; he was more often in Sister Beatrice's study now, rather than the garden. I'd wanted to talk to him about what Elisabetta had told me, her doubts, but as I approached, he looked hurried, jerked his head towards the orphanage, and quickly told me how he was helping to plan Elisabetta's return to the *santuario* and that he was due to see Sister Beatrice. My courage ebbed away. As I watched him leave, my mind returned to Dottor Visconti's words, that he'd believed that Giulio had always been able to walk.

'We know who won't be there,' said Elisabetta, filling the silence, 'and we won't miss that rotten old priest!' I turned away, not wanting to be reminded that I had been the one to alert Padre Bosco about what the doctor from Roma had thought of her.

Sister Beatrice had told Elisabetta a much gentler version of what had happened at Sunday mass. Ashamed of my part, I'd gone along with Sister Beatrice's story. She hadn't mentioned how Padre Bosco had waved a copy of the report by the doctor from Roma at the congregation, spitting with satisfaction that Elisabetta was mad. No mention was made to her that he'd forbidden parishioners to return to the shrine. Or that people had kept quiet at the time but had been talking of nothing else since and had been visiting the *santuario* in ever-growing numbers.

After Padre Bosco's outburst at San Donato, Sister Beatrice declared that if the people saw Elisabetta again, they would know that she was just an ordinary girl who'd been visited by the Madonna, not the manipulative liar Padre Bosco or the doctor from Roma made her out to be.

Elisabetta would return to the shrine, she'd announced, and she chose a date and time, insisting that was when it should happen.

Desperate to see Maria again, Elisabetta agreed to Sister Beatrice's plans.

Frail and thin as Elisabetta was, I didn't think it was a good idea.

~

'Ready?' Elisabetta gathered her rosary beads to her chest. I took her arm and felt a familiar comfort as she leaned into me to support her. Her steps were slow, hesitant but I held her strong.

Waiting inside the entrance of the orphanage were Signora Visconti, her hand resting on the curve of her pregnant belly, and Giulio. As soon as Signora Visconti glimpsed Elisabetta, she rushed towards her and shook the white lace mantilla from her head, fashioning a bow around Elisabetta's waist.

While she fussed around Elisabetta, I glanced at Giulio with an awkward smile. I'd never seen him in a suit before. His white shirt looked crisp and smart against his skin, golden from working in the garden. He returned my smile, his good eye resting on me before turning away. The dressmaker who made the nun's habits had taken my measurements, and although my new grey dress was a little old-fashioned, it was cinched at the waist with a thin black belt. With the darts and buttons, it fitted perfectly.

Sister Beatrice rushed out of her study, brushing a stiff new habit as she approached Elisabetta, who nodded obediently in response to Sister Beatrice's enquiries about how she was feeling. Pushing back her sleeve, Sister Beatrice tapped the glass face of a watch I'd never seen her wear. Giulio stepped forward and we took our places.

We filed down the orphanage steps in a tight, solemn procession. Sister Beatrice was at the front, head bowed in respect, followed by a small group of her most devout nuns and Signora Visconti, hands clasped tight in prayer. Next came Giulio, with Elisabetta following him closely. I brought up the rear just behind her, anxiously watching her step.

A hush fell among the people who had gathered in large numbers, as Giulio had predicted. Everyone was dressed in their Sunday best, straining to get a look at Elisabetta. In the silence, the steps of our little procession crunched on the loose gravel. Our route to the river seemed unfamiliar, crowds blotting out the grassy field, blurring the edges of the wood. Aware of people watching me, I concentrated on Elisabetta's back, thinking how frail she seemed, but I kept a finger on the belt of my dress and pulled myself a little taller.

As we passed, some onlookers made the sign of the cross, others bowed their heads or whispered to one another. Every so often, the voices of older women punctured the silence.

'She doesn't look well. *Poverina!*'

'What's happened to her? Padre Bosco should be ashamed of himself!'

Elisabetta stared straight ahead, her head raised towards Giulio's shoulders, her fingertips clasping her rosary beads. She was weak and walked slowly, but with each step, the crowd silently urged her on, willing her forward, their eyes trained on her pale face or tiny bare feet. I found myself moved by their devotion.

When we reached the shrine, the melody of 'Ave Maria' reached us on the breeze, sung in devoted rounds. The beauty of the sound caught in my throat.

The *santuario* now had a formal entrance hung with colourful blue and white banners. Stalls stacked high with bottles of holy water, medallions, and statues of the Madonna marked our way. On a table, there were several collection boxes, some stuffed so full, that banknotes spilled out of the top. I'd never seen so much money.

Gone were the picnic blankets, replaced by rows of chairs arranged in a semi-circle around the spring. They were all taken, with many people standing. The broken Madonna was still in place on the rock boulder, but my makeshift wall of pebbles was gone. Seated there were important-looking people wearing medals and sashes in the colour of the Italian flag. A sick feeling rose from my stomach.

Elisabetta turned to me, panic in her eyes. Reading our expressions, Giulio stepped forward and held out his arm for her. Relieved, she took it, and Giulio walked her to the seat next to Sister Beatrice. As Giulio sat beside me, just behind Elisabetta, my heart was racing.

The last round of 'Ave Maria' was carried away on the mountain air. Silence settled on the congregation. Into this came the sound of the river lapping downstream and the birds singing in the trees. The sky was an uninterrupted blue, like the cloak of the Madonna herself, and was crowned with a golden sun. For a fleeting moment, it was the place where Elisabetta and I had spent the early mornings together.

An old woman coughed near me, setting off an echo of coughing across the crowd. Once it had died down, Sister Beatrice rose to her feet.

'Today we come together to honour the Madonna of Atina. There are some who would have you believe She does not make herself known here. And that those who know different are not to be trusted!'

She drew a deep breath, looking to Elisabetta, and addressed the crowd.

'Let us pray that divisions are healed and that we may come to bear witness in our lives to the qualities of love and kindness that Our Blessed Mother wants us to share.'

Her simple words were measured, with no reference to Elisabetta or Padre Bosco. She didn't mention what had happened to Giulio, or Signora Visconti's pregnancy, and sat down, tapping her new watch. In the faces of the crowd, it was clear no more was needed. By the time Elisabetta stood up to lead on the first decade of the rosary, as had been agreed, the entire congregation was united in devoted silence.

We chanted our way through the *Ave Marias* and the *Gloria* in harmonious unison. All eyes were on Elisabetta. The sun was beating down on us.

At the *Misteri Gloriosi*, the rosary beads suddenly slipped through Elisabetta's fingers.

A gasp rose from the crowd.

With a broad smile, Elisabetta turned to Sister Beatrice, then to me, a triumphant glint in her eyes.

'She's here with me,' she announced. 'Maria's here!' Her voice was trembling.

Whispers ran through the crowd. People nudged one another, straining to get a look at Elisabetta. Then they turned their eyes to the sky, and then to one another.

Elisabetta raised her head towards the sun. For what seemed like an eternity, she stared at the sky, completely entranced, her smile widening as she opened her arms in an embrace. Nobody dared to speak as they looked up too, shielding their eyes from the brightness of the sun, its rays glowing bright at the edges like a shining crown.

My eyes were trained on Elisabetta. When I caught sight of the first barely perceptible shaking of her shoulders, I nudged Giulio. Together, we caught her as she fell.

The crowd gasped.

At that moment, as Giulio and I held Elisabetta, darkness fell on the shrine. The air grew cold. All around people were shouting, calling the Madonna's name, the noise growing louder and louder, eerie in the darkness.

Giulio had one hand out supporting Elisabetta, the other on mine, sending a shiver of warm pleasure through the chill.

The moon had covered the sun.

But I didn't understand what an eclipse was at the time.

14

Giulio

A harsh sun had baked the earth into a dry crust. Giulio was stripped to the waist, sweat shining on the muscles that had grown taut and defined. He was digging deeper into a ditch, where he was determined to lift all the persistent fleshy tendrils and nodules of bindweed that threatened the success of the garden. Surrounded by mounds of soil, he did not hear the girls approaching.

'Boo!'

Giulio recoiled with a strength that far exceeded the volume of Elisabetta's mischievous call. He quickly retrieved his shirt lying on the side of the ditch, trying to push away the fateful explosion that burst back into his mind.

'Sorry, I didn't mean to make you jump that much,' said Elisabetta, giggling at the success of her prank. She'd recovered well after collapsing at the shrine, buoyed by having seen Maria again and the crowds who'd experienced her presence too.

Adelina's eyes were on Giulio's naked torso. Reeling and flustered, he didn't want her to see the embarrassment of jagged skin and scars which covered the left side of his body. He tried to pull on his shirt, but his left arm got tangled in the sleeve. When he caught her eye, he thought she would turn away, disgusted by his body. But she didn't.

Elisabetta was still laughing at how she had caught out Giulio and didn't notice how Adelina was staring at him.

'You really got me there,' he said, his fingers fumbling with the buttons of his shirt. He was shaky still and trying not to look at Adelina. 'If I'd managed to frighten a grown up like that when I was in primary class, I'd be pretty pleased with myself too.'

'I'm eleven years old, I'll have you know,' Elisabetta replied, 'though lots of people think I'm younger, just because I'm small.'

'You're not eleven years old, surely?'

'She's telling the truth,' Adelina replied, glancing at Giulio briefly, her cheeks still flushed red.

'No, you can't be,' said Giulio, shaking his head at Elisabetta.

'She is.' Adelina was quiet, but insistent.

'I was born on midsummer's eve, 1938. That makes me eleven years old,' chirruped Elisabetta as if reciting her times tables.

Giulio looked at Adelina for confirmation. She nodded. He didn't have to ask Elisabetta to repeat her birth date.

It was a day that was etched in his memory.

~

Padre Bosco had made it sound so simple. Sixteen-year-old altar boy Giulio was to go on a mission, as he called it. To collect a baby from a fallen mother and uncertain future, and to deliver the child to grateful new parents.

'There's a little something in it for you too,' Padre Bosco had said, releasing a banknote from a fat wad in the pocket of his cassock, rather than the church safe.

'Midnight, at River Mollarino. Don't be late. When she's given you the baby, take the back road to the lemonade seller's house and mind no-one sees you. Hand the child over. When it's done, come back here.'

Giulio had swallowed hard, every instinct in his body warning him not to get involved. Maybe it would be straightforward, he reasoned, trying to ignore the tightness in his stomach. If he could slip the banknote into his mother's grateful hand, it would make feeding the family in the coming weeks a good deal easier.

Padre Bosco had waved the cash at Giulio with a knowing smile and put it back in his pocket, making it clear that payment would only be made on completion of the task.

His eyes fixed on the ground, Giulio had nodded weakly. Saying no to Padre Bosco was not an option.

Midsummer dusk was descending as Giulio had set off for River Mollarino. The last birdsong disappeared into the shadows of the trees, overlaid by insistent cicadas. He didn't need to get there so early, he kept telling himself, but he'd been nervous all day, getting into a petty argument with his brother Carlo over whose turn it was to feed the cows. It'd ended up with Giulio filling the troughs, shoving the hay at the disgruntled cows who'd shuffled and mooed in response. The door of the cow stall had shuddered on its hinges as Giulio had slammed it shut.

It was a languid night, barely a whisper of relief from the heat of the day. Sweat prickled Giulio's brow. He was still angry at himself for not standing his ground with Carlo. But most of all at Padre Bosco for making him do his dirty work.

He kicked at a few pebbles on the path down to the river, sending them bouncing ahead of him.

The call of a distant owl had pierced through the hot night. Giulio had thought about going back to ask Padre Bosco more about his so-called mission, and found himself imagining the woman and child, but he knew no answers would be forthcoming.

Close by, another owl responded. Giulio looked up into the trees and caught the flash of a pair of green eyes trained on him. He turned away quickly, hoping to evade his mother's superstitions, but the sight of the owl made him uneasy, and he hurried on.

Misfortune, that's what his mother always said about owls. Giulio told himself that it was to do with the fate of the mother and child, about to be separated. He had a job to do, that was all. But even as he tried to convince himself, a creeping sense of foreboding took hold. He thought of turning back, but he knew he had to go through with it.

As he approached the river pounding downstream, Giulio was startled by movement in the dark water ahead of him. At first, he thought it must be a heron diving for a fish, but just as he realised it was impossible at this time of night, a plaintive wailing came from the same direction.

Giulio rushed towards what sounded like a baby crying. He saw a woman struggling in the water, the sling holding the baby to her unravelling fast.

He knew if he didn't get there before it came away from her body, the baby had no chance.

He flung himself towards her and dived into the icy water.

With the intense focus he had developed over the years waiting for a pull on his fishing line, he snatched the baby from her mother just as the material fell away.

The baby spluttered but he held the child tight in one arm, raising its little body out of the water. With a strength he didn't know he had, he wrenched and pulled the woman to the surface with his other arm, all the while kicking frantically against the water.

She coughed and gasped for breath and let herself be dragged by Giulio onto the pebbles, while the baby shrieked with all its might.

'I'm so sorry, Elisabetta, I'm so sorry,' she repeated, brushing water from the baby's face as Giulio guided her, stumbling, to the pebbles. 'I don't know what I was doing. If I can't be a mother to you... Forgive me, my child... please forgive me.'

Giulio handed the baby back to the woman and she cradled her close to her chest, kissing her forehead. He leant forward, his hands on his knees, trying to regain his breath. He could barely bring himself to look at them, overwhelmed by the sadness of this mother who'd rather leave this world with her child than be parted from her.

What had he done by saving them?

~

In the garden, Giulio was left alone with his memories of that night, sadness weighing down on him. All around, the vegetable beds were bursting with plump tomatoes, fingers of long runner beans hanging in heavy clumps, fat peppers and zucchinis and tall leafy spires of maize. The garden he'd brought back to life with great care. Yet he'd failed to see what had been in front of him all the time. He stopped under the shade of the plum tree. All the fruit was gone, except for a few brown mouldy plums scattered around the base of the tree. As he pieced together his memories and what he now knew about Elisabetta, he prodded at one of the plums with his foot. It fell apart, covering his shoe with rancid juice and exposing a cluster of tiny maggots.

He'd never questioned why he'd been drawn to Elisabetta at the prayer group. Yes, he'd known there was something special, mystical about her. But he could never have imagined she was the child he'd saved at River Mollarino, bound to the mother whose love for her was so great she would rather life ended than that they be parted. He'd missed every trace of the invisible thread that connected him to Elisabetta.

When Elisabetta had told him the date of her birth, he saw again her mother's pleading eyes as she sought forgiveness from her baby daughter at the river. Their eyes were the same deep pools of light blue. Elisabetta's pale skin had the same translucent quality. Mother and daughter shared a certain aura – otherworldly, as if no one could ever come close.

Giulio hung his head as he remembered how the mother had clutched Elisabetta, keeping the baby's head close to her heart until the very last moment. He couldn't bring himself to look at her. She was wretched, tears streaming down her face.

'Take her, please, before I change my mind,' she had said, offering the child up to Giulio.

Hesitating, Giulio had stepped forward. His body was shaking but he accepted the baby gently from her reluctant arms, bringing her close to his chest, and holding her tight to him, afraid he might drop her. Her face nuzzled into the nape of his neck, her breath warm on his skin.

He walked away with the baby without looking back at the mother. If he had turned round, she would have seen he was crying too.

~

He'd only seen the woman one other time. Almost two years later, in May 1940, Giulio was in the back of an army truck, on his way to fight for Italy's glory. He'd spotted her among the crowds of crying mothers and wives gathered to wave goodbye to their loved ones at the market square. Suddenly aware that he may never return to Atina, he pushed his way to the front to see her better, and he waved at her frantically, his heart pounding.

Dressed in best funeral mourning black, she looked up and tried to make her way towards him, but there were too many people pressed up against one another. Too far away to speak to, he gestured towards the other end of the piazza, mimicking taking a drink to quench his thirst. She looked over her shoulder but when she turned back towards him, the truck was pulling away. Giulio could only hope that she'd understood his meaning, where she might find her daughter. The child he had he handed over as a baby to the family of the lemonade seller.

~

Under the cover of darkness, the key eased open the side entrance of San Donato and Giulio crept in. Early to bed, early to rise was Padre Bosco's mantra, but Giulio kept his movements small and careful, grateful that Padre Bosco hadn't asked him to return his set of keys. He'd probably forgotten his previously dutiful sacristan still had them.

The registers were ordered according to date and type. Red leather for baptisms, brown for confirmation, green for marriages and black for funerals. Giulio struck a match, the flame picking up the dust on the shelves, and he lit a candle. His fingertip ran backwards, skimming the gold embossed Roman numerals on the black run of registers. He lifted down the volume he was looking for. May 1940. On the day Giulio left Atina to begin his sentence in the Italian army, there'd only been one funeral. The funeral Elisabetta's mother would have attended.

Antonelli, Luisa. Seventy-two years of age.

Giulio's mind clambered back in time, to what he could remember of Luisa and the Antonelli family.

There would have been a good turnout for Luisa's funeral. The women of Atina, including his own mother and grandmother, paid Luisa regular visits, curious to learn about what the future held for them. Luisa's skill at reading the cards was well known. Crops were sown according to her guidance, relationships pursued or abandoned.

Luisa had never married and lived on the road out of Atina with her sister, Romana. Widowed and highly strung, Romana had three children, a daughter and two sons, Giulio vaguely remembered but they had all left years before. She had always fretted after her eldest, Franco, whose reputation in Atina had been as someone to best steer clear of, on account of his murky dealings and liking for settling scores with his fists. Believing her son to be unjustly vilified, Franco had been forced to seek a life overseas and rumour had it, Romana had gone mad as a result.

Giulio carefully replaced the funeral register, without stirring the dust. He reached for the red shelf, the baptism records of the new lives in the parish. 1938 had been a bountiful year, thanks to Mussolini's Battle of the Births, encouraging large families. His eyes scanned the many entries for June. Baptisms normally took place within the first week after birth. But in Elisabetta's case, an adoption, it may have been a little later. His finger rushed forward to July.

He knew the family name he was searching for – De Angelis – the family of the lemonade seller and his wife.

De Angelis, Elisabetta. Born 21 June 1938.

Her mother's name was registered as De Angelis, Grazia. She was the woman Giulio had handed baby Elisabetta to, grateful for a daughter she'd never been able to bear herself. She wasn't the woman who'd given birth to Elisabetta.

When Giulio had returned from the war, he'd found out little about the death of Grazia De Angelis. Collaborators of the Nazi occupants of Atina were only ever remembered in hushed whispers. The unspoken pact not to relive their darkest hours of suffering, so close to the front line and carnage at Monte Cassino, held firm. Giulio only knew that Elisabetta's adoptive father, a fellow soldier, had died early in the war in some distant field.

Giulio snapped the register shut. Elisabetta had a mother. It wasn't Grazia De Angelis. Only he and Padre Bosco knew this.

Wherever she was, Giulio made up his mind to find Elisabetta's mother. She was ill, she needed her mother, the woman who'd returned to mourn Luisa Antonelli. The same woman he'd saved from drowning herself and her baby in the river as a sixteen-year-old lad.

~

Giulio attended morning mass the next day. He'd always enjoyed the slow rhythm of the early mass, the meditative quality of communal prayer before the day became one of toil and labour. The bells for the blessing of the bread and wine rang clearer, the blood of Christ was sharper on the tongue.

The ageing widows of the congregation had always treated him kindly, mostly out of pity. Few of them were left, but he was touched by their warm, if surprised, greetings. He'd heard that attendance had dwindled since Padre Bosco set himself against the Flower Girl of Atina and was grateful that the old women still welcomed him, in spite of his outburst in the house of God.

Entering the church from the sacristy, Padre Bosco quickly spotted Giulio. *'You've come back. I knew you would,'* his expression seemed to say. Giulio bowed his head in reply. He'd let the priest believe for the duration of the mass that he was contrite. The power of the service would do the rest. He accepted communion from him with due reverence. At the final blessing, he knelt again to pray, allowing the old ladies to leave one by one, so that he was alone in the church. When he heard the last footsteps, he sat up and waited.

It wasn't long before Padre Bosco shuffled in, the holes in the elbows of his cardigan visible now that his vestments had been tidied away.

'It's good to see you return to San Donato,' he said, a self-satisfied look on his face.

'Padre Bosco,' he replied, bowing slightly. He'd keep up the pretence for as long as necessary.

'Won't you come and take coffee with me?'

Giulio nodded.

'You know your way,' said Padre Bosco, leading them back through the sacristy.

Giulio followed him through the labyrinth of doors and corridors which separated the main body of the church from the presbytery. A pang of unexpected nostalgia hit him. He'd missed the smell of lingering incense, and he searched out the carved wooden angel in an alcove and the statue of St. Francis of Assisi that he'd always liked, bowing his head in reverence.

The door of the sacristan's cupboard was ajar. It was a mess, stuffed with used collection envelopes and spent candle stubs. The stock of communion wine and wafers clearly needed replenishing. Gone was the careful order of Giulio's touch.

He'd always enjoyed the nature of his sacristan duties, the quiet care he brought to San Donato, and although Padre Bosco never uttered a word of praise or gratitude, he knew he had earned his respect. Even if he'd never match Peppe Morelli in Padre Bosco's eyes. Giulio's neighbour when he was a child, Peppe had been Padre Bosco's sacristan when he had been a younger priest and was mentioned from time to time in obvious admiration. No-one in Atina knew what had become of Peppe Morelli, who had left under a cloud as a young man.

In the hallway they stopped as Padre Bosco called out to his housekeeper. 'Signora Paola, an extra cup of coffee this morning please. Giulio's here.'

From the kitchen came an exclamation of surprise and a clattering of cups. Giulio smiled at the noise and looked towards the kitchen, half expecting Paola to pop her head round the door. His attention was drawn to the table with its white crochet cloth where post was placed, ready for Paola to take away with her when she had finished her duties.

He recognised the old-fashioned spidery scrawl of the priest. What he hadn't expected was an envelope addressed to a certain Monsignor Roberto at a Bishop's Palace far away in the north of Italy. Padre Bosco saw Giulio's eyes on the letter and turned it over.

'Come through,' he said, moving him on. 'Take a seat.'

Giulio had never cared for the parlour where Padre Bosco met parishioners. With its heavy, ornate furniture and display cabinets full of religious ephemera, statues, and formal coffee services, it had the air of an expensive museum, designed to remind parishioners who was in charge.

'How are you keeping?' asked Padre Bosco. 'I hear you are doing a grand job with the gardens of the orphanage.'

'You'd see for yourself if you came to visit,' Giulio replied in a matter-of-fact tone.

'Well, you know why that is.' Padre Bosco stirred two heaped spoons of sugar into his coffee.

Giulio looked him in the eye. 'Why exactly?' he asked.

'All the nonsense about the apparitions. You know what the doctor from Roma said. I don't want to be giving any credence to that girl.'

'The Madonna has visited Elisabetta again. The crowds saw her. I'm sure you've heard all about it.'

Padre Bosco turned away, staring out of the window with its view onto the piazza.

'And what about me?' Giulio asked. 'It's here for all to see. How I can walk properly again. You can't go on ignoring her, denying her.'

Padre Bosco turned back to him. The friendliness had evaporated.

'What is it you've come for?'

Giulio drew a deep breath. He'd been brought up to respect the authority of the church, of the man he was sitting opposite.

'We both know that Elisabetta is the child you asked me to take from her mother.'

Padre Bosco swatted at a fly that was buzzing around his head and landed on his bulbous nose.

'And?'

'Elisabetta has a mother, who never wanted to give her away. The child is not at all well…'

'You're right there, at least,' replied Padre Bosco, tapping his forehead. 'The child is mad, just as the good doctor from Roma confirmed. Soon this nonsense will stop once and for all.'

'What do you mean?'

A wave of nauseous apprehension came over Giulio as the old priest stood up, an arch smile on his face.

'I believe you have a garden to attend to,' he replied, reaching for the letter on the table and putting it in the pocket of his cassock.

15

An unkempt vine grew thick around the entrance to Romana Antonelli's home, the long tendrils and shrivelling grapes obscuring the door. As Giulio raised his hand to knock at a smooth spot between splinters of green paint, he wasn't hopeful of a response.

Nobody seemed to know or care about Romana, even though some of the older women still remembered her fortune-telling sister Luisa fondly.

It was a beautiful, crisp morning. From here, the sound of the mountain water racing over the pebbles was soothing, a bend in the river bringing it close to the Antonelli home. Thick bushes crowded in on what looked like a direct path to the water's edge.

He was about to leave when he heard a heavy bolt sliding back. He took a nervous step backwards, his breathing growing faster.

The door inched open, revealing a tiny, frail woman. Her stained dress sagged at her shoulders, and white hair escaped from a crumpled bun. Like many old folk, her eyes were clouded but gave a hint of a familiar light blue.

'There you are, Franco,' she said, scarcely making a sound.

Giulio hesitated.

'Well, don't just stand there.' A hand clawed with arthritis beckoned him in.

Inside it was dark, the air stale. Dirty plates and bowls seemed to cover every available surface. Giulio edged past crates of jars used for preserving tomatoes, stacked unevenly on top of one another, drawing in his nostrils as he went. Mouse droppings were clustered in the corners, and he stubbed his toe on a demijohn which held the thick sediment of what was once wine.

'It's difficult looking after yourself at my age when all your family has gone,' she said, squinting in his direction as she used the edge of the table to guide herself into a nearby chair.

Giulio knew she couldn't make out much of him. His altar boy conscience was on the verge of getting the better of him. He ought to tell her that he wasn't her beloved son returned from America, but then he thought of Elisabetta. Even though she'd initially been better after seeing the Madonna and her collapse at the *santuario*, she had become much frailer again and her visits to the garden had stopped. He had to help her.

He slid onto the opposite chair and remained silent.

'Why's it taken you so long to come back, Franco?' she sighed. '*Ti aspettavo.*'

Giulio coughed as he tried to think of what to say.

'*Eh, quel che è fatto è fatto,*' she continued. She wrung her mottled hands. One of the raised veins was throbbing beneath the loose skin.

'Your brother Antonio didn't return,' she sighed. 'I remember the day Marcello brought the telegram, like it was yesterday. *Bon alma* Antonio, he died in some frozen field in Russia. For that bastard Mussolini.'

Giulio nodded in agreement at the old woman's sentiment, still searching for words.

'As for your sister,' she said, her voice dripping with spite, 'see for yourself. Hasn't been back in years. There's a letter up there.'

She indicated with her head to the mantlepiece above the fireplace where ashes lay deep. Giulio stepped forward and picked up an envelope, his heart pounding.

The writing was neat, clearly a woman's hand. The stamp was of a king's head and the mark next to it suggested it'd been posted six months previously.

He prised the envelope open, holding his breath.

Inside was a letter, two banknotes with the same king's head and a photo. He turned over the photo.

When she heard his breath catch, the old woman picked up again in the same resentful tone. 'She knows I can't read. But I can see just about enough to know she has a baby. Am I right? Is it a son?'

Giulio looked at the woman in the photo he'd only met twice in his life, but who'd affected him so deeply. Her hair was cut shorter, framing the face which had lost none of its beauty. Full of maternal pride, she held a baby close to her chest, yet Giulio couldn't help but sense sadness in those blue eyes.

'Yes, his name is Christian,' Giulio replied, stumbling over the pronunciation of this foreign name written on the reverse of the photo.

'What sort of name is that?' the old woman asked.

Giulio turned over the envelope in his hand. She'd written her name and address on the back.

Mrs Maria Atkins, 15 Woodland Road, St. Albans, England.

'*Inglese,*' he replied. 'She's living in England.'

'I'm sure she's making a good life for herself. She always knew how to look after herself, that one. At least she had a boy.'

In his hands, the envelope felt like it was on fire. He now knew Elisabetta's mother's name. Maria. And he had her address, more than he'd hoped for. A mother again, surely she'd want to help the child she'd never wanted to give away?

'She's sent you some money,' he said, waving the notes at the old woman. 'I'll take it to the bank, get it changed,' he said, thinking on his feet, stuffing the envelope in his pocket. 'Then I'll come back. Tidy this place up for you.'

The old woman sat back in her chair and nodded.

'You're a good son, Franco.'

~

The words Giulio wrote to Maria didn't come close to the emotion he felt. They were brief and when he read them back, he was ashamed of his schoolboy language. Afraid too, that someone else could read the letter, though he couldn't imagine Maria's life in England or who might read his Italian.

For two weeks, he thought only of Maria. It'd been eleven years since he'd taken Elisabetta away from her, to deliver her baby to the lemonade seller's family, as instructed by Padre Bosco. Yet he could remember clearly. How she had watched every little movement of her daughter, as if committing all the details to memory. The kindness in her voice, not only as she spoke to the child but to him, as if she had known how much this incident would come to mark his life too. And of course, he had never forgotten her beauty, which had left an imprint on his sixteen-year-old mind. Marble skin, long dark hair, and light-blue eyes.

Waiting for a reply to his letter was agony. He feared it might never come. He re-read Maria's letter to her mother again and again. The way she described her English husband, Colin, unsettled him. He sounded cold and distant. But Giulio liked the look of the little boy, Christian. With his dark hair and piercing eyes, the resemblance to his mother was striking.

~

Each day Elisabetta was growing weaker and was unable to return to the garden. But Adelina found an excuse to return alone.

'Elisabetta's been having more fits… I don't know what to do… I've tried talking to Sister Beatrice…I'm not sure about what she sees…'

Adelina looked at Giulio beneath her long eyelashes for some reassurance, but Giulio remained quiet, gazing past her, towards the river. Initially he'd been pleased to see her, and he'd toyed with telling her how he'd come to discover Elisabetta's real mother. But as she spoke, voicing her doubts about Elisabetta's visions, he found he was annoyed at her. Elisabetta had saved him, of that he was certain. He decided to keep Maria to himself.

The next day, a letter arrived addressed to Giulio, with an English postmark.

It was the same day Signora Visconti went into labour.

16

Adelina

Elisabetta didn't want to go. Neither did I. But Dottor Visconti insisted.

'Mafalda can't take much more. And the baby seems to be giving up too. She believes only Elisabetta can help her now. *Please.*' His voice trembled as he pleaded with Sister Beatrice.

'Elisabetta isn't well enough to be going anywhere. You of all people should know. Yet you want to bring her to your wife, you want Elisabetta to save her, even though you and your doctor from Roma still don't believe her. Shame on you!'

Sister Beatrice turned away. 'It's only for Mafalda that I'm letting you take Elisabetta.'

He hurried us towards his black car. My chest grew tight. Elisabetta was clinging onto my arm, huddled in a blanket, shivering. She took small, uneven steps.

Dottor Visconti slammed the car door behind us and gripped the steering wheel with both hands as the car sped off, throwing up gravel towards a grim-faced Sister Beatrice.

The car smelt of antiseptic and juddered and bounced over the holes in the road. Nobody talked. Elisabetta slid out an icy hand from under her blanket and I pressed it tight, although I was nervous too.

As we crossed the threshold into their impressive home, Signora Visconti was howling in agony. Her screaming frightened me but as Elisabetta clutched at my arm and looked at me with hollow eyes, I held her steady.

'This way,' said Dottor Visconti, panic flashing in his eyes. We followed him reluctantly into their ornate bedroom. An elderly nurse stood up. My stomach lurched at the sight of her stooped back, but she didn't give me a second glance. She scrunched her lined face and shook her head at the doctor.

'Mafalda,' whispered Dottor Visconti, approaching the bed, his voice heavy with his love for her.

'I can't do it anymore, Alfredo,' she cried as he took her hand in his. Her hair was clinging in long, damp streaks to her face, which was contorted with pain.

'She's here, Elisabetta's here,' he said softly, 'and Adelina too.' He gestured towards us to approach. Dottor Visconti took Elisabetta's hand and placed it in his wife's. Elisabetta looked at me, her eyes wide with alarm. I rested my shaking hand on her shoulder to calm her, and she relaxed a little.

'I'm so glad you're here,' slurred Signora Visconti in a voice that didn't seem her own.

'It's the drugs,' said Dottor Visconti, reading my expression.

We stayed silent for what seemed like an eternity. The nurse sat away from us at the end of the bed, focused on the space between Signora Visconti's legs, which was covered with a sort of tent made of sheets. I tried not to look but my eyes kept returning to the old woman, wishing she wasn't here.

Elisabetta's little finger moved slowly back and forth over Signora Visconti's palm, tracing the arc of her lifeline until her breathing calmed and her face loosened. I kept the nurse in the corner of my eye.

Then Signora Visconti let out an almighty cry, howling as a wave of pain gripped her body.

The bossy nurse stood up and shooed us out of the room.

'That's it, Signora, now push. Push with everything you've got. It's time to see your baby.'

Elisabetta and I sat outside the bedroom. We listened to every grunt and curse, to the nurse shouting instructions, her voice cold and stern, Dottor Visconti encouraging his wife. We held each other close, as if our own lives hung in the balance.

When the first scream of the newborn rose from the bedroom,

we were exhausted.

'We have a son. Mafalda and I have a son!' cried Dottor Visconti. He scooped Elisabetta up in his arms with a giant bear hug. If he noticed we were crying, he would have put it down to joy.

But my tears were not for the safe delivery of baby Visconti.

The nurse helping Signora Visconti was the same woman who'd looked after Mamma when she'd had the fever. Signora Petruzzi. Who told me when I was seven years old that my mother was dead, without a word or gesture of comfort.

~

The night of Renato Visconti's birth was a long one for Elisabetta and me.

Curled up in Elisabetta's bed, we were so tired, but neither of us could sleep.

For me, the voice of Signora Petruzzi wouldn't go away. It was like a nest of crawling insects buried deep in my mind. Up they crept, bringing up long forgotten memories.

'You're to go to the orphanage. Nobody wants you.'

'Why would they want an angry, snivelling girl like you?'

Shaking, I repeated the words to Elisabetta, sparing none of the woman's harsh tone. Elisabetta listened and held me tight.

'When Signora Visconti was screaming in pain, I heard my mother,' Elisabetta said eventually.

'Grazia?' Mamma had been Grazia's friend, and I had a faint memory of visiting Grazia, baby Elisabetta in her arms.

Elisabetta nodded and started to cry.

'What did you hear?'

'My mother was pleading with the German soldiers.'

Elisabetta curled into a small ball, her head against my shoulder.

'I saw from the window what they did to my mother. It's what happened to Santa Maria Goretti.'

'Oh, no,' I replied, moving my head to rest on Elisabetta's.

'I saw it all. She looked at me as she took her last breath.'

I'd known that Grazia's death had something to do with the Germans, but not that Elisabetta had seen what had happened.

'Why didn't you tell me before?'

'I don't know. It's like you with the nurse. It's like I've always known. But until tonight I hadn't remembered.'

She snuggled in close to me.

'You're the only one who understands, Lina.'

'That's why we'll always be friends.'

I clung to her, the only person who knew me too.

Part 2

17

Padre Bosco

Padre Bosco leant back in his armchair, his hands clasped as in prayer, his forefingers tapping against one another.

Opposite him, Dottor Visconti was making light work of the bottle of grappa, which Padre Bosco suggested they share to wet the baby's head, barely a day after the birth.

'I never thought this day would come,' slurred Dottor Visconti.

'*Salute*!' replied Padre Bosco as he leant forward to refill his *cumpàgno*'s glass, barely having taken a sip from his own. The ageing doctor's face was flushed, the effect of the strong spirit accelerated by lack of sleep.

'Me, a father at sixty-five years of age! *Chi l'avrebbe mai detto*!' He laughed, raising his glass unsteadily towards his old friend, who returned the gesture before setting back down his own glass, untouched.

'Perhaps your son will carry on the family tradition and become a fine doctor here in Atina.'

'*Speriamo*,' nodded Dottor Visconti, 'Mafalda would be so proud!'

'And Mafalda, how is she recovering?' asked Padre Bosco with his air of benevolent concern. 'I understand it was a difficult birth. Signora Petruzzi stopped by to light a candle of thanks for the child.'

'Signora Petruzzi thinks it was down to her,' interrupted Dottor Visconti, 'says she knew that Mafalda and the child would make it, given all her years' experience. But she hadn't been saying that before I fetched Elisabetta.'

'Ah yes, she mentioned her,' said Padre Bosco, his tone light. 'Said the girl cried a lot. And her friend too.'

'Mafalda believes it was divine intervention. Nothing less.'

Padre Bosco smiled but was caught off-guard by the weight in the doctor's statement. He proceeded cautiously.

'And you? What do you believe?'

'I agree with my esteemed colleague's diagnosis as far as Elisabetta's diabetes and epilepsy are concerned.' He sighed. 'But last night, Mafalda was this close to dying,' he replied, holding a shaking thumb and forefinger up to the priest, barely a hair's breadth apart.

'Now I have a son and my wife has survived. Elisabetta was there. She held Mafalda's hand. They prayed together. Anyway, why are you asking me? You're the priest. You should know!'

Padre Bosco stood up and walked behind Dottor Visconti's seat.

'You're tired, Alfredo,' he said, patting Dottor Visconti on the shoulder.

'Sorry, Luigi, you know how I am... a couple of drinks... I speak as I find.' He rubbed his forehead. 'You're right, I'm exhausted.'

'I've been thinking about the girl,' Padre Bosco started tentatively. 'The diabetes and epilepsy... she isn't getting any better.'

'Yes, the specialist from Roma and I agree that both conditions need to be controlled better.'

'Perhaps she's not getting the care she needs. You know how stretched things are at the orphanage.'

Padre Bosco paused for effect. 'Sister Beatrice means well, but she leaves the girl's young friend Adelina to care for her most of the time.'

'Adelina is very devoted to Elisabetta,' replied Dottor Visconti, alcohol and tiredness slowing his words.

Padre Bosco moved in front of the chair where Dottor Visconti was slumped, struggling to keep his eyes open.

'My dear Alfredo,' he said, raising his chin in the way he always did before preaching his sermon, 'I fear you may not be considering all aspects of this situation.'

Dottor Visconti's dense grey eyebrows knitted into a frown, and Padre Bosco nodded.

'Adelina has told me of her concerns for the girl's health. How worried she is about her friend.'

Dottor Visconti yawned loudly, but Padre Bosco was hitting his stride.

'Put yourself in Sister Beatrice's place. I hear the collections at the so-called *santuario* are benefitting the orphanage. Re-decoration, new clothes and shoes for the children, better food. She may be overlooking the girl's medical needs for...'

Padre Bosco left the words hanging in mid-air.

'Adelina? Sister Beatrice?' Dottor Visconti rubbed his eyes.

'Adelina is a loyal friend, and in spite of growing up in the orphanage, she's a sensible and honest young lady. She'll have to leave there soon, given her age.'

'I hadn't thought about that. What will she do?'

Padre Bosco continued, leaving the question unanswered.

'I took it upon myself to make some enquiries, on behalf of Elisabetta. I have a few connections, as you know, in higher places,' said Padre Bosco, with no modesty. 'You remember, Monsignor Roberto, and of course, Bishop Morelli.'

'Peppe Morelli, your young sacristan from all those years ago?' said Dottor Visconti, scratching his head at the memory. 'But I thought he didn't want people to know where he came from. You've always told me, it was for his own good.'

'And there's no reason to start talking about it now,' said Padre Bosco, his tone final. 'But his private secretary, Monsignor Roberto, offered to help...There is a home run by a religious order in the hills near Roma. Near to Castel Gandolfo. Normally it is only for those who can afford the fees, but when I described the circumstances, they're prepared to take the girl.'

'They could provide the medical care Elisabetta needs?'

'Not being an expert, I sent them the report by the doctor from Roma and they agreed that their home would be a much better environment for her.'

'That's good of you, Luigi, given all the trouble the *santuario* has caused you,' replied Dottor Visconti, swaying as he rose from his seat. 'I'll give them a call to discuss her case, but it sounds like the ideal place for Elisabetta.'

'I think you'll find that they have all the information they need in the report, Alfredo. I'll make the arrangements with Sister Beatrice. You needn't concern yourself any further. Just enjoy the time with your son!' smiled Padre Bosco, ushering Dottor Visconti towards the door.

'Thank you, Luigi. Mafalda will be pleased to know that the church is taking Elisabetta in and caring for her.'

The two men shook hands and Padre Bosco let out a sigh, grateful that his old friend was too drunk to ask him further questions about the home for Elisabetta. Omission of detail was not a sin in the same way as a lie.

'You asked about Adelina,' said Padre Bosco, as he guided Dottor Visconti, a hand under his elbow. 'I wondered whether you might take her on now that Mafalda will be caring for the baby. You'll need someone to help you with your appointments and paperwork.'

Dottor Visconti laughed and slapped his friend on the back.

'My dear Luigi, you may have found the best solution for Elisabetta, but I'm afraid Adelina can't read or write properly. She couldn't even write a list of the foods that Elisabetta had eaten.'

Dottor Visconti stumbled on the first step down into the market square and Padre Bosco reached out to help him regain his balance, masking his disappointment. Adelina had always struck him as intelligent, mature for her years. He'd never considered that she might be illiterate.

As the fresh air hit Dottor Visconti's face, he straightened up and patted his old friend on the arm.

'You're a good man, Luigi. I'll talk to Mafalda. She likes Adelina; she's always saying what a good friend she is to Elisabetta. Adelina can help with the baby. I'm sure we can come to an arrangement.'

A broad smile lifted the old priest's wrinkled features and as he waved goodbye to Dottor Visconti, he said a swift prayer of thanks.

18

Adelina

In the few days after the birth of Renato Visconti, Elisabetta and I were closer than we'd ever been, *due piselli in un baccello*. We didn't speak of what'd happened to Grazia, or about the awful Signora Petruzzi. We didn't have to.

Although she was unwell, we snuggled together under the covers like we used to. When she was a little better, we played cat's cradle and laughed at our tangled fingers in the wool. She read from the damaged *Il Grande Libro dei Santi* to me, and since she found it soothing, I was happy to listen. We were back together, inseparable best friends. That was all that mattered to me.

In our own little world, we paid little attention to the excited chatter of the nuns who brought food for Elisabetta. Apparently, Atina was aflame with talk of Renato's miracle birth. Elisabetta didn't seem to care much about the baby, though I was happy for Signora and Dottor Visconti; they were always kind to me.

There was one subject that troubled Elisabetta, and I tried to push it away, afraid of losing our closeness once more.

'Why hasn't Sister Beatrice stayed and talked with me like she used to?' she asked.

'She must be busy.'

I'd also noticed that Sister Beatrice's visits had been brief but I didn't want to show Elisabetta that it suited me she was around less.

'Do you think I've upset her? What if I ask her to stop awhile when she comes next time? Maybe if I ask her to read to me about Santa Teresa di Lisieux?'

I shrugged, hoping she wouldn't.

~

When Sister Beatrice next came to our room, Elisabetta shuffled up in her bed and pulled herself onto her elbows.

'Pillow, Adelina,' she said, nudging me away, whilst smiling sweetly at Sister Beatrice. 'And a glass of water!'

'How are you feeling today?' Sister Beatrice asked. I stayed on my bed, knowing Elisabetta wouldn't miss her water.

'Better, thank you,' came the eager reply.

Sister Beatrice nodded but seemed distracted.

'Perhaps you might feel up to some special visitors tomorrow?'

Elisabetta perked up at the word '*speciale*'.

'Signora Visconti wants to come by with baby Renato.'

Elisabetta's brow formed into a question, but she thought better of it and tried not to look deflated. But I was pleased to hear they were coming and wondered if I might be allowed to hold baby Renato.

'Good, that settles it. Dottor Visconti will come too.'

Sister Beatrice turned on her heel and left the room before either of us had the chance to speak again.

'Why's Sister Beatrice saying they're special visitors?' asked Elisabetta as soon as the door was shut, sliding listlessly back into the bed.

'Maybe she meant that it's special because Renato is coming. Their first family outing?'

'Ah, yes,' nodded Elisabetta. 'They're coming to thank us. Maybe they'll bring us a little gift?'

We both smiled.

'Sweets?' cried Elisabetta.

'Maybe chocolate? Those Baci ones?' I replied, imagining the taste of the expensive chocolate covered hazelnuts.

That was all we thought of it. Little did we know how our world was about to change.

~

The Visconti family arrived in our room with the air of respectful guests at a funeral, accompanied by a serious-looking Sister Beatrice.

Elisabetta wrinkled her nose at the baby and looked to see if there was any sign of a gift and turned away, disappointed.

I assumed they were all quiet so as not to wake baby Renato, who was sound asleep in Signora Visconti's arms, his chubby face emerging from a swathe of tight blankets. I couldn't help myself and stepped forward to peek at him. Renato snuffled in his sleep, a twitch in his face showing off his pudgy cheeks. He had a button nose and plump lips.

A proud Signora Visconti smiled and looked to her husband, and he nodded in reply. Renato was laid with great care in my arms, smelling of milk and Signora Visconti's rose perfume. I smiled and held him closer, watching his chest rise and fall.

Dottor Visconti laid a hand on his wife's shoulder. As she placed her hand on his, Elisabetta coughed in a way I knew to be false. No one had yet greeted her, sitting up in a brand-new white cotton nightdress, her hair in perfectly matching plaits, which I had taken care to finish with ribbons of white lace. Baby Renato was left in my arms, as all turned to face Elisabetta.

'Elisabetta,' pronounced Dottor Visconti in a sombre tone, which had none of his usual friendliness. I looked up from the baby. Elisabetta's smile had turned sour, and she glanced at me and then at Sister Beatrice for reassurance. Sister Beatrice brushed at a mark on her black sleeve. A small cry from baby Renato broke the silence, but as I jiggled him, he drifted back to sleep.

'I'm concerned your health is not improving sufficiently,' said Dottor Visconti, slow and careful with his words. 'You need to go somewhere with doctors and nurses who can help you get better.'

My stomach lurched. Elisabetta looked at me, panicked. In my arms, Renato's face twisted into a grimace as if he was about to cry.

'It's been agreed that you'll go to a convalescent home near Roma where they'll be able to give you the care you need,' said Dottor Visconti.

'I don't want to go!' cried Elisabetta. She pounded the bed with clenched fists, kicking away the covers. 'I want to stay here with

Adelina. You can't make me go away on my own!'

Elisabetta was shrieking. 'I've got to stay close to the river. If I go, Maria might not come back to me!'

I gripped on to Renato, trying to control the shaking in my body. Renato was squirming in my arms like a slippery fish. I wanted to hand him back, but Signora Visconti sat on Elisabetta's bed. She had hold of Elisabetta's flailing arms and was shushing her in a gentle voice.

Sister Beatrice stepped towards Elisabetta, whose pale face drained of its last colour.

'It's what's best for you, Elisabetta,' she said, reaching towards her, but Elisabetta turned away. 'Padre Bosco has secured the place. We should be grateful to him.'

'It'll only be until you're better,' said Signora Visconti. 'We all want you to be well again. You'll be back here and able to go to the *santuario* as soon as you are recovered.'

Elisabetta sank back into her pillows, her chest heaving. She sobbed into the painful silence of the room, looking past Signora Visconti towards me.

My heart was pounding. I wanted to go to her, to tell her I didn't want us to be parted. But Sister Beatrice was beside me, dabbing at the corners of her eyes with her handkerchief, which she quickly returned to her pocket. She was looking at baby Renato, who had settled back into contented sleep in my arms.

'You'll be an excellent help to Signora Visconti, Adelina.'

'What?'

Signora Visconti had joined Sister Beatrice at my side.

'We've talked it through, Adelina, my husband and I.' She glanced over to him, and he smiled.

'Sorry, I don't understand…'

Renato made a gurgling noise and leaked a dribble of milk from the corner of his mouth.

'I've seen how well you've always cared for Elisabetta. We thought you might like to come and help me with the baby.'

I dabbed the softness of Renato's face with the handkerchief, which Sister Beatrice offered me, taking care not to rouse him from his sleep.

'It's time for you to leave the orphanage, Adelina,' said Sister Beatrice, taking the handkerchief back but not looking at me. Her voice was strong and clear. 'You're almost sixteen now, and with Elisabetta gone… I don't need to tell you this is a wonderful opportunity for you, and very kind of Dottor and Signora Visconti.'

'But Elisa…'

'You'll have your own room, of course, and with your help with Renato, I'll be able to manage the patients still. Who knows, I could even teach you what I do, and when Renato goes to school, you could help me with the administration,' added Signora Visconti brightly.

A tingle of excitement ran through me at the thought of being welcomed into the Visconti family, their beautiful home. I looked to Elisabetta, hoping she might be pleased for me, even though I didn't want us to be apart.

'No!' screamed Elisabetta. 'You can't take me away! You can't have Adelina! It's not fair!' she sobbed again, but her cries quickly grew weak.

Sister Beatrice sat beside Elisabetta on her bed and comforted her.

'Please, at least let me return to the river one last time before I go,' she sniffed. 'I want to see Maria again.'

'We'll hold a final ceremony, to pray for your full recovery,' promised Sister Beatrice, clutching her hand.

Behind her, Dottor Visconti brought out a syringe from his bag and Sister Beatrice nodded.

'Just to help you sleep a little,' said Dottor Visconti, piercing the skin on Elisabetta's forearm. She grimaced before her eyes flickered to a close.

~

Once Elisabetta was asleep, Signora Visconti turned towards me.

'What do you say, Adelina?' she asked gently. 'I know you don't want to leave Elisabetta, but she'll be well looked after at the convalescent home. It's what she needs, to get better. I'm sure you understand.'

'I do… but… Elisabetta…'

'It's an honour for you to be offered this position, in the home of the Visconti family,' repeated Sister Beatrice, making it clear that all was decided. 'And we'll make sure you get the help you need, to assist Signora Visconti with the paperwork and such like in years to come.'

Sister Beatrice nodded at me, letting me know that she'd understood my fear that I'd be shown up as not being able to read and write. She was giving me a future, the nun who until Elisabetta had her visions, had never called by my name and who'd only ever punished me.

'Yes,' I replied eagerly, addressing Signora and Dottor Visconti, relieved Elisabetta couldn't hear me. 'Thank you.'

A rumble rose from the bottom end of the bundle in my arms, and a flash of a smile passed across Renato's face.

'It's only wind,' I giggled, knowing that babies can only smile when they are a bit older. Signora Visconti and Sister Beatrice both laughed.

'I'm so pleased,' Signora Visconti said, lifting Renato from me. 'I need to feed him now, but I can see Renato's already taken to you.'

I handed him back, tucking in a flap of his blanket, which had worked loose. Signora Visconti smiled at my gesture.

'Thank you, Dottor Visconti, Signora Visconti.'

'It's our pleasure, Adelina,' replied Dottor Visconti. 'You'll be doing us a great service. In fact, it was Padre Bosco who made the suggestion, but a fine idea it's turned out to be!'

At the mention of Padre Bosco's name, an edge of guilt crept into my mind, but it didn't settle.

'I've agreed with Padre Bosco that there will be a ceremony at the shrine in a month's time,' stated Sister Beatrice in a matter-of-fact tone. 'Elisabetta will be there. She'll leave for the convalescent home after the ceremony.'

'I'm surprised Padre Bosco agreed. Will he be attending this time?' asked Signora Visconti.

'Yes, he'll be there. It makes him look good to be seen to help Elisabetta,' replied Sister Beatrice drily.

Silence fell between the women. Dottor Visconti closed the clasp on his bag and helped his wife and child from the seat.

I'd already begun to imagine looking after baby Renato and the excitement of having my own room in their beautiful house. But in front of me lay a frail, sleeping Elisabetta.

'May I stay here with Elisabetta until she leaves for the convalescent home, please?'

'Of course, Adelina. We knew you'd want to,' replied Signora Visconti.

She held Renato towards me, and I stroked his hand to say goodbye.

19

Giulio

He'd wanted to keep Maria's letter pristine, just like his memory of her. But Giulio had unfolded and replaced the letter in his garden overalls so many times that it had grown grubby from his soil on his fingers. He pushed the crumpled paper back into his pocket and continued his inspection of the vegetable beds. As he bent to lift the leaves of the zucchini, the dull pain in his left hip sharpened and he had to straighten up. A familiar rigidity had returned to his body these last few days, and he'd not been moving as freely.

He waited for the pain to subside, turning Maria's words over again in his mind.

15 Woodland Road,
St. Albans,
England

July 1949

Dearest Giulio,

My hand is shaking as I write, but that the news should come from you was my only comfort. How could you imagine that I might have forgotten you? I have thought of you often, wondering what happened to you, the man you've become, how what happened that night might have left you.

It may be eleven years, but what you did for us at River Mollarino has always stayed with me. Your compassion was the only light on my darkest day.

Learning what Elisabetta has gone through breaks my heart, again. To hear of her poor health, how she is suffering.

All these years, I believed Padre Bosco had kept his word, that she has been growing up with a good family. Now I know he is protecting his own and others' interests, yet again.

Although he is a man of God, and it is difficult to write this, you are right not to trust him.

Please don't feel guilty. He has used both of us. Back then, you were a young man in an impossible situation.

As soon as you receive this, please write again. Tell me everything you can about Elisabetta, what she's like, every little detail of how she looks, how she speaks. Stay close to her and do what you can for her.

My husband, Colin, knows little of my past, and I'm not sure what I can do. For him, my life started when I nursed him back to health after his injuries at Monte Cassino. He thinks he saved me, the English officer, taking home a beautiful wife from a godforsaken country. In some ways he was right, but it wasn't the war or German occupation I was mourning.

Dear God, forgive me for my part in all these lies.

Maria

Under the leaves mottled white with mildew, the zucchini had grown fat and shiny. Giulio took out his knife and sliced clean through the thick stems, thinking of Padre Bosco and Maria's warning about him. As he piled the zucchini into a basket, Adelina appeared with a shy smile.

'I'm sorry, I haven't been able to come before.'

Her hair was loose, which suited her. He couldn't help but notice that her chin was held a little higher too. She looked older than when he'd last seen her.

'I heard about Signora Visconti having the baby, and you and Elisabetta being there. What happened? How's Elisabetta?'

'So much has changed since I last saw you. I'm not sure where to begin!'

There was much Giulio felt he ought to share with Adelina too. But the more he had turned it over in his mind, the more he understood he couldn't tell her about having found Maria. Adelina wouldn't be able to not tell Elisabetta, and since he wasn't sure whether Maria could return, it seemed best to keep the knowledge to himself.

'Start with what's important to you,' he said, relieved at not having to do the talking.

Adelina brushed a loose strand of hair from her face and smiled at him.

'Dottor and Signora Visconti have asked me to live with them to care for baby Renato,' Adelina announced, her voice full of pride. 'Sister Beatrice says it's an honour to be asked, and a wonderful opportunity for me.'

'You're leaving the orphanage?' But what about…?' The news struck him like a swift blow to the stomach, confirmation of feelings he'd tried to push away.

Silence hung in the summer fug. A pair of white butterflies flitted playfully from branch to branch nearby.

'Sister Beatrice is right. It'll give you a good start in life,' said Giulio. The words were correct, but he pronounced them without enthusiasm.

Adelina looked to the ground.

'Elisabetta is leaving too, if that's what you're thinking about,' replied Adelina with a flat edge to her voice.

'What?' Giulio was thinking about Adelina no longer being at the orphanage, and it took a moment to register what she'd said.

'Padre Bosco has found a convalescent home for her, where there are doctors and nurses who can care for her. A special place, out in the hills near Roma. She'll be staying there until she gets better.'

'Padre Bosco? What's Elisabetta's health got to do with him?' Giulio replied sharply.

Adelina stepped backwards. 'Maybe he's just trying to help her. She isn't getting any better…'

She was upset and Giulio regretted letting his instinct about the priest slip out. 'You're right, if there is a place that can help... How's Elisabetta taken the news?'

'She doesn't want to go, and she wasn't happy that I'm leaving either. But there'll be a ceremony next month at the *santuario* before she leaves. Even Padre Bosco is going this time. Sister Beatrice says I can stay with Elisabetta until she leaves.'

'That's good. We've a month together still,' said Giulio. He was already thinking of Maria and how he must let her know about this latest turn of events. Given her words about Padre Bosco, surely this would bring her back to Italy.

'I'll do everything I can to encourage Elisabetta back out into the garden.' Adelina smiled, a look of relief settling on her face. 'It always does her good and she enjoys it so much when the three of us are together.'

'So do I,' said Giulio. 'And will you still come by, when you're living with the Viscontis?'

'Yes,' said Adelina, averting her eyes from Giulio as the colour rose in her cheeks.

~

Fork and spade were his preferred tools, not pen and paper. He screwed up two attempts before he wrote as if he was speaking to Maria in person. Padre Bosco's actions – the convalescent home, agreeing to a final ceremony when he'd been so dead set against Elisabetta. He didn't like the sound of any of it. He must persuade Maria to come for the ceremony. For Elisabetta's sake.

20

Adelina

E lisabetta immediately took against the wheelchair.
'I'm not using it! I'm not an invalid.'

I ran my hand along the smooth curved wooden handles and the fine black grain of the leather seat. It was new and expensive looking.

'Padre Bosco thought it might help you,' Sister Beatrice replied as she struggled to manoeuvre the wheelchair. Elisabetta turned away from it with a defiant look and Sister Beatrice slipped out of our bedroom as quickly as she could.

'This could be fun,' I said, releasing a pedal with my foot. It gave a rewarding clunk. The wheels rolled effortlessly across the floor. 'No wonder Sister Beatrice couldn't move it! Come on, let's go for a *passegiata*!'

'I don't want to!' Elisabetta replied, but she was eyeing up the chair.

'I'll push you as far as the garden. You can save your energy by not having to walk. Once we're there, you can get out and walk if you feel up to it.'

'You think so?'

Elisabetta pulled herself up in bed and as I reached her, bringing the wheelchair close to her bed, one leg was already poking out from under her blanket. She gripped the arm of the chair for support as I helped lower her in. She'd lost so much weight that the bones in her arms and legs made me think of twigs that could snap in my fingers.

'It's you in charge of the Flower Girl of Atina now,' said Elisabetta.

Elisabetta's voice had an edge, but I didn't respond. With my hands resting on the handles, ready to push off, I towered above her, looking down at the top of her scalp, parted evenly where I had arranged her plaits earlier. For all the talk of the *santuario* and her visions, it was me pushing a sick girl in a wheelchair. She'd be leaving soon and although I couldn't imagine life without her, my daydreams were taking me to my room in the comfortable Visconti household, my days spent with baby Renato.

~

The wheelchair glided along the corridors of the orphanage. Some of the little kids stopped as they saw us approaching, staring at frail Elisabetta in her gleaming carriage. They scooted to one side to make way for us. As we approached the steps, there was a commotion as Enzo and some of the other young lads scrapped among one another for the prize of showing off their strength. They all wanted to carry the chair down the steps towards the garden.

The noise brought Sister Beatrice hurrying out of her study, but when she saw the boys set the chair and a smiling Elisabetta onto the path, her anger melted.

'Bravo!' she clapped.

Enzo and the boys strutted off and Sister Beatrice came over to us.

'I'm so glad you changed your mind, Elisabetta. The fresh air will do you good.'

Elisabetta smiled sweetly.

'Lead the way, Adelina!' Sister Beatrice said, rubbing her forehead. 'I think I'll take a turn with you, now I'm outside. I could do with a break from the ledgers.'

She bent down beside Elisabetta, whose face lit up as she took her hand. 'Let's make sure you take some beautiful memories of Santa Scolastica's garden away with you.'

'But I'll be back before too long. It's only until I get better, isn't it?'

'You'll be back with us before you know it. And I'm sure Adelina will come to visit as often as she can, won't you?'

'Of course,' I replied. 'I'll be the first person to greet you when you get back.' I smiled, although I couldn't imagine a day without her.

'Maybe you'll bring baby Renato sometimes too!' said Sister Beatrice.

The words reassured Elisabetta, but I could tell from the face that she pulled at his name, that Elisabetta wouldn't care if she didn't see baby Renato.

Sister Beatrice walked alongside the wheelchair. She and Elisabetta chattered happily, and as we entered the garden through the iron gate, a bank of bright yellow *girasole* greeted us. Sister Beatrice stepped to one side to make way for the wheelchair and inhaled deeply, as if to take in all the scents of the garden at once. The heady honeysuckle was at its height.

'When I first came to the orphanage, I used to enjoy many quiet moments here,' she said, smiling at the memory. 'And to see the garden restored brings me such joy. Giulio has done a wonderful job!'

At the mention of his name, my heart made a little leap. She was right. Giulio's hard work had paid off for all to admire. Ahead of us, tall bean plants laden with long pods stood to attention in tidy rows, orange marigolds planted at their feet to distract any insects that might take a liking to the beans. As we made our way along the path, we took in neat arrangements of curly lettuces and shiny peppers.

'Oh! Look!' Sister Beatrice was pointing at the circular herb garden, divided like the spokes of a wheel.

'There's thyme, rosemary, basil, parsley, sage, oregano and garlic,' said Elisabetta proudly. 'We helped Giulio plant them earlier in the spring. I did get all the names right, didn't I?' she asked.

I nodded, remembering not just the names of the plants but the way Giulio dug the soil, his body leaning on the spade, the angle of his face as he smiled at us.

Sister Beatrice was beside herself with joy. 'I'd told him about the herb garden I'd started there. When Giulio came, it was just a mound of weeds. Now look at it!'

In the far corner of the garden, Giulio appeared from behind the door of his shed. He was shirtless and Sister Beatrice turned away to preserve his modesty and I did the same, but only after I'd taken him in. Giulio ducked back behind the door, only re-emerging when he was fully clothed again.

'Forgive me, Sister Beatrice, it's been a hot afternoon in the garden,' said Giulio, a look of concern on his face as he took in the sight of Elisabetta in the wheelchair. He looked to me, but Elisabetta was beckoning him towards her.

'What do you think of my new carriage?' laughed Elisabetta. 'Padre Bosco gave it to me as a gift, just so I can come and see you!'

'Padre Bosco?' Giulio's serious tone cut Elisabetta short, and it was Sister Beatrice who picked up the story.

'I think he's trying to make amends. He's had a change of heart. He knows he's not treated Elisabetta as well as he should've.'

Giulio nodded, but I could see he was not convinced. He crouched down to Elisabetta and took her hand.

'Since Padre Bosco has seen fit to give the Flower Girl of Atina a carriage, I think we should make the most of it, don't you?'

Elisabetta giggled, and I stepped aside.

'I've got something to show you,' he said, steering her towards one of the outer walls of the garden.

'Ooh, what is it?'

'You'll have to wait and see!'

Sister Beatrice and I followed a few paces behind them.

At Elisabetta's eye level, on a section of the wall that was already baked in the sun, a large black scorpion appeared. It was completely still. Giulio didn't take her too close at first, but Elisabetta was leaning forward to get a better view, so he edged the wheelchair towards it.

'They're quite something, aren't they?' said Giulio.

Elisabetta nodded as she took in the impressive creature. 'I like the shape of it,' she said, holding out her arms in the shape of the claws, 'the ridged body and the kink in the tail.'

'You're not scared of it?'

'No, should I be?'

'The sting in the tail is poisonous. It could be painful, but it wouldn't kill you.'

131

I edged forward a little, closer to Giulio, to get a better look at the scorpion's shiny shell.

Sister Beatrice recoiled at the sight of the scorpion.

'Makes me think of Padre Bosco,' said Elisabetta, snapping her fingers in a pincer movement.

'Padre Bosco? Why?' asked Giulio, looking straight at me. I dipped my head as my cheeks flushed red. I'd never admitted to Giulio that I'd been the one who'd told Padre Bosco of my doubts about Elisabetta, but in that moment I swore he knew.

'Maybe it's the black body, or the claws.' Elisabetta clamped her fingers tight shut in a gesture that made Sister Beatrice jump. She turned and walked away.

'What did I do?' Elisabetta asked Giulio. 'Did I say something wrong?'

'I think she just doesn't like scorpions,' replied Giulio as he moved the wheelchair away from the wall. I could feel his eyes were still on me, but I didn't look his way, too scared he would see my betrayal of Elisabetta written across my face.

'Or Padre Bosco,' said Elisabetta quietly.

August 1949

Dearest Giulio,

I've read your letters over and over, trying to make sense of what has happened to Elisabetta.

I keep coming back to a memory that will never leave me.

Do you remember when you waved and beckoned me towards the piazza from the back of the army truck, you on your way to war, me returned to Atina for the one and only time for my dear Aunt Luisa's funeral? I got your meaning straight away and rushed straight to the stall of the lemonade seller.

I saw Elisabetta, a toddler, with her family. I did what I shouldn't have, but I couldn't help myself. As I bought my drink, I spoke with her, took the doll she offered me, stopped and played with her. Nerves seized my body, but together we pretended that Elisabetta was going swimming with her doll at River Mollarino, just as I had played with my own ragged doll as a child.

Somehow, Elisabetta seemed to know I wasn't a stranger. She joined in the game, giggling and chattering away, a lively beautiful child. The way she smiled, just like her father.

My heart was broken. Yet it was full of joy. I've never forgotten that moment.

I'll do my best to return to Italy in time for the ceremony. Colin is difficult. He won't want me to go, even if I pretend my mother is ill and needs me. They say Italian men are jealous, but Colin barely lets me out of his sight. Perhaps he's right not to trust me.

I pray for the courage and strength to do what is right for Elisabetta.

Maria

21

Adelina

L etters and numbers had always been a jumble on the page for me. They stretched, shrank and slithered away so that I couldn't catch hold of them. It'd only been Elisabetta helping me and memorising, over and over, again and again, that had spared me from Signora Rossi's stick more often.

'I know it'll be hard for you, Adelina. But working for the Visconti family, it's important that you can read and write properly, and manage numbers,' said Sister Beatrice in her study, her rod stiff back turned to me.

'Lessons with Signora Rossi… on my own…?' The skin around my thumbnail was raw, but still I pulled at it, terrified at being alone, me and my dumbness, with Signora Rossi.

'You may not like this now, but believe me, you'll thank me one day.'

'But Elisabetta?'

'You needn't concern yourself. I'll take her out into the garden every morning in the wheelchair and the other sisters will take it in turns to stay with her.'

My feeble excuse to wriggle out had been anticipated. It was settled. I was to go to Signora Rossi's home every morning for lessons until I moved in with the Viscontis.

~

'You'll see, Signora Rossi isn't so bad,' said Elisabetta. Her mood lifted instantly at the news that Sister Beatrice would accompany her every morning to the garden.

'How would you know? She likes you. She treats me as if I'm stupid.'

'You're not stupid. Just not very good at school lessons, that's all,' said Elisabetta, barely hiding the smirk on her face.

I threw the reading book Sister Beatrice had given me onto the floor. The smug boy and girl on the cover stared back at me. They looked about five years old.

'Sorry.' Elisabetta was still grinning. 'You know what I mean.'

'Do I?'

'Don't be upset with me. Sister Beatrice is only trying to help you.'

'But what if I'm past helping?' I replied, burying my head into the pillow.

'You're not! You'll see. Signora Rossi's a wonderful teacher.'

'You'd know that, wouldn't you?'

'What's that meant to mean?'

'Signora Rossi, Sister Beatrice, Signora Visconti… Giulio. The whole of Atina is always there for their barefoot little flower girl.'

'Why are you being so mean, Adelina? It's you Sister Beatrice is helping. It's me they're sending away. Far from you, and Giulio.'

Elisabetta patted the space next to her on her bed. Without looking at her, I slowly picked up the book.

'I'm scared too,' she said.

'What of?' I put the book back on my bed and lay beside her.

'Going back to the river, going away, everything…' She sighed. 'What if Maria doesn't come back to me? What if I don't get better?'

'Then I'll come and get you and look after you,' I replied without hesitation, staring up at a patch of heart-shaped mould on the ceiling.

~

Knowing how angry Signora Rossi got if anyone was late to school, I set off so early that I arrived in the market square well before the arranged time. I perched on the rim of the fountain at the centre of the piazza and ran my fingers around the dimples and bubbles on the surface of the water, creating little waves like those in my stomach.

Atina was stirring to life. The widows in their mourning black stood gossiping outside San Donato after early morning mass. Some headed for the bakers, where a delivery boy, probably about my age, loaded a bicycle with sturdy loaves. The bar had its first customers, older men who looked like they were having their first break from work in the fields, sleeves rolled up, cigarettes being passed round.

In front of me, the palazzo stood proud, the sunlight settling on its honey-coloured exterior and arch shaped windows. A maid with a stiff broom appeared at the front gate, leaving it open to reveal a beautiful courtyard with tall palm trees.

I got up, strolling past slowly so that I might get a better view.

'*Buongiorno,*' I called as she swept the cobbles in front of the gate. I dawdled as she replied, looking beyond her to the green paradise behind the gate, red and yellow flowers set like jewels among the trees.

The glimpse of the palazzo's hidden courtyard helped push aside my nerves as I took one of the narrow, cobbled streets off the piazza.

San Donato struck its first chime for eight o'clock as I arrived at Signora Rossi's front door. I waited for the brief gap before the second chime to bring the head of a lion against its backplate. A chair scraped against a tiled floor, and it took a few moments for the old teacher to reach me. Her breath rasped as she opened the door.

'*Bene, bene.*' She smiled, approving of my punctuality, and ushered me into her home. At once, I was struck by its refined air, heavy ornate furniture polished to a sparkle and dark paintings lining the walls. Above an elegant sideboard, covered in a lace cloth, a portrait of the Madonna in her blue robes, cradling baby Jesus, had pride of place. Framed photos, tinged brown, were of men with groomed moustaches and military uniforms, women with fine clothes and stern expressions.

There was only one child who appeared, first with chubby cheeks and a mischievous glint in her eye. She progressed to a young woman who looked ill at ease in her frilly lace collared blouse and large fussy brooch and matching earrings. Alone, and to one side, was a photo of a group of young nuns on the steps of an important-looking church. At their centre were the same eyes as in the solo portrait of the uncomfortable young woman, but they looked much happier.

Signora Rossi pointed to a seat at the table where a pencil and paper were waiting for me, alongside the same book Sister Beatrice had given me, the reading book for pupils first starting school. My heart sank, but my eyes were still on the photos.

'Yes, the young lady and the nun are both me,' she said, picking up the group photo of the nuns, stroking the glass with tenderness.

'Sorry, Signora Rossi, I didn't mean to stare. I never knew…'

'That I was a nun once?'

I nodded, my eyes on the book which had its childish illustration of a boy and a girl holding pencils, poised to write. I hated them instantly.

'I rarely bring any visitors into this room,' she said, waving towards an impressive piano whose fine wood shone. The worn music book was open as if it had just been played. She set the photo down with a sigh.

'I woke up this morning, and I thought we should have our lesson here.'

'Why?'

The word had left my lips before I could pull it back, but Signora Rossi didn't seem to mind my impertinence.

'When Sister Beatrice asked me if I would give you some individual instruction, I thought back to the years you've been in my class.'

How many times had she rapped me across the knuckles with her ruler, I found myself thinking, while always praising Elisabetta?

'I don't expect you to understand, Adelina. It's difficult to hold discipline and teach so many children with such varying abilities. But if you're willing to start again at the beginning with me, I think we can make some good progress with your letters and numbers.'

'Really?'

'Yes, I do. I've been looking back, and I think I know what the problem is. I want to try a different way for you.'

I nodded and sat up straight in the chair. Signora Rossi lowered herself with some difficulty into the seat opposite me and smiled.

I was starting to appreciate why Elisabetta had always liked her so much.

'What happened?' I ventured, my head inclining towards the photo of the carefree young nuns.

'I was young when I joined, confused about my feelings,' she replied with candour. 'I knew I'd never marry and have a husband. I liked women and the idea of living among other women seemed like the ideal solution.'

I swallowed a large gulp of air.

'It didn't work out. But they did train me to become a teacher, so all was not lost,' she smiled. 'Shall we begin?'

~

In three weeks of mornings in Signora Rossi's piano room, the letters untangled and rearranged themselves into words that formed into neat script on the page and flowed from my mouth.

Signora Rossi sat back in her armchair as I worked, her hands loosely clasped in her lap. She nodded from time to time, a light smile lifting the wrinkled corners of her mouth. We never spoke again of her having been a nun, but it gave way to a comfortable ease between us, and I was eager to learn and please her.

For numbers, Signora Rossi wrote out lists of fruit and vegetables and prices and had me organise imaginary bills with changing quantities for all the families along her street. Kilos of potatoes and tomatoes became my friends and grams of cherries and hazelnuts were the treats I distributed among each of the homes with accuracy.

'I underestimated you, Adelina,' was the most comment she ever made on my progress, but it was enough to send me back to the orphanage with a spring in my step.

Each afternoon, Elisabetta and I looked forward to telling each other the small details of our short time apart, snuggled together on her bed.

'I knew Signora Rossi would help you,' said Elisabetta when I rushed back to show her my neat handwriting or read a few sentences out loud to her. I told her about Signora Rossi's long-haired cat, Leonora, and how she lived indoors and had her own red velvet cushion that she left covered in fur, when she wasn't sitting on Signora Rossi's lap, clawing at her knees. The cat was the subject of endless fascination for us both, as we'd only ever known thin, rangy cats that belonged only to the outdoors. The elegance of Signora Rossi's home was a frequent topic, and I described the photos on the sideboard. But I left out the picture of the group of nuns and the story that went with it.

For her part, Elisabetta imitated the sound of the wheelchair on the garden path, told me of the colours and markings of butterflies she'd seen and the creaminess of her milky coffee at the end of her passegiata with Sister Beatrice. Giulio made them coffee each day on his little stove in the shed.

'Oh, and today these yellow daisy flowers came into bloom for the first time,' she said, pointing to two glasses, one on her bedside, and one on mine. 'Giulio wanted you to have a bunch as well, so I asked Sister Beatrice to put yours in water too.'

'That was kind of him,' I said, a flush of warmth rising in my cheeks.

'He misses you,' said Elisabetta in a matter-of-fact way.

'Me?' I laughed while my heart thumped in my chest.

'*Certo!* As much as he likes Sister Beatrice, it's not the same as it used to be, when the three of us were together.'

'We had fun, didn't we?' I sighed.

Elisabetta nodded, her eyes downcast.

Neither of us spoke for a while. At my bedside, a couple of the bright daisy flower heads had buckled on their thin stems and were drooping, while Elisabetta's were standing tall. Leaning forward, I could see just a thin line of water at the bottom of my glass, which some stems did not even reach, while Elisabetta's was full to the brim.

'What's going to happen to me, Lina? We've only got a week left together. Nobody knows how long I'll be gone. Dottor Visconti, Sister Beatrice, they all they say it's only until I get better, but how long is that going to be? Will I see Maria at the convalescent home? It's so far from the river!'

I didn't know what to say. I'd tried to reassure her so many times.

'We won't ever be together again like this.' Elisabetta was crying. 'When I come back, you'll be gone. You'll have your own life with the Viscontis.'

Elisabetta crumpled, the words caught between sobs.

She was right, and I didn't reply. I could read and write properly for the first time and I had a new life to look forward to.

22

A buzz swirled around the orphanage. The excitable nuns had gathered a ragtag choir to include most of the children, and despite the off-key notes of the early practices and some initial reluctance, the children had risen to the occasion. As the day of the ceremony at the *santuario* grew closer, their voices wove together in sweet harmony.

For their last rehearsal, each child received a blue satin sash, trimmed with white lace, which had been lovingly sewn by the nuns. When they tried them on with their uniform of a white shirt, grey shorts for the boys and modest grey pleated skirts for the girls, the walls of the orphanage were fit to explode.

It was a relief to slip out of the building and leave a crotchety Elisabetta with Sister Beatrice. She'd not slept well and was refusing to eat any breakfast.

'It's only natural,' said Sister Beatrice, laying a damp flannel on Elisabetta's forehead to cool her down. 'A few nerves, this insufferable heat.' She turned to me with a quick wave of dismissal.

'Give my thanks to Signora Rossi. Tell her I'll call by after all this is over. She's done a remarkable job with you, really she has!'

It rankled that Sister Beatrice didn't think to praise me for what I'd achieved, rather than Signora Rossi, but I was happy to get away as quickly as I could. The last days with Elisabetta had been difficult. Neither of us knew how to smooth the path to our goodbye. She'd taken a turn for the worse in terms of her health, her lack of energy mixing with anger and fretfulness into a sulky stew. When I was sympathetic, she pushed me away. But the slow withdrawal suited me too.

I hadn't told her, but the fact that I was Elisabetta's special friend had seen me become the centre of some attention in Atina. Ever since my first morning lesson, I still had the habit of arriving early in the piazza hoping to catch more glimpses of the secret courtyard of the palazzo.

At first, it was just a friendly smile or *Buongiorno*, but before long, people approached me for news of Elisabetta and her health. The enquiries were always polite, and I responded in kind. Sister Beatrice had always drummed it into the children of the orphanage that we had to be well behaved in public. 'Don't give them any excuse to treat you as second-class citizens. Hold your heads high!' she would say.

Before long, the baker offered me a panini after my lesson. At the bar, I was encouraged to choose an ice-cream.

'How was your last lesson with Signora Rossi?' asked Gianni, the bar owner. He'd already served up my favourite chocolate ice-cream, but now he was adding a generous second scoop to my *coppa*.

'It went well, thank you. Signora Rossi is an excellent teacher.'

'You deserve this after all your hard work!' He smiled, as he handed over the ice-cream, adding a wafer in the shape of a fan. I'd never had an ice-cream with the treat of a wafer and stood at the counter, contemplating whether to nibble it from the top down or to lift it out of the chocolate and lick it.

'Vanilla for me.' Padre Bosco was beside me.

'I think I'll have two scoops today as well,' he said, looking directly at me. I covered my mouth hastily with my hand as ice-cream dribbled from the wafer to my lips.

Gianni waved away Padre Bosco's coins and the old priest motioned for me to walk with him towards San Donato.

'You look well, Adelina, it's been a little while since I've seen you,' he said as he shuffled away from Gianni's earshot. His movement was so slow that I felt awkward trying to match my pace to his. The piazza had almost emptied of people, lunch having already beckoned them out of the heat.

'I hear you've made the most of the opportunity with Signora Rossi. She tells me you've been a very good student.'

'Thank you, Padre Bosco.'

We walked silently in the shade of the plane trees which encircled the piazza. A young boy on a bicycle came flying towards us from the opposite direction, as if trying to get back home before his lunchtime *pasta con fagioli* got cold. Padre Bosco waved him down and he stopped obediently, head bowed, ready to accept words of reprimand. But when the old priest handed him his untouched ice-cream, the boy didn't quite know how to react. He hesitated as he took the unexpected gift but as he steered away, one hand on the bicycle handle, the other clutching the ice-cream, a huge grin lit up his face. Padre Bosco wiped his hands against one another with a slight look of disdain.

'Signora Rossi speaks highly of the progress you've made,' continued Padre Bosco, picking up his thread as if there'd been no interruption. He paused under the shade of a plane tree and smiled at me.

My ice-cream was melting into a soupy puddle in the paper cup.

'Eat up!' he said, indicating the ice-cream with his head. 'You'll be starting with Dottor and Signora Visconti in the next few days,' he continued, while I nodded and tried to lick my dripping ice-cream without slurping. 'So much in life to look forward to!'

'I'm very grateful to Dottor and Signora Visconti for the opportunity,' I replied when the last traces of chocolate were no more. 'And of course, to you, for recommending me to them.'

He smiled, indicating for us to continue our way. 'You'll miss your friend.' His tone was sympathetic.

I nodded as we walked together. 'It's natural,' he said. 'You've spent so much of your lives together. It'll be the first time you've been apart.'

'Hopefully it won't be for long.'

Padre Bosco looked past me towards San Donato.

'Perhaps I might suggest to Sister Beatrice that you're given the responsibility of accompanying her to the ambulance alone tomorrow. The chance for you to say a proper goodbye.'

'Do you think Sister Beatrice will allow it?' I asked, hoping that we might be allowed some time alone together, to put the last few awkward days behind us and be the friends we had always been. 'Surely Sister Beatrice will want to be there herself?'

'Leave it with me. Your loyalty to the church hasn't gone unnoticed.'

'Thank you, Padre Bosco.'

'Off you go.' He waved me away with a smile, but I was unsettled by his words about the church and what he meant. 'I have an important guest arriving for tomorrow, and I must make sure all is as it should be,' he said, nodding towards San Donato. Even if I had been brave enough to ask, he didn't give me the chance to find out who the person might be.

As he turned to leave, I heard a familiar cough nearby. Padre Bosco turned in the direction of the sound and his face hardened. Without a second glance, he headed back towards San Donato whose twin bell towers rose stark against the cloudless blue sky.

When Padre Bosco had closed the presbytery door behind him, Giulio stepped out from the shadow of the plane trees.

'What are you doing here?' I whispered, looking quickly around me. The sun-baked piazza was empty but for a stray dog stretched out, panting heavily in the heat. For a split second, I allowed myself to imagine that Giulio had come to walk me back to the orphanage after my lesson, even though it would set tongues wagging in Atina and meet with Sister Beatrice's stern disapproval.

Giulio shifted his weight from one leg to another.

'What did he want?' he said, raising an angry chin towards San Donato.

'We talked about me saying goodbye to Elisabetta, that's all. He's going to ask Sister Beatrice if I can take Elisabetta to the ambulance tomorrow, on my own.'

Giulio's features darkened, and he shook his head, muttering something under his breath. We'd always avoided talking about Padre Bosco and I'd hoped he'd come round to seeing the better side of him, like Sister Beatrice.

I swallowed hard. Maybe Giulio had known all along that it was me who had raised doubts about Elisabetta, that I told Padre Bosco what was going on.

'What's the matter?' I asked, hoping I was wrong.

'I'm sorry,' he said, returning to the Giulio I knew, but he kept glancing over to the other side of the piazza. 'I'm a little distracted right now, that's all.'

The bell of San Donato chimed a heavy one o'clock in the oppressive heat, causing a lazy pigeon to flap at the disruption of its siesta.

'I've got to go,' said Giulio, running his fingers through his dark hair, setting back a stray lock which had worked loose from the hair oil which I'd only ever seen him use when he helped at the *santuario*.

'Where are you going?' I asked, looking at the ground. He had shined his black leather shoes so much that they gleamed in the sun.

You stupid, dumb girl. The hair oil, the shiny shoes. A smarter pair of trousers and a crisp shirt too. Here was a man, clearly dressed to meet a woman. How could I have missed the signs?

He turned away without replying.

'Adelina!' he called after me, a note of frustration in his voice bouncing off the walls of the ancient palazzo as I hurried away, tears welling inside me.

23

Giulio

Sweat prickled on Giulio's brow as he watched Adelina flee. Part of him wanted to go after her, but he limped off in the opposite direction towards *Cimitero San Marco* as fast as his bad leg would carry him, late already.

Every so often he had to stop, as he waited for the pain in his leg to ease. The sun was beating down on him. A rivulet of sweat ran down the line of his spine, sealing his shirt to his body. He mopped his brow with his handkerchief, cursing at himself.

Padre Bosco was up to something. He knew it in his bones and had stopped when he saw the old priest charming Adelina with his ice-cream and well-honed ways. But he'd only upset Adelina and now had lingered too long.

By the time he was at the rusted entrance gates of the cemetery, the bell of San Donato had chimed for the quarter of the hour. He stopped, bent double in pain, but he had to continue.

The steps down the steep hillside to each successive haphazard terrace of the cemetery ground into his hip, but as he passed the quiet marble sentinels, dotted with the photos of their occupants, and family mausoleums sheltered under the tall pines, he calmed a little. He glanced over to the tucked away corner of his own family's plots and vowed he would stop by next time. A refreshing breeze whipped across his face, which he accepted as a sign of encouragement. He took a deep breath and wiped his forehead with the back of his hand.

The last layer of the cemetery was yet to be used and had the air of an unkempt meadow waiting to be tilled. It was in the far corner that they'd agreed to meet, where bushy cypresses formed a natural screen from prying eyes. He looked down towards the clump of trees and sensed a little movement, which he took to be birds in the branches, but as he drew nearer, he saw the bottom half of a pair of chubby white legs, clearly belonging to a young child, weaving in and out of sight. His heart lifted as he smoothed down his hair.

Giulio didn't want to scare the toddler, Christian. Or Maria.

His heart was in his mouth as he approached. He'd rehearsed this moment so many times in his head and now that it was here, he was afraid. He hesitated, rubbing his hand on his aching left leg.

Maria stepped out of the darkness of the trees towards him, the young boy close behind. Her smile crumpled into shock, a hand to her mouth, as she took in the molten skin on the left side of his face and the eye that was sealed shut.

'I'm sorry, I should have warned you… in the letters,' he mumbled. 'The war wasn't so kind to me.'

Maria shook her head and approached Giulio, her eyes glistening.

'I looked after many young soldiers just like you.' She drew him towards her with a motherly embrace, and although she barely reached the top of his chest, Giulio allowed himself to be held for the first time since he'd been injured. All at once, the walls he'd built around himself fell away. He cried into her shoulder, sobbing for his dead friends, the years in the prisoner of war camp, his family. For the life he'd lost. Christian started to cry too.

'I'm so sorry… I didn't mean to…'

'There's nothing to apologise for,' replied Maria, who kept him in her arms until his heaving chest subsided. Giulio wiped his eyes and nose with the back of his hand, unable to look at her.

She pulled away from him gently but kept one hand on his arm and scooped up her little boy with the other.

'Christian, this is Giulio,' she said, smoothing her son's dark hair. Christian stopped crying as soon as he was back in her arms and gave Giulio a toothy grin. Giulio brushed his face and found himself returning the child's smile.

'You've got your mother's eyes,' said Giulio, raising a hand towards Christian, 'and your sister Elisabetta's too.'

Pride at what he'd said flashed across Maria's face, but then her head dropped and Christian wriggled in his mother's arms to be set free again, spying some butterflies fluttering around them. She set him down and Maria and Giulio watched him chase after the butterflies with glee.

'I'm glad you're here,' said Giulio tentatively. He sensed Maria was nervous, not that he knew where to begin or what to say.

'I've thought about Elisabetta constantly,' she replied, her eyes trained on Christian. 'How is she? What's happened since you last wrote to me? Has she any more visitations?' The questions came fast, one after another.

A silence fell between them as Giulio weighed up his words. Maria's face couldn't mask her turmoil, and although Giulio wished he could comfort her, he knew he had to be honest.

'Her health isn't good. She's been getting weaker and has been in a wheelchair these last few weeks.'

Maria raised her hands to her mouth. 'She's not able to walk?'

Giulio shook his head. They followed the line of cypress trees, watching Christian as he got close to the butterflies and swiped a pudgy arm at them, squealing with delight.

'She doesn't want to go to the convalescent home that Padre Bosco has organised for her. These last few days, she's been very quiet. It's been hard to get her to say much. She doesn't even want to talk to Adelina.'

He turned to look at Maria and when he saw that she'd stopped a pace behind him, the memory of how he'd saved Maria and Elisabetta rushed to him as fast as the waters of River Mollarino that night eleven years previously.

Giulio hung his head in shame.

'I don't know if I did the right thing that night,' he said, 'or if I should have found you, or written to you.'

'You don't have to apologise, Giulio,' she replied, laying a gentle hand on his forearm. 'What's done is done… I should know.'

With that small gesture, the warmth of her touch on his arm,

Giulio relaxed.

Maria crouched down to Christian, who was presenting her with a string of purple campanula flowers, ripped from their stem. She accepted them graciously, tucking them in the hair above her ear, and gave him a hug. He trotted back to the same patch where the flowers had come from, in search of more.

'I think somewhere deep inside I always knew this day would come,' she said.

'You did?'

Maria nodded but didn't offer more.

Christian's ruddy red cheeks came running back towards them. He looked to his mother and then deposited a fistful of torn petals and grass stems at Giulio's feet and waited. They both couldn't help but laugh, and Christian's little face beamed at their reaction.

'You're a bit of a character, aren't you?' Giulio pinched the little boy's fat cheek between thumb and forefinger, and Christian chuckled with gusto.

'I never allowed myself to dream of having another child, knowing that I abandoned Elisabetta, yet here he is,' said Maria, her love for Christian palpable. She whisked Christian off his feet, pretending to eat him, so that he giggled even louder, before setting him back down. He ran back to his patch of flowers.

'He's a good boy, and he means the world to his father. But every day I carried him, I thought of Elisabetta. And every day I give him the love I haven't been able to give to my daughter.'

Giulio's breath caught in his throat. He'd wanted to ask Maria about why she hadn't been able to be a mother to Elisabetta, but somehow none of his questions were important now.

'You didn't come just because I asked you to?'

Maria shook her head. 'I came because Elisabetta needs me.' She looked at Giulio, blinking back tears. Christian rushed towards them, this time with a collection of sticks, which he handed to Giulio.

'Bravo!' clapped Giulio and off Christian ran in search of more natural treasure.

'When you wrote to me about the goodbye for Elisabetta at the river, I felt it here,' said Maria, pressing her hand into her stomach. 'I just knew that I had to come.'

'What will you do?'

'I don't know,' she replied, shaking her head. 'I've spent so long thinking about what would be best. I pray for guidance from our Blessed Madonna. She's helped bring me here. She'll help us.'

At her words, Christian let out a high-pitched scream. He was pointing at a patch of grass and Giulio got to him first, lifting him up swiftly and clutching him to his chest.

A startled viper slid back into the tall folds of grass before it could harm the little boy.

24

Adelina

On that morning of the ceremony, I was awake before the sun rose, snatches of upsetting dreams leaving me anxious and jittery. Elisabetta was breathing heavily in her sleep, so I got up to fetch a glass of water and wandered towards the side door of the orphanage for a little air. The draught left a delicious cool whisper on my face.

Sitting on the doorstep, I waited. Soon, a huge red circle of sun emerged from the treetops by the river, heralding a beautiful day. My first thought was that I wanted to tell Elisabetta about the magnificent sunrise. But later she'd be gone, to recover in the convalescent home. Better to get used to not having her around.

Or Giulio. How stupid I'd been. He'd been dressed up to meet a woman yesterday. How could I have ever thought he might be interested in a girl like me? I blushed and looked down at my feet, stabbing at a rock with my right foot.

A swift lizard cocked its head and immediately slid back into the gap.

Signora Rossi's words came to mind.

'Concentrate only on what's in front of you,' she'd said so many times as she'd taught me to master the words on the page. 'Don't run ahead of yourself. One step at a time.'

My list. I'd drawn it up carefully, following instructions from Sister Beatrice. Down one side of the paper I'd written times, and neatly alongside my responsibilities to help get Elisabetta ready for the day. Item one, I told myself, forcing away thoughts of Giulio. Wash Elisabetta's hair.

Signora Visconti had prepared a special hair lotion, made with lavender and rosemary from the garden. She'd delivered it in a beautiful jar and said that Elisabetta would take Santa Scolastica with her. The smell was deep and comforting. Elisabetta said it reminded her of Giulio and we'd laughed.

My mind was on the second task on the list, to collect Elisabetta's dress from Sister Beatrice's study, when a heavy clunk of car doors came from near the entrance to the orphanage. Curious, I moved behind a tree where I could get a clearer view.

A gleaming long black car, the likes of which I'd never seen. A uniformed driver was holding open one of the rear doors. Out stepped an elderly man, dressed in fine purple robes. Despite his age, he had a sprightly air. Unlike the second figure, who emerged from the other side of the vehicle, clearly pleased at having the door opened for him. Padre Bosco.

Sister Beatrice appeared and bobbed in greeting to the purple-robed priest. He passed into the orphanage without looking at her, while Padre Bosco smiled in a way at odds with his usual self. She looked to the ground in response, and I found myself pulling at a sharp edge of nail with my teeth, even as I imagined that Padre Bosco was probably just checking last arrangements with Sister Beatrice and making good on his promise that I should be left alone with Elisabetta at the ambulance to say goodbye. Here he was with his important visitor, just as he had told me.

As soon as they were inside, the driver struck a match, lit a cigarette, and made a circuit of the vehicle, inspecting closely. Here and there he dabbed at a smudge with a cloth. I had a wild urge to drag a stick along the shiny car.

Between long drags of his cigarette, he whistled *O Sole Mio*, the same melody over and over again, so that it became more and more irritating. I wondered how Sister Beatrice would be reacting to being told that I should have the chance to be left alone with Elisabetta to say goodbye. Annoyed, probably.

The driver had just started on his second cigarette when he jumped to attention, grinding the cigarette into the gravel with his foot. The purple priest approached the car in haste, without a backward glance at Sister Beatrice, who stood small and with dropped shoulders on the bottom step of the orphanage. Padre Bosco followed like an obedient dog.

The car engine purred to a start. As it rolled away, Sister Beatrice hurried back into the orphanage, her face pinched. In the pit of my stomach, I recognised what she was feeling from the day before with Giulio. Trying to hold back tears when your hope has gone.

~

Outside Sister Beatrice's study, I hesitated, even though my excuse was ready. She'd been kind to me since the start of Elisabetta's apparitions and she'd done me a good turn, arranging for my private lessons with Signora Rossi. But I still couldn't shake off my nervousness of old. If she shouted at me, I'd tell her I couldn't sleep with nerves and just wanted to check the timings again, to make sure that I'd got everything right for Elisabetta on such an important day.

'Enter.'

Her voice was almost as quiet as my knock and when she glimpsed me through tear-filled eyes, she didn't even hide the fact that she was crying.

'I thought it would be one of the other sisters.'

A silence fell where I expected her to scold me, or at least ask me what I was doing there. But her gaze was distant, and she reminded me for a moment of a new child arriving at the orphanage, utterly bewildered, and lost.

'Would you like me to fetch one of the sisters for you?' I asked tentatively.

'It makes no difference now,' she said, pulling a handkerchief from the sleeve of her habit. Her voice was thin and weak, and she blew her nose.

'I saw the car.'

She raised her head to look at me and I tried to gauge whether it was safe to continue or whether the full wrath of Sister Beatrice was about to be unleashed.

'Padre Bosco and his guest, I saw them arrive… And I saw when they left too.'

Sister Beatrice buried her head in her hands. 'I should have known,' she said, addressing herself not to me but to the statue of the Madonna which had pride of place on her desk. 'What a fool I've been to think that they'd listen to the voice of a young girl and we women of the church.'

My mind reeled backwards to the words which Sister Beatrice had pronounced with such love and courage on many occasions at the *santuario*. How she reminded those gathered that the Madonna brought a change of consciousness. After all the years of hurt and loss of the war, she gave us hope, a reminder to live simple lives dedicated to love for one another.

'They see us as a threat, these old grey men of the church,' she continued, as if remembering some of her fight and spirit, but her head sank back into her cupped hands.

'But you always told us that women and girls hold the future in their hands. We nurture, we know that to love and be loved is what the Madonna wants for us all.'

A wan smile raised a crease in Sister Beatrice's face.

'I never thought you were much of a believer.'

I looked at my feet. 'I liked what you said, though, about the Madonna being there, for women and girls especially.'

'I'm pleased I made an impression on you,' she said, slowly raising herself to her feet. 'But unfortunately, the Church doesn't much care for Elisabetta or for what I have to preach.'

'Was that why they came?'

Sister Beatrice nodded and turned her back to me. 'Padre Bosco will lead mass today with his guest of honour, Monsignor Roberto. I won't be allowed to speak and Elisabetta will be a participant at mass like every other person present.'

'Why are they changing all the plans you made?' I could hear my voice rising in anger. 'Surely Elisabetta deserves everyone's prayers to help her recover?'

'I have to do as they say,' she sighed. 'As if it isn't enough that our dear Elisabetta is leaving today.'

'What shall we tell her? She'll be so disappointed!'

'I'll tell her the truth,' said Sister Beatrice, recovering some of her resolve. 'For people to understand the messages of the Madonna, they need to see how the Church represses those who hear her.'

'You mean if people see how they treat Elisabetta, her message becomes more powerful?'

Sister Beatrice rested her hand on my shoulder. 'You've grown up a great deal recently. You should be proud of yourself.'

I walked taller back to our room. The unexpected praise from Sister Beatrice made me determined that I would do my very best with the Visconti family, as a way of thanking her. And it helped me face what I knew would be a difficult goodbye with Elisabetta.

~

Running a brush through Elisabetta's long wet hair, we both grimaced as I came up against a knotty tangle, but Elisabetta didn't seem to have the strength to complain. Since she'd woken, she'd been quiet, and we'd barely talked. The knock at the door came as a relief.

'Where's that lovely smell coming from?' asked Sister Beatrice in a light tone, sensing the air of tension.

'Signora Visconti made it for me, from herbs in the garden,' replied Elisabetta without emotion.

'What a beautiful gift.' Sister Beatrice twirled the glass bottle in her hand, glancing a fingertip over the swirling ridges of glass before setting it back down.

'How are you today, Elisabetta?'

'I don't feel well. I'm tired.'

Elisabetta's bottom lip stuck out in a sullen pout. The colour of her skin was grey, like a dull winter's day.

Looking towards Sister Beatrice, I indicated with my head a bowl beside Elisabetta's bed. A thick skin had formed on the untouched bowl of milk. A bunch of dark grapes lay intact.

'You really need to eat something,' said Sister Beatrice, clearly concerned. 'Perhaps you'd like something else? Some bread and ricotta? Or a little honey?'

Elisabetta shrugged and gave Sister Beatrice a weak smile.

'I'll tell Padre Bosco that you're not up to it today,' started Sister Beatrice. 'He can carry on with his plans for mass.'

'Mass? Padre Bosco?' Elisabetta turned to Sister Beatrice, even though her voice was weak and her movement slow. I lifted the brush from Elisabetta's hair and lay it beside the mirror without making a sound and moved aside for Sister Beatrice.

'Well, it wasn't so much Padre Bosco,' she said, taking Elisabetta's hand in hers. 'He's acting on orders from a certain Monsignor Roberto. They came first thing this morning to tell me that Padre Bosco will conduct a traditional mass at the *santuario* today, not the celebration I'd planned.'

Elisabetta's eyes flashed between Sister Beatrice and me.

'They don't want you to speak, do they?'

'No.'

'And what about me?'

'I've been told that you're to attend the mass like everyone else.'

'They're really trying to keep us in our places, aren't they?'

Sister Beatrice blinked, but it was Elisabetta who continued.

'It's me that everyone's coming to see. It's me and Maria. Her messages. Not two old priests!' Elisabetta looked brighter for a moment. She turned to Sister Beatrice.

'Maria's coming today. I can feel it. She's so close.'

'Really?'

'I'm sure,' Elisabetta said. 'The old priests think they're in charge, but they have no control over her.'

'Very well,' said Sister Beatrice, clearly pleased. 'We'll be beside you all the time, looking after you.'

'I know you will,' said Elisabetta. 'If only you could both come with me to the convalescent home, everything would be so much better.'

'That's not possible,' sighed Sister Beatrice, repeating the same lines she'd tried to convince Elisabetta with so many times. 'You need care we can't give you. The orphanage and the other sisters need me. Adelina has a new life to start with the Visconti family.'

'But this is my life, here,' she said, turning towards me. 'With you. In the garden with Giulio, going to the river, Maria visiting me.'

'You'll be back before you know it. They'll get you better, you'll be walking round the garden with Giulio, no more wheelchair,' said Sister Beatrice, forcing a note of optimism into her voice.

'You both keep telling me the same things.' Elisabetta's face was forlorn. 'But if you're right, why do I keep feeling that I won't be coming back here for a very long time?'

25

I pushed down hard on the brake of the wheelchair and swerved round to crouch in front of Elisabetta. She was dwarfed by its huge metal frame, which looked to be swallowing her. At the far end of the corridor, Sister Beatrice was waiting, her back rod straight. Panic tightened in my throat and chest.

'Are you sure you want to do this?' I said, resting my hand on her cheek. Her skin was cold and clammy at the same time. 'You don't have to go.'

She placed an icy hand on mine and patted it gently. 'Maria's coming for me.'

'I'll tell Sister Beatrice you're feverish… This isn't a good idea. You're not up to this today. I know you…'

'You mean well, but you don't understand. I've got to be at the river today.' Her voice was firm, and the corners of her mouth lifted into a weak smile. 'She's coming especially for me.'

'Please, Elisabetta, listen to me. I don't have a good feeling. I've been trying to tell you all morning. It's not too late to stop this. We can stay here until the ambulance comes. Just you and me, we can talk about all our favourite times together. I'll take you out into the garden.'

Elisabetta's eyes moved away from me, drifting off to a place that I couldn't reach and pulled her hand away from mine. 'Let me go now. Please.'

'Ready?' shrilled Sister Beatrice. She brushed at a mark on her long black habit.

'Yes, we're coming now!' Elisabetta replied. 'Adelina was just checking my dress!'

~

We approached the front door of the orphanage, one wheel squeaking along the terracotta tiles.

'How do I look?' asked Elisabetta. She smoothed the satin in her lap.

'A little pale perhaps,' said Sister Beatrice. 'You're sure you're well enough?'

'Yes, I'm sure. What's all that noise?'

'I had a look out of the window before. Let's just say more people have come to pray for you than we imagined. Giulio has laid wood down for a path for the wheelchair and made sure it's kept clear. All is as it should be.'

'Where's Giulio?' said Elisabetta, peering round the sides of the wheelchair. 'It's not like him to keep us waiting!'

'Giu-li-o!' she called playfully, as if it was a game of hide and seek.

'Giulio isn't here.'

'Why not?'

'Padre Bosco said that Adelina and I are to accompany you.'

'Did you know about this?' said Elisabetta, turning in the chair towards me.

'Adelina was under instruction from me not to tell you. I didn't want you more upset.'

Relief had swept over me when I'd learnt Giulio was to play no active part. After the embarrassment of the previous day, at least I wouldn't have to feel awkward walking alongside him as he wheeled Elisabetta towards the *santuario*. According to Sister Beatrice, Padre Bosco had been adamant that Giulio was not required.

'But he'll be there, at the river, won't he?' asked Elisabetta, clearly upset.

'Of course. Padre Bosco can't stop him from being there and saying goodbye to you.'

'No more about Padre Bosco,' replied Elisabetta, waving her hand in dismissal. 'Let's go.'

~

As Sister Beatrice eased open the door, the din of the crowd dropped. She stood before them, stock still, until the last voices petered away. My hands gripped the wheelchair tight.

'Ready?'

Elisabetta nodded, kissing her pearl rosary beads with great solemnity.

The squeak of the wheelchair was the only sound. A blur of bodies stood six or seven deep, pressed up against one another in an eerie silence. They craned and stretched to get a better view of the tiny figure in front of me in the wheelchair, huddled in a blanket, trying to pull herself a little more upright. Sweat sealed my grip on the handles even tighter.

Elisabetta raised her hand weakly from the arm of the wheelchair to acknowledge the crowd. The rosary beads dangled from her fingers, shimmering in the fierce sun. She looked down and drew the beads towards her heart.

Close to us, women in headscarves dropped to their knees, followed by their children and then men drawing the sign of the cross in front of them. Sister Beatrice came forward to lift the wheelchair down the steps. Some men rushed forward to help, and they set us down on the path to the *santuario*.

Although my hands were on the wheelchair and we were moving forward, it was the crowd that pressed us on, straining at us from behind the cordon, which marked our way.

As we passed, heads bowed. 'Pray for us,' called one woman, her voice quivering in the silence. Some children were holding flowers, and when a little girl ran out in front of the wheelchair to give hers to Elisabetta, I had to stop abruptly. Elisabetta smiled at the little girl, around four or five years of age, dressed in her Sunday best. She accepted the long white lily stems with grace and held the lilies close to her, breathing in their heavy perfume. A murmur of approval rose from those who could see what was happening and the little girl moved to the edge of the path, beside a proud mother who reached a hand to her child. Both bobbed as we moved on.

Before long, flowers were being thrown in the wheelchair's path. As we rolled over them, I thought was how sad it was that they should be crushed and trampled.

All the while, Sister Beatrice walked alongside us, her presence calm and dignified. She kept a close eye on Elisabetta, like an anxious mother looking out for a fretful child, placing a hand on Elisabetta's shoulder from time to time. Elisabetta looked back at her gratefully. The snip of jealously I often experienced when I was alone with the two of them returned, but much weaker, and I was glad to have Sister Beatrice beside us. If the crowd on either side of us moved too close, she instructed them with a stern look to keep back.

As we approached the *santuario*, the sweet sound of the orphanage children singing 'Ave Maria' greeted us. Sister Beatrice had told me that even Padre Bosco didn't have the heart to deny the children their moment of glory and had consented that they could still sing the entry to the mass. Their innocent voices caused Sister Beatrice to wipe away a tear. It was good to see them, scrubbed clean and standing proud in their blue sashes of the Madonna. I kept looking at them, rather than the crowd gawping at us as we moved closer to the altar.

Signora Visconti stepped forward, indicating the space that had been reserved for Elisabetta. But Sister Beatrice and Signora Visconti struggled to keep the path clear in front of us as people pressed ever closer for a view of Elisabetta. We slowed to a halt. Hands reached out to touch her as she recoiled in her seat. Frozen with panic, I was relieved when an angry Giulio pushed his way through the sea of faces.

'Give them some space, *per l'amore di Dio*,' he exclaimed. Some people stepped back, but Giulio was not satisfied.

'Leave her be! Is this how you treat her?'

Heads bowed, people fell back. Giulio looked at me and, without hesitation, I handed the wheelchair over to him.

'It's ok,' he whispered to me, before leaning down to Elisabetta as she clung to her rosary and blanket. 'Don't worry, I'll stay with you now.'

I didn't look at him, still upset at what had happened the day before. But it was good to have him beside me.

A last lily stem was hanging forlornly from a spoke of the wheelchair, the others having been lost in the press of people. I pulled it away and threw it to one side with some force.

Giulio steered Elisabetta to an empty space next to the broken Madonna. She'd been simply but elegantly surrounded by vases of white flowers. The most perfect specimens of lilies lay at her feet. It was clearly Signora Visconti's handiwork.

With Sister Beatrice, I took my place and kept my eyes down, grateful for Dottor and Signora Visconti alongside us, baby Renato asleep in his pram. With my palms, I smoothed down my skirt and kept them there, pressing down, trying to stop my legs from shaking and concentrated on the rounded pebbles at my feet to calm myself.

Elisabetta sat in the wheelchair, her eyes closed, tucked under her pale blue blanket. A memory came back to me of how Elisabetta and I had found a baby bird not far from here, ousted from its nest and struggling to breathe. Elisabetta had insisted we stay with it until the end, while the thought of watching it die had been unbearable to me. She'd made it a little raft of sticks to send it on to 'a better place' down river, while I looked away.

She prayed for some time. Occasionally her eyelids fluttered a little, but otherwise she remained absorbed. The crowd seemed to hold its breath, an occasional cough interrupting the sound of the river flowing over the pebbles.

Behind Elisabetta, Giulio stood, eyes closed, hands clasped in prayer. From beneath my eyelashes, I took him in, smart in his suit. A familiar surge of feeling returned. His face, although damaged and blemished, still drew me. All the while, I was telling myself that I had to forget him. He opened his eyes and looked in my direction with an embarrassed smile. I returned it shyly, feeling warmth rising in my cheeks.

But his eyes were looking past me. I turned and glimpsed an older woman, her face framed by a heavy black lace mantilla. She inclined her head slightly towards Giulio. I craned to get a better look at her, but she'd taken a step back, disappearing behind two elderly women who took advantage of her front row place.

Unsettled, I looked at Giulio. Was this the woman he'd met yesterday? Surely, she couldn't be the object of his desire? I'd only glimpsed her, but she had the air of a more mature woman. Why would Giulio be interested in an older woman? I hung my head.

The bell for mass startled me.

Elisabetta made a slow sign of the cross. Turning to Giulio, she indicated he should adjust the wheelchair more towards the altar for mass.

Monsignor Roberto appeared like a peacock in purple, followed by a procession of young altar servers, who were clearly enjoying showing off their brand-new cassocks and surplices. At the rear came Padre Bosco, whose unsteady feet struggled with the pebbles. Away from San Donato, he looked older and when he approached the altar, bowing stiffly and slowly to Monsignor Roberto, it was clear that the man who held so much sway in Atina was a mere servant to this more important priest. A sigh of disappointment trickled through the crowd as they realised that a standard mass was about to be conducted by Padre Bosco.

Padre Bosco worked his way through mass at a slow pace. At first, the congregation was respectful and chanted their responses diligently, distracted from Padre Bosco's predictable delivery by the man in purple. With a full head of white hair, round gold-rimmed glasses and a stern expression, Monsignor Roberto had the air of a headmaster. He kept stroking the heavy jewelled crucifix on his chest while scanning his audience, looking pleased with himself. I disliked him immediately.

As Padre Bosco plodded through the gloria, Sister Beatrice's leg was jiggling beneath her habit. She looked across to Elisabetta, who stared at Padre Bosco without flinching. Giulio's gaze was also trained on the old priest. Baby Renato chose that moment to bawl with all his tiny might. Shushing him brought Signora Visconti no reprieve, only harsh stares from Monsignor Roberto. She unbuttoned her blouse and Renato pawed at her angrily as if to say, 'what took you so long?' He took her nipple and fed greedily, showing his displeasure at having been kept waiting with more loud crying before snuffling to her breast again. Monsignor Roberto wrinkled his face in disgust.

Away from his stronghold of San Donato and out in the open air of the river, Padre Bosco was shrinking. The wind spirited his voice away. He shouted, which only made him come across in angry, half-heard bursts. The wind picked up and the leaves of the trees rustled louder. The river streamed with force over the pebbles, gushing like a heavy downpour of rain in the middle of a thunderstorm.

Impatience was brewing in the crowd. There were stifled yawns and questioning looks. Why was the old man in charge when they'd all come to see Elisabetta? They'd hoped there'd be another miracle before she left, and if not, they'd come to pray for her restored health, that the Flower Girl of Atina would soon be amongst them again, fully recovered, ready to bring the Madonna back to them.

The colour in Monsignor Roberto's face was close to matching the colour of his robes. Exasperated, he rose to his feet and was about to take Padre Bosco's place at the altar when a movement caught the corner of my eye.

I swivelled round to Elisabetta.

She was raising her outstretched arms to the sky.

The crowd held its breath as all eyes turned to her.

Her head arched backwards against the wheelchair. Her eyes wide-open, Elisabetta's face took on a radiant smile.

Sister Beatrice dropped to her knees beside me and took my hand and pulled me down too. I wanted to go to Elisabetta but all around us the crowd was falling to their knees, some looking at Elisabetta, others looking up at the sky, lifting their arms. A hum of excitement rippled around me.

Elisabetta brought her hands to her face, then to her heart. Her hands remained there for some time before she brought them up to her lips, releasing a kiss towards the crowd.

'She's here with us today.'

Elisabetta's voice rang clear across the *santuario*.

Murmurs and gasps all around me soon settled into a reverential silence. A tight squeeze to my hand reminded me that Sister Beatrice still had hold of me, but like everyone else, I was watching Elisabetta, transfixed.

She was happy, as if she was being released from all her pain.

'You are loved.'

Her voice was full of joy. She leant forward in her wheelchair, her arms outstretched in readiness for an embrace.

People turned to one another. Some clasped hands, families drew closer. There was a quiet hush. Sister Beatrice's hand was shaking in mine, but her eyes focused on Elisabetta. I glanced across to the Viscontis. They were the picture of the perfect family: Dottor Visconti with his arm across his wife's shoulders, Signora Visconti cradling Renato to her breast.

My urge was to go to Elisabetta, to be at her side as I'd always been. But it was Giulio kneeling closest to Elisabetta's wheelchair. The Last Supper, hanging in the refectory at the orphanage came to mind as I looked at him. Even though he was right next to her, Giulio seemed withdrawn, just like Judas in the painting.

Behind the altar, Monsignor Roberto and Padre Bosco remained still. They looked at one another and then to the crowd, unsure what to do.

Nobody was paying them attention. All eyes were directed at Elisabetta, and she spoke again. Her words came slowly, the intensity of her emotion growing.

'I am always with you.'

Elisabetta inhaled deeply.

'I want you to have a different life. One without pain and suffering. A life full of happiness. It's time to make the life you deserve.'

As the crowd puzzled at her words, Elisabetta fell back into her wheelchair, limp.

Giulio leant towards her and reached for her hand. He flicked his head towards me, and I shook myself free from Sister Beatrice's grasp.

'Elisabetta, Elisabetta!'

I was screaming, my hands tangled in her rosary beads, when Dottor Visconti lifted me away from Elisabetta. A sea of faces swarmed in like flies.

'Giulio!' I cried from where Dottor Visconti had deposited me. A jostling fray had formed around Elisabetta. People were pressing at me from all around, pushing towards Elisabetta. Monsignor Roberto elbowed his way past me.

'Giulio!' A mob was closing in. My feeble voice was drowned by the commotion around me. 'Giulio, *aiutami!*'

'Let us through!' Giulio was shouting with such force that people stood back for him to reach me. On his heels, there was a distressed woman clutching a red-faced toddler to her chest. Her heavy black lace mantilla had slipped from one side of her pale face. I stared at her. Before me were the blue eyes that I'd looked into so many times. Elisabetta's eyes.

In the crush, Giulio took my hand and kept a protective arm behind the woman, pressing us up against each other. The toddler in her arms had the same blue eyes too. There was a flicker of a smile in the woman's features, even though her face told me she was in as much anguish as me.

'You're safe, Adelina,' she said in a soft voice.

A shudder ran through me, my mind tangled with who she was and how she knew my name. But Giulio was shouting, 'Out of the way,' forcing people apart. He barged our way through until we were at Elisabetta's wheelchair.

Elisabetta's eyes closed as Dottor Visconti pulled a needle from her arm.

'We need to get her out of here as soon as possible.' He turned to Giulio, who immediately lifted Elisabetta into his arms, holding her slight figure across his body. Elisabetta's eyes flickered open, and I moved towards her, but she looked past me, until she came to the woman holding the baby boy.

She lifted a weak hand towards her, and the woman stepped forward. The mantilla slipped from her face, revealing a woman in her early forties, still beautiful, with shoulder-length dark hair and pale skin.

'You're here,' said Elisabetta, her eyelids drawing down. 'I knew you'd come for me.'

The woman clasped Elisabetta's hand and drew it towards her and the boy. The cries of those around us masked her wretched tears.

Dottor Visconti waved his arms at her angrily. 'This is not a circus. She needs medical attention. Step aside, please.' He gestured sharply at Giulio to move on, not giving the woman a second glance.

With careful tenderness, Giulio eased her hand from Elisabetta's, until only their fingertips were touching.

Bodies pressed in against me, sharp elbows and flailing arms, reaching out for Elisabetta. Dottor Visconti struck out at them as Giulio edged away, carrying Elisabetta. I wanted to follow, but the woman was swaying as if about to fall. The toddler was still in her arms, and I propped her up for long enough, the child caught between us, for Sister Beatrice to reach us and take the child into her arms. The boy thumped clenched fists against her, writhing to return to his mother. Sister Beatrice took firm hold of him, and he gave in.

In my arms, the woman had steadied, but was still shaking. She was shorter than me, with the same pale skin as Elisabetta, even a familiar way of looking both grateful and lost at the same time.

People continued to press in on us, menacing in their eagerness. The purple robes of Monsignor Roberto stood firm as he glanced sideways at the woman. 'Nothing to see here,' he called, the authority clear in his voice. 'Go home now. You've seen what you wanted to see,' he continued, waving them away. He swatted people away like annoying flies, sneering as he did so. Heads down in deference, they fell back as ordered.

My hands were still on the woman's arms. As Monsignor Roberto spoke, she shrank from my hold, her trembling reaching my palms.

Monsignor Roberto stood with his back to her. He waited for the crowd to disperse, stony-faced. He didn't look at or speak to her. But when a red-faced Padre Bosco reached us, he looked her up and down and then spat at her feet.

In shock, I stepped back, pushing up against Sister Beatrice, who was still holding the boy. He shrieked and seized the opportunity to wriggle free of Sister Beatrice. He barged into Padre Bosco at full pelt, and the old man buckled as the little boy ran back to his mother's waiting arms.

'Quick!' I whispered to her as Monsignor Roberto and Sister Beatrice bent down to see to Padre Bosco. 'Come with me.'

She nodded, and I pushed my way through the crowd, which parted to make way for us. The boy's laughter, excited at the game he thought we were playing, drowned out Monsignor Roberto's insistent calls for us to stop.

In the distance, the ambulance ready to take Elisabetta to the convalescent home was in sight, parked in a quiet spot near the orphanage garden, out of bounds to the crowds. I ran as fast as I could, glancing over my shoulder to check she was close behind. The boy was squealing with delight as she caught up with me.

'I've spent so many years running from them,' she said, gulping for air, putting her little boy to the ground for a moment. 'But really I've been running away from myself and Elisabetta,' she said between breaths. 'I hadn't realised until today, Adelina. I've been running scared all these years.'

'Are you Elisabetta's...?' There was a part of me that couldn't quite say the word. Mother.

She nodded. 'I'm Maria,' she said, breathing deeply. She took my hand. 'I've come from England. I'm not going to run away again.'

Her palm was soft, her hold tender. Her face relaxed, as if she could finally let go of a burden that she'd carried for a very long time.

There were so many questions I wanted to ask Maria, but my first thought was that I wanted to please her, to help her.

'I don't think we have much time,' I said, not letting go of her hand, until we caught up with her little boy, who had continued to run towards the orphanage garden. Maria scooped him up, and we ran as fast as we could.

~

Ahead of us, Giulio was laying a motionless Elisabetta onto a stretcher, held at either end by men in white uniforms. At her head, Dottor Visconti was speaking and waving his hands at a man in a suit, who bent down towards Elisabetta, his stethoscope poised.

Giulio caught sight of us and stepped away from the stretcher, urging us to hurry. The little boy wriggled away from his mother's arms and got to the ambulance first. He ran straight to Giulio as if he were a long-lost friend, and Giulio responded in kind, holding the little boy to him. Maria reached them before me, a stitch in my side forcing me to stop a few paces back.

'They're about to leave,' said Giulio as he approached Maria with the little boy in his arms. 'The doctor from the convalescent home says they've got the medication she needs in the ambulance.'

The two men slid the stretcher into the vehicle, and I rushed forward to see Elisabetta, but the other doctor climbed in beside her and blocked my view.

'Where are they taking her?' pleaded Maria. 'I've come all the way from England. I can't let her go again!'

She banged on the closing rear doors of the ambulance. One of the stretcher bearers poked his head out of the door.

'Where are you taking her? I need to know. Tell me now.'

The young man cowered. 'The asylum,' he blurted. Realising what he'd said, his hand reached for his mouth, too late. The doctor in the ambulance pulled him back inside and slammed the door behind them. Tyres screeched as the ambulance pulled away.

An open-mouthed Dottor Visconti stood in the parting trail of dust. 'What asylum?' he stammered. 'She's meant to be going to a convalescent home. Padre Bosco organised it.'

At the sound of his name, Maria wailed and dropped to her knees.

Her hands covered her face as her body rocked backwards, then forwards.

Dottor Visconti looked to Maria, then Giulio and me. Giulio was shaking his head, muttering a swear word and Padre Bosco's name under his breath. All I could do was stand there, covered in hot panic.

'What's going on?' said Dottor Visconti. His grizzled, creased face was showing his age. 'Who's this woman?'

Before anyone could answer, Sister Beatrice arrived, pushing Padre Bosco in Elisabetta's wheelchair. She let go of the wheelchair and stood alone in the space left by the ambulance.

'They've gone already? But Elisabetta… What's happened?' she asked, but nobody replied.

'Will somebody please have the courtesy to tell me what's happening here?' said Dottor Visconti, growing redder in the face. He turned to Padre Bosco, furious.

'Luigi? Why is Elisabetta being taken to an asylum? You said you'd arranged a convalescent home.'

The old priest waved a scornful, indignant hand in the air.

'Asylum, convalescent home? They're all the same to me,' he shrugged. 'The girl's mad,' he crowed. 'The Madonna has never appeared here. It's just a girl with fantasies and a lot of deluded people. Not even her best friend believed her!' he sneered, turning towards me. 'Ask her yourself!'

Giulio turned sharply towards me.

I couldn't meet the shock and disappointment in his eyes. My body was shaking. I heard a surprised intake of breath all around me.

'You evil man!' roared Sister Beatrice, letting fly.

Nobody was looking at me now.

'You and Monsignor Roberto had this all planned, didn't you? I was such a fool to believe that you cared about Elisabetta. You're only interested in yourselves.'

Giulio moved beside Sister Beatrice in a show of support and glared at the priest. I was grateful that he wasn't still looking at me.

'Where is your important friend, anyway?' asked Sister Beatrice.

Padre Bosco looked away, as if he too was wondering what had become of Monsignor Roberto, but Sister Beatrice hadn't finished.

'You denounce Elisabetta, then when you see people believe in her and her visions, you try and make yourself look good, with the wheelchair and the story of the convalescent home, all the time planning to get her out of the way and lock her up in an asylum.'

I walked over to Maria and gave her a hand up from where she was still kneeling on the ground, distraught. The little boy, who had been sitting quietly beside her, got up too. Sister Beatrice was still shouting at Padre Bosco.

'How many more lives, besides Elisabetta's, have you wrecked? Call yourself a man of God? You and Monsignor Roberto should be ashamed of yourselves.'

'At least I don't go round spreading lies about visions and female priests,' Padre Bosco snapped back, looking to Dottor Visconti for support.

Dottor Visconti shook his head and looked to the ground. 'Elisabetta's a child. She needs medical help.'

'And she'll get it, along with help for her madness,' Padre Bosco replied.

'You're everything I despise about the male church,' said Sister Beatrice, turning on her heel back towards the orphanage. Giulio took Maria's arm, and they walked away, as did Dottor Visconti.

For a moment, I stood there, not knowing what to do. Padre Bosco was stranded in the wheelchair, boiling with rage. He turned towards a rustle in the trees.

'You can come out now. It's all over,' he said wearily.

Monsignor Roberto emerged, brushing leaves off his purple robes. He shot me a look to send me back to the orphanage too. I pressed down hard on a pearl of Elisabetta's rosary, which was still dangling from my fingers, and followed the others.

Part 3

26

Giulio

The heat of the day had stewed into a dull, stormy torpor, which kept people at home, spurning their usual passegiata. Giulio was grateful for the dark cloud cover, which allowed his distinctive gait to disappear into the shadows. He made his way to the outer edge of Atina, past tall dark fields of ripening maize and picked his way down a weed-strewn path towards Romana Antonelli's home.

Behind a bead curtain which had seen better days, the threads visible, the front door was open. His heart beating fast, Giulio tapped the metal pole supporting the nearby washing line three times, the signal they'd arranged if there was any news of Elisabetta.

Maria appeared immediately, wiping her hands on a cloth. With a quick glance over her shoulder, Maria put a finger to her lips and beckoned towards a low wall hidden by thick oleander, away from the house. In the shaft of light from the house, Giulio couldn't help but notice that the top buttons of her blouse were open, the pale skin of her neck and upper chest glistening in the heat.

'You have some news?' she whispered, rubbing at the worry lines in her forehead.

He frowned and shook his head. Her face crumpled in disappointment, and he put out his hand, guiding her to sit on the wall.

'Can we talk? Are your mother and Christian sleeping?'

'Yes, they're both fast asleep,' she sighed. 'With Christian, it's like she's gone back in time and calls him Franco or Antonio, as if he's one of her baby sons. He happily sits on her knee while she plays peekaboo with him, and he repeats back the words of the nursery rhymes to her. They're as thick as thieves.'

'And you?'

'One minute she treats me as if I've never been away, and in the next breath, she gets angry, asks me who I am.' Maria shrugged her shoulders. 'My mother and I, we never quite saw eye to eye, even at the best of times.'

The noisy cicadas filled the silence.

'Adelina,' Giulio started, his voice hesitant.

'Has something happened to Adelina?' Maria replied, her eyebrows sharpening with concern.

'No, no,' Giulio replied, shaking his head. 'Adelina came to visit earlier with the Visconti baby, she said…'

Nerves nibbled at Giulio, but he knew he had to finish what he'd started and couldn't tell Maria that Adelina was beside herself, distraught at the loss of Elisabetta.

'Adelina… she suggested I ask you about Monsignor Roberto,' he said, drawing out the words, 'If you know him? Whether he might know where they've taken Elisabetta.'

Maria bowed her head. Her shoulders slumped in a way that made Giulio think of a flat bicycle tyre.

'Adelina saw him the morning before everything that happened. He went with Padre Bosco to see Sister Beatrice.' Giulio's bad leg was throbbing. 'Adelina said you were tired of running away from them.'

Maria swallowed hard.

'Monsignor Roberto.' She pronounced his name with a note of weariness. It hung in the stormy air of the night.

'That man,' she said, looking down into her lap, 'has a lot to answer for.'

'You can trust me.'

'Dearest Giulio,' Maria replied, anguish clouding her face. She took his hand, and a shiver ran through his body. 'You're the *only* person I trust. But I'm afraid your opinion of me will change.'

'I'd never judge you,' he replied, looking up into her eyes as she patted his hand as if he were a child.

'There's someone I need to see, to find Elisabetta. Will you help me?'

At those last words, Giulio would have done anything that Maria asked. He wanted so much to make amends for having taken Elisabetta away from her as a baby, to reunite mother and daughter, the child he loved, who had cured him.

Whatever she was about to ask him to do, it wouldn't touch what he'd had to deal with as a soldier on the front or the agony of his injuries. He could handle it, he told himself, if it meant that they could find Elisabetta. Together.

27

The train hugged the deep wooded hillside, cutting a swathe through trees brandishing their early autumn glory. The regularity of the slow *ddum-ddum* of the wheels on the track helped to soothe Giulio, dampening thoughts of what was to come. He'd never been to this part of Italy, known for the finer things in life – art of the masters and food and wine for the most discerning palate. It was all far from his experience as a humble gardener from the impoverished, forgotten south. But he could appreciate the bounty of nature. All around reds, golds and oranges besieged him.

A vast blue lake appeared in pockets between the trees. A weak sun glistened on its surface, picking out gentle waves.

He looked across at Maria sitting opposite, clutching Christian. They were both dozing. He'd have to wake them soon, but for that moment he could take her in without reserve. Her chestnut hair had worked free from her loose bun, her eyes were fringed with delicate lines, her lips parted. A clear, simple beauty, like nature itself.

The conductor walked through the carriage, upright and proud in his dark blue uniform. 'Santa Croce next stop!' he pronounced, pausing by the three of them. His voice jolted Maria and a fractious Christian awake. As a proud veteran, the conductor had taken the injured ex-soldier and his supposed family from the South under his wing for the journey, assuring him he wouldn't let them miss their destination. Giulio's facial disfigurement made his age difficult to gauge and, although fifteen years younger than Maria, he could pass as her husband without a second thought. He was enjoying the pretence.

'Let me help you with that,' said the conductor, pulling down two light bags from the luggage rack.

'That's very kind of you,' replied Maria. She yawned and brushed loose strands of hair from her face as Giulio lifted Christian from her lap. Even Christian seemed to have fallen into the game and accepted Giulio cajoling him into his coat.

'Where are you headed? Do you have someone meeting you at the station?' enquired the conductor. Giulio knew he was just being friendly, but he sensed Maria tense and stepped in with a reply.

'No, we'll be needing a taxi at the station. Is there likely to be one there?'

'I'm sure there will be, but if not, just ask at the counter and they'll help you.'

'Thank you.'

The conductor made a performance of descending the train steps with the bags, offering a hand to Maria, then Christian. He gave Giulio the time to take the steps at his own pace. It was a mark of respect which touched Giulio.

'Have a pleasant stay,' the conductor said, and the family of three returned his wave as one.

~

They'd agreed they would rest overnight. He hadn't questioned her about who they were going to see and had trusted that Maria had her reasons, but he wondered if it had something to do with Monsignor Roberto. When they arrived at the small pensione in the village, the unspoken assumption that they would have separate rooms had been superseded by their little masquerade with the conductor. The old woman who owned the house showed them to a large room with a double bed and a cot in a nook away from the bed, separated by a curtain. Christian had recovered his good humour and immediately took a liking to the hiding place of the cot behind the curtain.

'Maybe I should ask her if she has another room?' ventured Giulio as Maria dropped her bag on the floor.

'And provoke her curiosity? I don't think that's a good idea in small place like this.'

The double bed loomed large in front of him, and he stepped back from it as if it might be about to burn him. 'I'll sleep on the

179

chair,' he said, nodding towards an uncomfortable looking armchair. He stood awkwardly with his back to her, looking for all the world like he was interested in the view from the window. He was staring at the dull wall of the adjacent building.

'How's your leg?' she asked. 'You looked uncomfortable when you were walking before.'

Maria was sitting on the bed, unlacing her shoes. She looked across to the cot. Christian was behind the curtain, but he was sucking on his thumb loudly, exhausted after the journey. He would be asleep in a matter of moments.

'Have a rest. You'll feel better for it,' she said. With motherly care, she plumped a pillow and patted it.

With his back to Maria, Giulio lowered himself onto the bed, his left leg sore and aching. The mattress was comfortable, and he was dog-tired. He slowly took off his left boot and shuffled onto the bed. Laying on his back, he closed his eyes and took a deep breath. The bed creaked as Maria sat beside him, keeping a clear space between them.

'Do you want to tell me what happened?' she whispered, resting a protective hand on his, the one that had carried a stick for so many years. A shiver ran through him as a deep sigh left his body.

'I was on guard duty,' he started, his eyes still closed. 'The day the Italian Army surrendered to the Allies in September forty-three.'

Giulio's face drew into a grimace, his cheeks burnt red.

Maria swallowed and pressed his hand gently.

'When the Italian officer in charge gave the boys the news that Italy was no longer fighting alongside the Germans, there was chaos. Nobody knew what to do,' he stuttered. 'It was every man for himself.'

In a quick, desperate huddle with his friends from Atina who were part of the same squad, they decided the best thing was to make a run for it.

'We tried to hide, get rid of our uniforms, but the German soldiers were thirsty for revenge. They aimed their rifles and grenades at us.'

A shudder ran through Giulio's body.

'My friends died right in front of me. Four young lads I'd grown up with, known all my life, blown to pieces. Body parts in my face, their blood all over me.'

He was shaking, and swiped his free hand across his face violently, again and again. Maria gripped his other hand tighter in hers until he stopped, and his body started to soften. His voice came back quieter, strained.

He told her of long days stuck in a filthy bed in the distant prisoner of war camp, as he made a slow recovery from the injuries that robbed him of his youth, his movement and the sight in one eye. Alone, without any of the friends he had fought with, and as far from Atina as he could be.

Giulio sobbed hard and deep. But as the sobs started to ebb, his mind felt a strange lightness, a relief he hadn't expected from speaking about what he'd kept locked inside for so long.

For her part, Maria told him that during the war she had been mobilised to nurse the injured Allies at Monte Cassino in the battle which had proved decisive to the Allies' fortunes but had cost so many lives.

'There was so little medicine or equipment, there wasn't much I could really do,' she sighed.

'So, I listened. I heard those young men yearning for home and their loves in countries I didn't know, whose languages I couldn't really understand.'

Her eyes were glistening. 'It was the only comfort I could offer. I still see their faces. I remember every one of those poor men.'

In between the long pauses, the two bared, wounded souls listened to each other breathing. Giulio stared at the dusty trail of spider webs hanging from the ceiling, until his right eyelid started to flicker shut. When Maria got down from the bed and found a blanket for the armchair, Giulio's last thought before he drifted to sleep was how he wanted to spare Maria any further loss.

He'd do all he could to reunite her with Elisabetta.

28

At the far side of a cobbled courtyard dotted with ancient moss, an unprepossessing arched doorway awaited them.

Christian insisted on holding both his mother's hand and Giulio's. After a few paces, he wouldn't move until they gave in to him. '*Sì, sì!*' Christian cried in the Italian he'd been hearing his mother speak, planting his feet on the cobbles in a way that made it clear they had no option but to give in to him. Maria made a mock face, as if to deny him his wish. Christian looked up at Giulio. With perfect co-ordination, Maria and Giulio swung Christian off the ground upwards, to squeals of delight.

As Christian's legs kicked the air, Giulio saw a row of three stern holy statues above the doorway, set deep into the honey-coloured walls. Each was enclosed in a tight protective alcove. They were hidden from the light, their niches dark. *What are you doing here?* they goaded, staring down at him.

Giulio's arm went limp. Christian fell heavily and cried. Maria helped him up, but her eyes were trained on Giulio, who was looking up at the statues, his weight shifting from his good leg to his bad leg.

'We've come all this way,' she said, taking Giulio gently by the arm. 'Let's keep to what we discussed. We have to… for Elisabetta's sake.'

He nodded weakly. It should have been him reassuring her, not the other way round. The tight collar of his shirt chafed at his skin, and he pulled it away from the flush of heat spreading up his neck and into his face. Damned tie, he thought to himself, unaccustomed to having to make himself look serious and presentable. He'd so wanted to get everything right for Maria.

'You're sure?' he asked, his voice sounding like a child's.

She placed a calming hand on his arm. He straightened up but the feeling was back, stronger than before. A creeping foreboding.

Maria flashed him a reassuring smile and linked her arm in his. At this, Christian stopped crying and snatched his mother's free hand. Together they approached the threshold as they had intended, as if they were a family.

~

The contrast between the pockmarked exterior of the building, with its missing plaques of plaster which looked to have crumbled away centuries earlier, and the impressive marble columns inside, could not have been starker.

'Ooh!' gasped Christian, the sound echoing across the hall, which made him stop in his tracks and look up at his mother.

Designed to magnify the status of its occupant and keep the lowly in their places, it had the desired effect on Giulio, whose nerves grew as he fumbled with a coin in his pocket. If she was overawed, Maria did not let it show. She shushed Christian and he instantly obeyed, staring at each of the austere statues of the saints in turn.

Beneath a carved marble tableau of the Madonna on her knees praying to her baby son, a simple brass handbell stood on an elegant half-moon table.

Maria looked to Giulio, and although Giulio's heart knew he would come to regret this moment, he nodded.

The bell rang loud and clear. Christian's eyes lit up at the sound and he looked expectantly towards the back of the hall where an open door gave a glimpse of the cloisters and courtyard beyond. Soon enough, there came the sound of footsteps on the marble tiles and an elderly priest scurried towards them. Giulio saw his look of surprise as he appraised them. The edge of pity was there that Giulio was familiar with whenever a stranger encountered his injuries for the first time. Today it was about to serve them well.

'How may I help you?' the priest asked, his tone respectful. He inclined his head towards Giulio. Maria and Giulio bowed slightly in response.

Holding Christian slightly ahead of her, who flashed a coy smile at the priest, Maria stepped forward. The priest returned Christian's smile, giving Maria the courage she needed.

'I understand this is most unusual,' Maria said, balancing charm with a note of assurance, 'but we wondered if it would be possible to see Bishop Morelli?'

The priest gave her a quizzical look, but Maria continued before he could reply, confident in the story that Giulio had willingly agreed to.

'During the war, Bishop Morelli met my husband at the Ospedale Santa Caterina after he received his terrible injuries. He prayed with us and gave us hope when the situation was very bleak. We returned for a final check-up this week and as you can see—' Maria paused, looking to Giulio and then to Christian '—he has made an incredible recovery.'

'I see,' nodded the priest, looking Giulio up and down. Giulio managed a weak smile, playing along with the story Maria had invented.

'We just wanted to thank him, personally. This will be the last time we will travel here. We come from the south, in the Apennine Mountains. He told us he grew up there. That's why I think he understood us so well...'

'Yes, Bishop Morelli is from a village in the mountains, a man of the people,' said the priest, 'as I am myself.' He sighed with a hint of wistfulness. 'You never forget where you come from.'

Maria and Giulio let their silence do the work.

'It is most irregular to call unannounced,' the priest started, but his tone soon softened. 'Wednesday is our quiet day. Most of the staff have their day off to coincide with Bishop Morelli's. His private secretary, Monsignor Roberto, is not here today, but the bishop is. Perhaps I might...'

The absence of Monsignor Roberto encouraged Maria, and she gave the elderly priest a respectful smile.

'If you could assist us, we would be most grateful.'

Flattered, the priest returned her smile. 'If you could let me have your name, I'll see what I can do.'

'Maria Antonelli,' she replied, her head held high.

Giulio sank down onto the gleaming wooden pew where the priest indicated they should wait. Without the need to bypass Monsignor Roberto with their pretence of being a family using Giulio's name, his role was gone.

~

Christian squirmed and wriggled on the pew. His movements made Giulio even more nervous. His bad leg jiggled. Next to him, Maria was staring into her lap.

The priest hurried back with a proud smile on his face. Gracious, Maria let him believe he had indeed persuaded Bishop Morelli of the virtues of this God-fearing family. She followed him along the cloisters at two steps removed, clutching Christian by the hand. Giulio dragged behind them, his bad leg making a scraping sound, which reverberated around the cloisters.

Knocking with a quiet, reverential tap, the priest listened for the instruction to enter. The voice on the other side of the door sounded a little hesitant to Giulio, but he wasn't sure if he was imagining it. The priest opened the door, stepping aside for the three of them before withdrawing discreetly.

~

Giulio recognised the man in front of him immediately. Peppe Morelli, now Bishop Morelli, hadn't changed much. Older, naturally, and a little fuller of face and figure. Slivers of grey in his lush head of hair gave the impression of a man in his prime, the adolescent glint in his eye still there, shining like the fat gold ring on his finger and the heavy cross at his chest, set with what looked like rubies, matching the red buttons and trim on his black vestments. Giulio couldn't help but bow, struck dumb at seeing him again in such splendour.

Bishop Giuseppe Morelli had been Giulio's neighbour when he was a young boy. The older teenager had taught Giulio and his twin brother Carlo to skim stones at River Mollarino when they were mischievous young scallywags. Peppe had left Atina under a cloud, not long after. Something to do with the *contadini*, the farmworkers, making their voices heard against the landowners, but those years at the beginning of Mussolini's reign now seemed so long ago.

Peppe, Bishop Morelli, remained standing behind his desk as he beckoned his guests to seats opposite him.

His eyes devoured Maria. He appraised her carefully, urging her to look at him, but her gaze remained on the polished tiles beneath her feet. Unable to witness what was clearly an old intimacy unfolding, Giulio turned away.

Sensing the tension in the silence, Christian grizzled on Maria's knee. Giulio whistled to catch Christian's attention, and the little boy slid from Maria and allowed himself to be hoisted onto Giulio's knees. At least he could do that, distract him, so that Maria could say what she had come for.

Peppe's eyes darted between Maria and Giulio and the little boy, back to Maria again.

For a split second, Giulio saw panic in Peppe's eyes. Christian chose that moment to wriggle off his knee and he toddled over to a window that framed a perfect view of the lake and ran his fingers through the golden tassels of the heavy curtains. Giulio followed Christian, his back to Maria and Peppe. He was grateful for the sight of the still blue waters.

'Why have you come, Maria?' Peppe whispered. Giulio could tell he had moved from behind the desk and was close to her.

'You know why,' she said, her voice resolute and calm.

'You could have come alone...'

'I needed a way to get past Monsignor Roberto. He'd stop me from speaking to you. That's why I asked Giulio to come with me.'

'Giulio?'

'You don't recognise him, do you?'

'Should I?' Bishop Morelli's voice had an edge of impatience.

'Have you really forgotten who you were? Before you became

a priest? Don't you even remember where you lived, who your neighbours were?'

Giulio turned round, his heart beating hard in his chest, and Peppe stepped towards him, narrowing his eyes.

'It can't be, surely?' he exclaimed, 'Little Giulio Conti!' Peppe extended his hand towards him, the gesture warm and sincere but Giulio shrank from him, embarrassed. 'I had no idea, forgive me,' Bishop Morelli said, trying not to let his eyes rest on Giulio's disfigured face.

'The war,' replied Giulio, shifting his weight uncomfortably.

'I'm so sorry.' The Bishop reached out and tapped Giulio's arm in genuine understanding.

'There's no need for you to feel pity for me.'

Giulio wanted to hate him. But he had only ever looked up to Peppe Morelli. His swagger had made him popular as one of the '*ragazzi*', but he was equally comfortable as a sacristan at San Donato, the apple of Padre Bosco's eye. As a child, Giulio had wished Peppe was his older brother.

Giulio took his seat. Peppe looked lost for a moment and turned towards Maria.

'Giulio's not my husband.'

Maria's quick retort hurt Giulio. He'd wanted to savour that moment where the man he had worshipped as a child might feel a little jealous of him. He slumped back into the plush upholstered seat.

Peppe took up his position behind his desk, a quizzical look on his face.

'I don't understand.'

'My husband's name is Colin. He's English, I live in England with him. Christian is Colin's son.'

At the sound of his name, Christian rushed over to his mother and took her hand. He glared suspiciously at the man tapping the desk with a slow index finger.

'England, how did you end up there?' Peppe asked, his brow

knitted in a string of questions.

'Colin was an English officer at Monte Cassino. They needed nurses, and I had learnt a little English. Anyway, that's got nothing to do with you and it's not why I'm here.'

Peppe recoiled, clearly unused to anyone speaking to him directly. He looked at Giulio, perhaps seeking an ally, but Giulio didn't respond.

'There's a lot you don't know,' said Maria, fixing Peppe with a determined look.

'So it would seem.'

Peppe leant back in his chair. His face disappeared behind his hands, his fingertips kneading his temples. Eventually, he drew them together in the sign of prayer. He stood up and addressed Maria.

'What do you want?'

In his manner and speech, he was Bishop Morelli again, who had clearly achieved his position by knowing how to deal with delicate matters. Giulio suddenly remembered how, before the war, he had once found a newspaper cutting from *Corriere della Sera* in the back of Padre Bosco's missal, announcing the ordination of a Bishop Morelli, feted as Italy's youngest bishop. It was heralded as a new era of young, senior clergy. But with such a common surname, he had never imagined that Bishop Morelli could ever have been Peppe Morelli, his childhood neighbour.

Giulio and Maria exchanged a glance. Giulio was willing Maria to hold her ground, not to be overawed by the Bishop.

'I want you to tell me where they've taken Elisabetta,' said Maria firmly. '*Our daughter.*'

Giulio's breath caught in his throat. Stunned, he turned towards Maria.

But Maria was barely even aware of his presence, her eyes boring into Peppe's guilty conscience. Giulio gripped the arm of the chair, trying to hold himself steady as he struggled to understand what he had heard. Maria and Peppe? But neither of them had been to Atina in years…

Peppe turned his back to them and walked over to the full-length window with its view over the idyllic lake. A fancy clock on the mantlepiece struck the hour, its twelve chimes vibrating in the silence. When it had ceased, it was the bishop who addressed them.

'A solution is needed first.'

'What do you mean?' Maria's voice was rising, anger replacing composure. 'Elisabetta's grown up without a family, despite what Padre Bosco and Monsignor Roberto promised me! She shouldn't be in an asylum. She's just unwell… lost.'

'She's caused quite a stir with her visions though, hasn't she?'

'I think the visions might have something to do with me, the one time she met me in the piazza when she was little, some sort of memory… I'm not sure,' Maria gulped. 'I told her my name, how I used to play at the river as a child. Maybe…'

Bewildered, Giulio stared at Maria. He rubbed his left leg, trying to understand what Maria had just said, what she meant.

But Peppe was talking again, walking towards Maria.

'The history of the church is littered with girls and young women who claim to see the Madonna,' he said, waving a dismissive arm.

'But she does seem to have caught the imagination of the people, I'll grant her that. A sign of the times we live in, I'm afraid. War, then poverty. A nation needs hope and who better to provide it than a fragile girl who brings messages they can change their fate?'

Giulio wanted to speak out, to tell them he believed in Elisabetta. His head was spinning.

'If the cult of Elisabetta were allowed to continue to grow, it wouldn't be much longer before they go rooting around to find out more about her,' said Peppe, his voice gentler, addressing Maria. 'That's what Padre Bosco had been trying to do, to put a stop to it all, that no connection was ever made with me. He needed a little more help, so Monsignor Roberto stepped in.'

'On your behalf? How can you be so cold and cruel?' Maria was shaking with anger. 'You're talking about a child, *our child.*'

Peppe turned away from Maria.

'Not only did you deny her when I wrote to you, telling you I was pregnant, now you're willing to lock your own daughter in an asylum!'

She fixed him with tears in her eyes.

'What happened to you, *Peppe*?'

At the sound of his name from her lips, Giulio saw the bishop turn back into the teenager he'd held in such high regard. Who'd so obviously been in love with the young Maria. Looking at him, he could see his feelings hadn't changed.

'I don't understand,' stammered Peppe. 'You wrote to me before she was born?'

'Of course! You couldn't have been happy in the church, otherwise we wouldn't have…' Maria blushed.

'I gave you the chance to choose if you wanted a life with me and our child. Finding each other again, all those years after we had both left Atina, it felt like we were being given another chance. But you ran away again and got Monsignor Roberto to write back on your behalf. He made it very clear that you didn't want to hear from me.'

'But I never saw your letter. Monsignor Roberto kept it all from me. He made all the arrangements for her adoption with Padre Bosco. I only found out on the day I was ordained Bishop. It was Padre Bosco who told me, thinking I'd known all along.' Peppe sank back in his chair, rubbing his forehead. 'By then it was all too late.'

Giulio watched as Maria and Peppe exchanged a look that left him feeling as if he should no longer be in the room.

'I was a coward.' Peppe waved a limp hand towards the fine furnishings and high ceiling of his office. 'I owe all this to Monsignor Roberto and Padre Bosco. I couldn't let them down.'

A heavy silence fell on the ornate room, magnified by the ticking of the clock. Only Christian seemed comfortable, sucking his thumb as he sat on his mother's knee, his eyelids flickering shut. Giulio shifted in his chair, aware of Maria trying to make sense of what she'd heard. The bishop was looking out of the window onto the blue void of the lake.

'You must understand my position, Maria,' he said. 'I've worked hard to be here. You know where we came from, the poverty, the lack of opportunity. I gave everything for this, including you. Please don't take it away from me now.'

Maria drew her son closer into her body. 'Tell me where Elisabetta is.'

'But I need to know…'

'I'll take her back to England with me. I'll be the mother to her I always should have been.'

The determination in her voice was as clear to Giulio as it was to Peppe, and although Giulio wanted Maria and Elisabetta to be reunited, he wasn't prepared for this.

'She'll learn English. Elisabetta's a bright girl. She'll get a second chance at life,' she sighed.

Peppe leant back in his seat again, taking his time to reply.

'You're sure? What will your husband say?'

'Leave that with me.'

Peppe rubbed his chin, considering the options.

'I can make sure that people forget about Elisabetta here in Italy, a story of serious illness followed by…' he looked out of the window across the lake '… but it means that neither you nor Elisabetta will ever be able to come back to Italy. You understand that?'

'I should never have allowed the church to take Elisabetta away from me. You and your hypocrite church and this damned country.'

'I can provide a little financial help,' he said, looking at Maria and then turning to Giulio, who immediately understood that payment would extend to him too. Hush money to keep Peppe's secret. Giulio nodded before looking down at his feet.

'I don't want your money.' Maria stood up. 'It'll make no difference to me to never set foot in Italy again.'

Peppe picked up an expensive pen and took a sheet of thick cream headed paper with the bishop's seal from a desk drawer. He wrote quickly, signing his name with a flourish. An envelope was addressed in the same manner.

Maria looked on. The sense of dread Giulio had been carrying with him as he had travelled the length of the country with Maria and Christian now twisted into a hard knot of realisation in his stomach.

29

The journey was long and tiring. Christian was fractious much of the time, sensing his mother's anxiety and Giulio's desperation. He refused to give in to sleep or to eat the panini or cheese his mother offered him. His insistent cries made the passengers around them arch their eyebrows and tut disapprovingly, so much so that even when Christian stopped, Giulio could only whisper in snatches with Maria.

'It doesn't have to be like this,' he pleaded under his breath. 'You don't have to go back to England with Elisabetta.' Maria stared out of the train window, watching the vineyards and cypresses flash past.

'I have a husband, Giulio, he's Christian's father,' Maria replied eventually, trying to avoid eye contact with the other train passengers. 'I've a home in England. Elisabetta will join a ready-made family. Stability is what she needs, a fresh start where nobody knows her history.'

'But Italy is her home, and you know how much I care for Elisabetta...'

'Giulio, you are a good man. But I'm taking Elisabetta to England. There's nothing more to be said.'

~

The taxi driver was reluctant and looked at Christian with an air of pity.

'It's no place to take a child. You realise that?'

'I'll make it worth your while,' said Maria, tapping her handbag. Giulio climbed in wearily beside her.

The driver took the road out into the deeply wooded countryside slowly, as if to underline that they really ought not be taking a child to their intended destination.

He turned into a long driveway with an imposing white building waiting at the end. 'Santa Maria della Pietà,' he announced, glancing over his shoulder at them with a sorrowful look.

Ahead of the car and in front of the large building with arched windows sealed with thick iron bars, were two large groups of people separated from one another, one of women, the other of men, arranged in uneven lines. The women were wearing identical shapeless grey dresses, the men in rough navy jackets and trousers. As they approached, they could hear a drum being played by a man in a white coat. The women and men responded to the dull beat by moving wooden batons which they all held. Some looked intent on their activity and kept with the rhythm, while others looked anguished and confused, their batons at sixes and sevens.

'The poor people in here,' muttered the taxi driver, 'what good is that meant to do them?'

Maria stuffed a generous quantity of banknotes in his outstretched hand without looking at him. Giulio followed her up the stone steps to a large porticoed entrance. He didn't dare a backward glance towards the exercising patients, who unsettled him with their empty stares and awkward movements. Yet he was aware of the eyes of several women on Christian, who dragged his feet, curious and wanting to please his audience. Giulio pulled at Christian's arm with a little too much force and he responded with a sharp yelp. Ahead of him, through the glass entrance doors, Maria was already addressing an officious nurse. She didn't register Christian's cry.

The bishop's seal granted them immediate entry to the principal's office. An elderly, distinguished-looking man with a formal suit under his white coat greeted them. He peered through heavy, dark-rimmed glasses.

'You're here for the Flower Girl of Atina,' he pronounced, indicating the phone on his desk. 'I received advance notification.'

'Yes.' Maria looked straight at him, her resolve unwavering.

'Very interesting case,' said the principal, stroking his neatly clipped goatee beard. 'As a team, we've not reached a definitive conclusion on her diagnosis. She's rather split opinion between us. Usually, visions of this kind are associated with repressed impulses from childhood, but in her case, we don't have sufficient information. She was extremely distressed when she first arrived, more so than we had been led to believe by…'

He picked up a buff-coloured folder of notes. 'Ah, yes, Monsignor Roberto,' he said, flicking through the pages in the folder, 'I remember now.'

'Of course, she was distressed,' said Maria, her words gaining speed. 'She'd been led to believe she was being taken to a convalescent home, not a mental asylum. She was ripped away from the people who love her, her friend Adelina, Giulio here.'

Giulio softened at hearing Maria talk of him in relation to Elisabetta.

'May we see her now?' Giulio asked. 'We understand the arrangements may take a while.'

'I don't think you quite understood my meaning when I talked about her level of distress,' said the principal, interrupting Giulio. 'You'll find her somewhat changed.'

With one finger still on his beard, he allowed his words to take effect.

'Electric shock treatment can be highly effective,' he said, picking up the notes as he turned away from them. 'It's been successfully used in many cases. Pioneered in this very institution by my predecessor…'

'What have you done to her?' said Maria, her hand reaching for Giulio's.

'At times, it can have unpredictable side effects,' he said, holding the notes against his chest as a barrier. 'Memory loss can be quite short-lived, or it can be extended.'

There was a moment of silence before he delivered his final blow. 'She currently has no recall of what led to her admission or her previous circumstances.'

Maria was shaking. She looked at Giulio, her eyes pleading for him to say what she lacked the courage to ask.

'She doesn't remember the orphanage. Her life there?' Giulio ventured, holding Maria's hand tight, while Christian clung to his mother's leg.

'No.'

'The apparitions… the shrine?'

'No.'

Maria's glazed eyes looked past the principal to a painting of the Madonna behind his head. Giulio wasn't sure whether she'd understood what he'd said.

'A new start in England could give her just what she needs,' the principal announced, his tone authoritative. 'It's strange how these things work out…'

Giulio's gut twisted in anger, but he knew he was in no position to question the doctor.

'Then we agree.' Maria took her hand from Giulio's as she pronounced the words, her eyes still on the Madonna.

'Naturally, we'll give you guidance on how best to deal with Elisabetta's condition,' he said, shaking Maria's hand as if he'd just sealed a business deal. 'Though our strong advice is that you limit mention of her past here in Italy in case that should cause her to relapse into hysteria.'

Maria nodded. 'May I see my daughter now?'

'Of course, of course,' said the principal, ushering her towards the door with a patronising smile. 'Think of Elisabetta like an unformed piece of clay. With your careful attention and care, you may craft a fine piece of pottery.'

He smiled, clearly pleased with the image he'd conjured and the way he'd flattered Maria. He held the door open for her, commenting on how well-behaved Christian was, how it would do Elisabetta good to be around a younger brother.

Giulio remained in his seat and watched as they walked away. Christian held his mother's hand but turned on his heels to give Giulio a cheeky wave. Giulio managed a thin smile, hoping the little boy wouldn't notice his eyes glistening. When Maria stopped at the door, Giulio couldn't look at her, afraid that his last bit of composure would break. She stood with her eyes fixed on him but didn't move.

The principal cleared his throat, slicing through their silent communication.

'Ah, yes. I was told you're taking her back on your own,' he said, addressing Maria, his hand outstretched for her to pass through the door first.

When she finally walked through, the principal turned to Giulio. 'You're doing the right thing, not seeing Elisabetta now. Remember her as she was,' he said, a hint of apology in his features. 'One of the nurses will see you out.'

Giulio nodded weakly at the ground as a tear escaped down his right cheek.

~

A low autumn sun peered over the top of the orphanage, forcing Giulio to shade his eyes. He set down his bag. Although it only contained the hated suit and shirt he'd worn to the Bishop's Palace and a couple of changes of clothes, it had weighed him down like the thoughts he had carried all the way back to Atina. His leg ached, the pain extending up his spine into his knotted shoulders and stiff neck. He'd only been gone a few days, but it seemed as if he had lived another life in that time.

A couple of the boys playing jacks with stones spotted him.

'Hey, Giulio, did you have a good holiday?'

He raised his hand half-heartedly in reply.

'What happened to you?' shouted Enzo. 'Why are you walking like that? I thought the Flower Girl of Atina cured you!'

'Long journey,' Giulio mumbled as he passed them, heading towards his shed in the garden. But Enzo's loud voice had carried and brought Sister Beatrice rushing out from her study. Giulio sighed. He'd had long enough to think through the story he was going to make up for her about the old army comrade he'd been to visit. Now he'd returned to the orphanage and knew he would never see

Elisabetta or Maria again, he lacked any enthusiasm.

'You're back!'

Sister Beatrice approached him with a spring in her step, but as soon as she saw how he was walking and how he avoided looking at her, she stopped. She steered Giulio away from the curious glances of the boys and gave him no option but to follow her back into her study. His boots scuffed the dirt of the driveway as he dragged himself behind the whirl of her long black skirt.

With the door shut behind them, Sister Beatrice stood in front of Giulio, her eyebrows raised. Giulio remained close to the threshold, clutching his bag, concentrating on the motes of dust dancing in a shaft of sunlight on the floor between them.

'You went to find Elisabetta, didn't you?'

Giulio nodded at the floorboards. He heard a sharp intake of breath.

'Did you see her?'

'No.' That much was true.

He couldn't tell her what he knew, the agreement between Maria and Peppe. The effects of the electric shock treatment on Elisabetta. These were secrets he now had to carry. For Elisabetta. For Maria.

He was grateful that Sister Beatrice's anger swept any other questions aside. She barely stopped to draw breath.

'They've hidden Elisabetta away. How very convenient,' she said, her voice heavy with sarcasm.

'It's always the same,' she railed, barely acknowledging Giulio. 'Those men always find some way. All they're interested in is themselves.'

She sank into the chair behind her desk, dismissing Giulio with a flick of her wrist. 'How did I ever think it could've been different?'

Giulio's leg dragged behind him as he left the room, the bag on his shoulder almost as heavy as his heart.

30

Adelina

Signora Visconti told me the news of Elisabetta's death, perched on my bed in her comfortable home.

I nodded like a dumb animal, unable to put my pain into words. She held my hand, barely able to hold back her own tears. As she closed the door behind her, my heart was throbbing in my head and I got up, thinking I was about to be sick, but I heard her speak to her husband, who must have been waiting just outside my bedroom door.

'Poor Adelina,' sniffed Signora Visconti. 'I'm not sure she's taken it in.'

An uncontrollable shaking took hold of my body and I leant against the doorframe, trying to hold myself upright.

'We need to give her time, *amore*,' said Dottor Visconti in his soothing voice. 'Patience and understanding, that's what she'll need from us.'

A muffled sob came from Signora Visconti, and I pictured her leaning into her husband's chest for comfort, while it hit me that I would never hold Elisabetta again, never twiddle her hair after one of her nightmares. She would never hold me again. Bile rose up from stomach, burning my throat as I swallowed it back down.

'I can't help thinking about what it must have been like for Elisabetta. Without Adelina, without all of us who cared for her so much.'

'We always knew her health was fragile. The report from the asylum said it was a combination of her diabetes and epilepsy. When I contacted the principal, he confirmed she had a reaction to her medication. Her body just wasn't strong enough.'

'But no funeral here, no-one to mourn her. Just a letter out of the blue after no news in all this time. It doesn't seem right.'

'The principal said he wrote out of courtesy, having seen my name in her medical notes. The burial took place there. Standard procedure, as she had no family.'

'*I was her family!*' I wanted to scream, but no sound came out.

Signora Visconti gave out a loud sigh. 'But Elisabetta belonged here, in Atina. It doesn't seem right.'

'I know, *amore*, but we can't change what's already happened.'

'You're right,' sniffed Signora Visconti, 'of course.'

~

Lying in bed, I ached for Elisabetta. My head, my heart, my arms, my legs, everything hurt. And yet I was numb, so numb and empty.

My room, the one that only a few weeks before had seemed so welcoming with its beautiful furniture, fresh flowers on the bedside table and scented sheets, was cold and lonely.

Determined not to cry, because I didn't want to upset the Viscontis further, I did the only thing left to me.

Sister Beatrice always said that the Madonna doesn't need fancy words. *'All she wants is for us to believe in her, and she will give her love freely.'*

My prayer to the Madonna of the *santuario* was simple.

I don't deserve that you listen to me.

If I hadn't doubted Elisabetta and run to Padre Bosco, none of this would have happened.

Please forgive me for this and all the times I was envious of Elisabetta.

I've never been much a believer, but I pray for Elisabetta's soul. I ask that in the next life you will reunite me and Elisabetta. I miss her so.

I paused and the words flowed from before I could pull them back.

If you are truly there for me, please can you forgive me and look kindly on me.

And on Giulio too. He's the only one who understands what Elisabetta meant to me. He'll be hurting too.

Amen.

~

A light tap at the door woke me. I turned to my right, expecting to see Elisabetta, but there was just the hulking shadow of the dressing table and the now familiar smell of cleanliness and order of the Visconti household. A thin sliver of light from the shutters only made the room seem emptier and colder.

'Sorry, Adelina, I didn't want to disturb you,' said Signora Visconti, stepping tentatively into the room, cradling a sleeping Renato in her arms, 'but the first patients will arrive soon.'

'Oh, I'm sorry,' I stammered, pulling myself up in bed. 'I don't normally sleep late, I must have...'

'There's no need to apologise,' she said sympathetically, resting on the edge of the bed. Renato fidgeted a little but sighed contentedly. 'How are you feeling?'

'I couldn't get to sleep at first, I just kept thinking of Elisabetta...'

With a kind nod, she encouraged me to continue.

'So, I tried praying to the Madonna of the *santuario*... and I felt a little better...'

Signora Visconti gave me a gentle smile and patted my leg beneath the blanket.

'You look a little brighter,' she said, rising to her feet. 'When you're ready, there's some warm milk waiting for you in the kitchen.'

~

Signora Visconti was happy to let me take Renato out for a morning stroll in his gleaming pram.

'It'll do you good,' she said, delighted by Renato's chuckles as I teased him into his outfit for the day. I'd chosen a cornflower blue two-piece, which set off his pudgy cheeks and dark eyes.

'Would you mind if we stopped by at the orphanage to see Sister Beatrice?'

Signora Visconti nodded, but then she hesitated. 'Are you sure it's not too soon?'

'It's fine,' I replied, tucking Renato into the pram. 'Perhaps I might introduce Renato to some of the babies in the nursery? It would mean that we would be out a little longer, but I'll be sure to bring him back in good time for his feed.'

Renato yawned, raising loosely clenched little fists to his dimpled face.

'*Va bene.* Tell Sister Beatrice I'll come by to see her soon.'

We'd barely left the house, and Renato fell fast asleep.

Along the cobbled streets of Atina, passers-by nodded at me with lowered eyes and whispered asides. When a couple of the old women approached me, clearly wanting to speak of Elisabetta's death, I raised a finger to my lips and inclined my head towards the pram, grateful for the excuse. They backed away, not wanting to be guilty of waking Dottor and Signora Visconti's baby.

At the sight of the tired and shabby orphanage, I gripped the chrome handle of the pram tighter and pushed us forward. Signora Visconti was kind to be concerned about my return to the orphanage, but it made no sense to avoid it, as even at the Visconti's house, all I could do was think about Elisabetta.

I visited Sister Beatrice's study as my first stop. She was bent over the ledger once again, her face drawn. Although she asked how I was, she didn't acknowledge my reply.

She took off her ancient glasses, held together with the fraying string and looked me straight in the eye.

'I'm leaving, Adelina.'

The words didn't immediately make sense, but as I realised what she had said, anger rose up in me.

'But you can't leave! Not now… Elisabetta…'

She glanced across to the tattered book of saints on her bookshelf and sighed.

'I'm being transferred to another orphanage. Overseas, apparently.'

'But what about the *santuario*… the prayer group?'

Sister Beatrice looked out of the window towards River Mollarino but didn't answer my question. Renato snuffled in his sleep, and I peered into the pram to check on him.

'At least Padre Bosco did right by you, suggesting you care for the baby. It suits your temperament. And you're in good hands with the Viscontis. They'll look after you.'

Elisabetta had always loved Sister Beatrice and she'd helped me, making sure I had lessons with Signora Rossi to read and write properly.

'But with Elisabetta and you both gone…'

'You're stronger than you imagine, Adelina. Never forget that.'

She walked towards the pram and smiled at sleeping Renato before resting her hand lightly on my forearm.

'When you feel weak, pray. The Madonna is always there for you.'

~

Autumn had descended on the garden. The tomato plants were curled and spotted, a few stunted fruits clinging on for a last burst of sun. Golden leaves gathered in sheltered corners and Giulio had uprooted the zucchini plants, their mottled remains piled in a tidy heap, waiting to be cleared away.

He appeared on the path, a fat bundle of bean canes under his arm, making for his shed. As he spotted me, his head dipped, and a couple of the sticks slipped from his grip and clattered to the ground. We both moved to pick them up, but Giulio bent forward stiffly, the canes in his arms pointing at me like arrows. I pulled myself and the pram back quickly.

'Sorry,' he said, not meeting my eye, pulling the canes together. Our silence had an uncomfortable edge before he offered, hesitating, 'Would you like a coffee?'

I nodded, pushing the pram with sleeping Renato. A wave of sadness swept over me.

Elisabetta had always looked forward to the end of their morning walks, when Giulio pushed her in the wheelchair, accompanied by Sister Beatrice. Milky coffee for her, strong for Sister Beatrice. When I returned from Signora Rossi's lessons, Elisabetta would tell me how he always made it just the way she liked it, not too hot, and how they would talk of the butterflies and insects in the garden.

'How are you?'

Giulio held a small cup half filled with coffee towards me.

'Thank you.' I took the cup, my hand shaking.

He lowered himself onto the bench beside me, his movement awkward.

'I can't stop thinking about her,' I said, staring ahead of me at the trees losing their leaves.

Giulio remained still, his attention on the leaves rustling at our feet.

I rubbed my fingers against the chill of the autumn air. 'I wasn't there for her when she needed me.'

'Don't torment yourself, there's nothing you could have done.'

'But I miss her so much…'

He nodded without looking at me. The silence between us seem to stretch backwards, as if we were both remembering the times the three of us had spent together.

His shoulders started to shake.

'I went to find Elisabetta… with Maria, before she went back to England,' he said, glancing at me sideways.

'I…'

Giulio hesitated. He looked as lost as I felt.

I took his hand.

His skin was rough, but I liked the feel of his strong hand in mine.

'You tried… that's what matters.'

Giulio nodded and looked at me.

Beneath my hand, Giulio spread his fingers a little, watching me as he did so. Heat ran through my body and I laced my fingers in his. Mine long and thin, his large, engrained with soil, dark hairs reaching for his knuckles.

They fitted together perfectly.

Part 4

1999

31

Atina, Apennine Mountains, Italy
Palazzo delle Colombe

Adelina

Drawing his cardigan towards my face, I breathe in deep the last traces of my husband. That smell of earth and hard work had always been the sign of a good man.

Our bed creaks beneath me as I sit to steady myself. My head is light, swimming and swirling. The pack of blood pressure tablets on my bedside table looks up at me, unsplintered.

It's been six long weeks since Giulio's funeral.

The grey wool of his cardigan is rough to the touch, tiny flecks of dried plane leaves caught in the weave. 'We should never forget where we came from,' Giulio insisted, taking care of the gardens of our elegant palazzo himself, as if our home and his position as respected Mayor of Atina were pieces of undeserved fortune.

Deep breaths, I tell myself, but it's no use, my heart is racing, tangled with questions and tainted memories. I push my left palm deep into the cold bedspread, gripping his cardigan in my other fist.

'Why didn't you tell me? All these years…'

Giulio's white pillow offers no response.

I throw his beloved cardigan at the wall, and it slides down into a ragged heap.

Beside the opened archive box from the town hall.

~

In the fog of grief, the cardboard box had slipped from my mind.

Giulio's long-serving secretary, Signora Marinello, had delivered it, unannounced.

'When you're ready,' she'd said in her officious manner, not meeting my eye and refusing the coffee I'd offered.

I'd let her go without asking what was inside. What did I want with more paperwork? Didn't the woman understand that death brings an endless queue of documents and letters to sign? I'd shoved the box into a corner. Records of Giulio's long, devoted service to Atina could wait. I wasn't going to play second fiddle to his sense of duty any longer.

Dust had settled on the untouched box until today. And on Giulio's final to-do list, sitting on the desk in his study. *Lina gift – jewellers?* Was the last item in his untidy handwriting. My husband for forty-eight years had been planning for my birthday, not expecting life to come to a sudden close.

~

Earlier, I'd set out for the Church of San Donato to return to daily mass for the first time since Giulio's death. I'd barely left our palazzo the previous few weeks and the spring sky took me by surprise. A gentle breeze whispered through radiant cherry blossom beside the market square. On the other side of the elaborate fountain that always reminded me of a wedding cake, a couple of Atina's gossips waved at me. Bags laden with fresh loaves of *pane rustico*, the ladies were wearing light jackets in pastel shades. My black coat weighed heavily. The old custom of mourning clothes was one I would be expected to honour as wife of Atina's respected former Mayor.

I nodded in acknowledgment without stopping, past the *Tricolore* and European flags fluttering above the honey-coloured town hall where Giulio had spent so much of his time. A respectful carpet of pink petals had settled at the foot of the war memorial.

At early morning mass, my place in the front pew was waiting. Prayer book to the right, the leather kneeler dipped to the shape of my knees. Ahead the altar was covered in its crisp white Easter cloth, embroidered with delicate golden vines. The cross above was polished to a sheen.

Our small congregation of the elderly and devoted settled into the calming rhythm of the prayers. We took our time to rise at the soft chime of the altar bells. Incense lingered in the air. The familiar, soothing balm of the ritual of mass was slowly bringing me back to myself.

'The joy of the resurrection.' Padre Alberto's words stayed with me as we sang our final hymn. The priest and my fellow parishioners greeted me warmly at the end of mass, and I was grateful for their kindness at my return. They left me to pray in the side chapel of Our Lady, as was my habit.

Beneath the statue of the Madonna tenderly holding the Christ child, I lit my first votive candle to remember Giulio. As I placed it on the top row of the ornate golden stand, my hand was shaking. I knelt to pray and gave thanks for the comfort and understanding of our long marriage, for a good man who I'd loved and who'd always loved me.

Beside Giulio's candle, I placed a taper to another candle. In memory of Elisabetta. As I'd done almost every day of my adult life.

On my knees beneath the Madonna, I fumbled with the clasp of my handbag for the pearls of the rosary beads. More than fifty years had passed since Elisabetta, my only true friend in life, had died. In so many ways it seemed like it was only yesterday, two girls together at the orphanage, sharing secrets. It was impossible to believe it had been half a century.

As I prayed for Giulio and Elisabetta's souls, a glint of sun through the stained-glass window shone on the cross dangling from my hand.

In that flash of gold came an untouched memory. Eleven-year-old Elisabetta at the *santuario*, the shrine by River Mollarino. In her beautiful white dress, holding the same rosary now in my hands. The adoring crowds were looking up at her, on her platform in front of the statue of the Madonna. She bowed her head, but her pale blue eyes caught mine. As if we were the only people there, she smiled, a hint of mischief in her eyes.

~

Comforted by my return to church and the memory of Elisabetta, back at our palazzo I ground some coffee beans, tamping the powder into the pot, watching the steam rise, the rich aroma filling the air. Pouring the coffee into Giulio's favourite chipped cup, I remembered, with a touch of guilt, how often I'd tried to persuade him to throw the old thing away.

The base of the cup fitted the scorched ring mark on his desk perfectly. Opening a drawer, I started on the task I'd been avoiding. Piles of bank statements in my husband's name, going back years. The figures were more than I'd imagined and showed I'd have little to worry about. Not that I ever doubted him. His gift for investing and trading in religious paintings, 'a little hobby' as he'd called it, seemed to have paid off well.

'How are you getting on, Signora?' asked Cristina, as she popped her head round the door.

More family member than housekeeper, Cristina was a few years younger than me, in her late fifties. She'd treated our two sons, Daniele and Carlo, as her own and she'd missed them as much as I did when they'd left to make their own lives, Daniele moving to the United States and Carlo to England. They'd both stayed for as long as they could after the funeral. It was Cristina who cried loudly as they left. While I remained quiet, desperately trying not to let the slightest hint of deep sadness escape. A reflex I had learnt long, long ago.

'Not too bad,' I replied, scooping up the statements and putting them into a plastic folder. 'Perhaps I might make that appointment to see Avvocato Locatelli now.'

'*Bene, bene*,' she replied, knowing how I'd not been returning the solicitor's regular and insistent phone calls.

'That one next?' She indicated the archive box from the town hall with her head.

'You think so?'

'Well, since you've made such good progress, it might be an idea. Anyway, mustn't be late,' she said, pointing to her watch. 'I've got an appointment at the hairdressers.'

~

Lifting the lid from the cardboard box, my hand went to the first of several bundles of letters, each held together with a thick elastic band. Many of the envelopes looked to be from the same stationery set or were of the zig zag blue and red borders of thin airmail paper. Addressed to my husband at the town hall, in the same neat hand. Each one carefully sliced open at the top edge with a knife.

With the distinctive stamps of the Queen's head, I knew they were from England. Carlo rarely sent anything in the post, preferring to call on the phone, but from time to time his wife Isabella would send us photos of the grandchildren, each time looking taller and brighter. Proud Nonna, they quickly found their way into frames.

I thumbed backwards through the date stamps. The Queen turned from solid matriarch back to attractive young woman. The oldest letters bore the image of her father, the same regal nose evident. My heart thumping, I eased the oldest letter from its envelope.

January 1950

Dearest Giulio,

I was foolish to think that Colin would take Elisabetta in and accept her. He resented her from the start, how my love for her took me away from him. We've separated.

The psychiatric hospital has given us a future. I'm a live-in nurse, which comes with a small house in the grounds, a place for Elisabetta, Christian and myself, our little family. The hospital is large, built of solid red brick. Yet it is tucked away in the English countryside, and green fields and ancient woodland surround us. The trees remind me a little of those rising from River Mollarino.

I get so much pleasure from seeing the children together. Elisabetta is a natural big sister, caring and kind. Christian loves to tease her and is forever getting her to play chase and hide and seek. Even when they fall out and argue, I feel blessed.

Life isn't easy for her. She's learned English well, but the girls at school make fun of her accent. One day she came home crying, asking me why they would tease her about where she lives. Girls can be so cruel.

But it is good for us to live here. We have access to excellent doctors who treat her with the latest medications for her epilepsy and talk with her. Sometimes she joins a group with the younger patients. They sit in a circle and talk about how they feel. She likes it and says it makes her feel safe. Her diabetes is now under better control and although she still has the occasional fit, her health is improving.

There've been no more visitations or talk of the Madonna. We do still go to church here and she seems to feel comfortable, although the English version of the Catholic Church seems a world away from the

212

likes of Monsignor Roberto and Padre Bosco.

I pray she makes progress. We share a bond that gives us both so much happiness and comfort. But I know what she's missing and what I can never make up to her. The guilt is a very heavy burden.

The other day, after one of the group meetings in the hospital, she came back so excited and found me in the kitchen.

'I've remembered, Mamma!' she cried, so happy.

'My friends. We were in the garden together, picking tomatoes. Giulio had grown them, and Adelina was holding the basket.'

The knife I was holding, a long spiral of potato peel falling from its tip, slipped through my fingers and blood ran down my palm.

'Fetch me a plaster!' I shouted so fiercely that she flinched and ran off in search of the first aid box, in tears.

I'm ashamed of what I said to her.

'Your life is in England now. Don't go dragging up the past.'

She nodded, the obedient child, eager to please. But I know I am only storing up problems for the future.

Dear God, forgive me for all these lies.

Maria

Sitting at my walnut dressing table, my palazzo bedroom is reflected back in the mirror. Dark ornate furniture and fine paintings, hung at pleasing intervals. And across the fine linen of our marital bed, forty years of letters lie opened, scattered.

I see myself, a woman of sixty-five years of age, hair still predominately dark. Well-defined eyebrows, a touch of light powder on skin that has aged well and full lips. Expensive pearls, just the right length, draw attention away from the lines on my neck. I set down my silver hairbrush on the dressing table and stand up, slowly.

Everything my adult life has rested on has gone.

When I rise from the upholstered seat, I am the 'giraffe' again. Fifteen years old, ungainly and excitable.

I skirt past the bed which Giulio and I shared for so many years, and head out of the bedroom towards the dramatic sweep of the palazzo staircase. My fingers fly along its gilded handrail as I look down onto the Renaissance painting of the Madonna and Child, which Giulio always insisted he'd never part with. Beneath it, on a highly polished court cupboard, the telephone awaits.

~

'Carlo?'

'Mamma?' At the other end of the line, I hear a chair being drawn closer to the receiver. 'What's wrong?'

My youngest son, always sensitive, just like his father.

'I need your help.'

'Wait a moment.'

He places the receiver on a surface and a door is closed. The chair sighs under his ample weight before he picks up the receiver again.

'What can I do for you, Mamma?'

I've always appreciated that about Carlo. Direct, no fuss. We have an easy relationship, where only a few words and a slight change in intonation are needed. It's no surprise he's become so successful in his work, even though I understand little of the world of information technology.

'It's a little complicated to explain the full story on the telephone, but I want you to find someone for me. In England.'

I've never placed demands on my sons in the way of so many Italian mothers, but I know he'll respond.

'Who?'

'Elisabetta De Angelis.'

'Elisabetta De Angelis?' Carlo turns over her name. 'Sounds familiar, but I can't place it. Do I know her?'

'I knew her, over fifty years ago, in the orphanage. The Flower Girl of Atina.'

'But she died years ago, didn't she? Why would she be in England?'

'That's what I'm trying to find out, Carlo.'

'Ok. What information do you have?'

I list the scant details pieced together from the letters.

'It's not much to go on, Mamma, but I'll do my best.'

'I know you will, son.'

A crackle on the line interrupts the brief silence.

'I don't know… but there's someone who might help you.' I hesitate at the memory. 'Do you remember that English girl, Dorothy Bianchi, who used to visit her grandmother here years ago?'

'Always asking questions about The Flower Girl of Atina and why everyone had forgotten her?'

'That's the one.'

'Didn't she make eyes at Papà? And wore funny clothes?' He laughed.

Wearing heavy boots, ripped fishnet tights beneath the shortest leather skirt, and panda make-up eyes, Dorothy had caused quite a stir among the young men of Atina in the late '70s. Armed with grief for her dead Italian father who years before had emigrated to England, and a bee in her bonnet, she'd barged her way through the town hall functionaries and charmed Giulio, who was then at the peak of his powers as Mayor of Atina. In her stilted accent and jumbled Italian, she'd wanted to know why the Flower Girl of Atina had been forgotten. When she was little, her father had told her about Elisabetta, the girl who'd captured the spirit of the times and gave them hope of a better future with her messages from the Madonna. Fired by her imagination and her natural inclination for disruption, she became fascinated with stories of the power of the Madonna.

'Wait a minute,' said Carlo. 'It can't be.'

'What?'

'*The* Dorothy Bianchi? Always on television, doing documentaries about history and religion?'

'Is she famous then? It doesn't surprise me. She was always a smart girl.'

Carlo lets out a small laugh at the other end of the line. 'Leave it with me, Mamma. I'll get back to you.'

~

Giulio's soft spot for Dorothy had been immediately obvious to me. Beneath Dorothy's tough and spiky exterior was a lost child looking for the comfort of an older father figure. And it turns out, Giulio was a man with a guilty conscience.

Dorothy stayed the best part of a long summer with her elderly grandmother. During that time, she regularly attended mass at the Church of San Donato and badgered Padre Emilio with questions about the Flower Girl of Atina, which he duly answered with a shrug and a host of platitudes. After Padre Bosco's retirement, the diocese had always installed priests from outside, with little knowledge or interest in the past. At times, Dorothy tried to ask some parishioners about their memories, but most took one look at her make-up, hair, and clothes and made out they couldn't really understand her, leaving her even more frustrated.

By then, only a small heap of pebbles remained of the shrine by the river. The orphanage was a building site, abandoned by the order which had dwindled in numbers and resources. It was about to be turned into a state-of-the-art teaching facility.

Yet Giulio accompanied Dorothy there. She was flattered by his attention and laughed at his lame jokes. They got on famously.

One time he brought her home to our palazzo for a meal, taken by an instinct to impress her. She arrived in a checked skirt that barely covered her bottom, slashes in her top, and holes in her tights which revealed far too much young flesh. She eyed up the gilded décor, the art hanging on the walls, the marble busts adorning the entrance.

'I didn't realise this was how communists lived,' she declared in her accented Italian, the barb delivered with a smile. Giulio didn't respond, ushering her in with a hand hovering above the small of her back. But I could see she'd touched a nerve.

She picked at the meal which I'd carefully selected, presented in our finest service.

'I'm vegetarian,' she said, pushing away the finest *vitello*. The plate of *pasta con sugo* I quickly offered as an alternative was left, half-eaten.

'Tell me about Elisabetta, the Flower Girl of Atina,' she demanded, turning to me. 'You lived with her, you knew her well.'

'It's all so long ago,' I replied clearing up the plates with hasty efficiency. 'I don't remember that much at all.'

I had no intention of sharing the memories I'd buried deep within me, and certainly didn't want to give *her* the satisfaction of my knowledge.

'But surely you can tell me something about her?' she insisted, but as I left the dining room, I glanced across to Giulio, and he immediately asked her about her studies in London.

When I returned with the tiramisù, the conversation had thankfully moved on, but she stared at me as I served her, and her portion landed in the bowl messily, cream running down the side as my hand shook. She smiled and turned to Giulio, talking of her history and theology studies at university, the music scene she was part of and how her Irish mother disapproved of everything she did. Giulio lapped it up. He switched to practising the English he laboured over at evening classes. This caused her much hilarity, as she made him repeat words and phrases which had no meaning to me. I barely said a word. She ate every last bit of the tiramisù.

As I poured myself another glass of wine, Giulio told her how he hoped to travel to England one day, especially since Carlo was showing interest in studying there. She looked at me with an edge of mocking pity, a middle-aged mother about to lose her youngest son.

She's immature, I told myself, trying to reason away why I didn't like Dorothy. It had nothing to do with how she got on with Giulio. What rankled was the fact that she had her own mind. A young woman who wouldn't go along with what life handed her. Unlike me.

Giulio never brought her back to the palazzo again, which suited me fine. She spent time in Atina's archive, looking at newspaper clippings and photos of the Flower Girl of Atina. By that time, her grandmother was nearing her end. The last I'd heard of Dorothy Bianchi was when she attended her grandmother's funeral. I didn't go, but out of respect, Giulio did.

August 1960

Dearest Giulio,

It brought me such pleasure to receive the photo of you and
Adelina and your boys, Daniele and Carlo. Gaeta in the sunshine looks
beautiful, seeing you together on the beach, the boys so proud of their fine
sandcastle. It looks like you had a hand in building it. And Adelina,
so lovely in her swimsuit, she reminded me of Sophia Loren! She always
was a swan, waiting to emerge.

You deserve this happiness. Adelina only ever had eyes for you.

Be proud of such a wonderful family. And your achievements
as Mayor. You clearly enjoy being able to help others and I know that
Adelina's talent and spirit have been invaluable in helping you and
preserving the palazzo.

Never feel guilty. Peppe's helping hand is the least he could do for
you and Adelina, to give you a comfortable life. I don't want a single lira
from the church, but there's no reason for you not to accept his 'gifts'.

Maria

218

32

'You're looking peaky, Signora,' says Cristina, her forehead furrowed with concern. *'Tè alla camomilla?'*

From my favourite drawing room armchair, the sound of water from the fountain in the courtyard soothes me.

'Signora! Shall I fetch Dottor Visconti? I'm sure he'll come as soon as he can for *you.'*

'There's no need to disturb Renato,' I reply. Perhaps I've been watching the blackbird ruffling his feathers in the water longer than I'd thought.

'May I?' says Cristina, indicating with her eyes the seat opposite mine. It's become hers these last few years, the seat cushion now shaped to her rear. She's the closest I've come to having a friend since Elisabetta.

'Of course.'

I could've so easily been Cristina. The housekeeper, instead of the lady of the palazzo, respected as wife of the Mayor. Depending on your viewpoint, fate or the Madonna herself had dealt me a good hand from a poor start.

She sits down, slipping off the housecoat she wears to do the chores and folds it into a neat square to sit on the brocade arm of the chair. She's wearing a black skirt, a little old-fashioned, the waistband lost between the roundness of her stomach and her heavy breasts which hang low, straining at the buttons of her white blouse.

'Signora, what's happened?'

She sighs. 'You looked through the box from the town hall, didn't you?'

I nod wearily. 'Cristina, I should have said to you years ago, please don't call me Signora. Just Lina.'

Cristina's back finds its comfortable position on the seat, and she rests her hands in her lap. 'Signora... sorry, Lina. Take your time. I'm not needed at home.'

~

The silence is comfortable with Cristina. Through the open window, the blue tits in the plane trees seem to sing and chat louder than usual.

Cristina stares past me and the marble jardiniere with my favourite ferns, onto a sculpted figure of the Madonna cradling her son. A present from Giulio so many years ago.

'What do you know of The Flower Girl of Atina?' I ask.

'Not much.' She shrugs. 'My mother told me she was there, the last time at the river when the girl collapsed and got taken away. Said that everyone believed her. But after she died, and the orphanage closed... You know how it is. Life moves on, people forgot about her.'

'What if I were to tell you she didn't die, but went to England, and that Giulio knew all along?'

Cristina rubs her chin and looks out at the fountain. She takes her time to reply but fixes me with her eyes.

'Signor Conti was a good man. He had a kind soul. If he did something like that, there must have been a reason.'

Cristina listens respectfully to the story I've started to untangle via Maria's letters and when I've finished, placing the bare facts before her, she appears unmoved.

'Signor Conti did what he thought was best for the girl and her mother, that's all. You've had a good life together, raised your sons, this place,' she says, waving her hand around the comfortable drawing room. Don't go thinking ill of Signor Conti now. Nothing's changed. Believe me, if you work for a family, you know them better than they know themselves.'

There was no arguing with her simple logic. She was right. We'd enjoyed almost fifty years of marriage. He'd been a decent, loving husband, a devoted father, he'd seen to us having a comfortable life.

But how could you keep Elisabetta from me?

In the hallway, the phone rings.

'I'll get it,' says Cristina, a hand on the arm of the chair.
But I am already out of my seat.

~

Flint Cottage,
Well Barnes Hospital,
St. Albans,
England.

October 1962

Dearest Giulio,

*Ours continues to be a simple but happy life here at the hospital.
Elisabetta is much more settled now. She loves working at the old
people's home and enjoys her job as a cook, even though I know she's
capable of so much more. At first, the elderly folk didn't know what to
make of pasta. They'd never tasted it before, but now they love all the
different shapes, with the sauces I taught her to cook. She enjoys chatting
with them, making them the sweet crostoli I grew up with on feast days.*

*It's good to see her and Christian go off to the library in town
together. The teachers tell me Christian has the potential to go to
university, if only he would stop fooling around so much and concentrate
on his work. She seems to have taken on making sure he fulfils his
potential, but when they return from the library, she's the one with the
heavy bag full of books that she always seems to be lost in.*

*I know she writes too. She keeps a diary. So many times, I've
been tempted to read it, but I would never want to break her trust. Or
perhaps I'm afraid of what I might find. The burden of guilt is not easy
to bear. We both know that…*

Maria

33

'Pronto?' I snatch at the receiver, hoping to hear Carlo's voice, but Avvocato Locatelli replies, clearly relieved at not having to deal with Cristina again.

'Ah, Signora Conti, how glad I am to speak with you.' How I hate his manner, his superior tone, but I leave him to offer his condolences once more.

'I'm expecting an important call. Perhaps we might speak another time?' My hand moves towards returning the receiver to its cradle when he interrupts me.

'What I must discuss with you is pressing. I'll be at the palazzo within the hour.'

He hangs up before I can reply. The insolence of the man, I think to myself.

~

'*Tutto bene?*' asks Cristina, heading towards the kitchen with my empty teacup.

'That solicitor won't give up.'

'You know what he's like,' says Cristina. 'A dog with a bone, that one. Probably just some document that needs signing.'

'He's coming soon.'

'I'll see him in and make him his usual coffee. Strong, three sugars.' She smiles, knowing how particular he is.

'Thank you. But please, go home after that. I've taken up all your afternoon with my talking.'

'It's the least I could do. I'm glad you told me,' she says, placing a comforting hand on my forearm. 'I'm sure Carlo will call as soon as he has any news of Elisabetta.'

~

Giulio had always admired Avvocato Locatelli for his tenaciousness and skill in dealing with complicated legal issues for the town hall, so it was natural that he should engage him to deal with our personal affairs too. An oily character, whose eyes always seem to rest on my breasts and my hips rather than my words. I left the room as soon as he came for his regular meetings with Giulio.

Avvocato Locatelli arrives with a bulging black leather briefcase.

'So much paperwork for a few signatures?' I ask, hopeful of dispatching him as quickly as possible, in case the call from Carlo should arrive.

He perches on the edge of his chair and drains his coffee in one gulp. Coughing to clear his throat, he hasn't undressed me with his eyes for once. His words appear well-rehearsed.

'I take it you've read reports of the disappearance of religious works of art in the newspapers. The shame it has brought to the church?'

I shake my head. Giulio was the one who'd become interested in religious art during our marriage, much to my initial surprise. He'd attended auctions, bought and sold well, so much so that it paved our way to life in the palazzo. It had been his hobby and interest, and I'd left him to it.

'There've been investigations into certain high-ranking church officials who sold precious works of art to line their own pockets.'

'Why would that be of any interest to me?'

'My dear Signora Conti, have you never asked yourself how the Mayor of Atina came to live in such a wonderful palazzo?' says Avvocato Locatelli, his upper lip curling into a snarl of mockery. 'Cardinal Morelli was very careful, and since he did not personally benefit, there was never any suspicion attached to him. And Signor Conti never held on to paintings for long.'

'What are you talking about?' But the word 'Cardinal' hits me in the stomach.

'Signor Conti's mistake was to keep the Renaissance Mother and Child, the one you have hanging in the hallway. The authorities are hunting for it. A substantial reward is being offered. We need to work out a plan.'

Giulio had told me the painting was valuable to him, but not in terms of money. And I knew why, even though we never discussed it. The Madonna's eyes, light blue and piercing, full of the loss she already knew she would suffer, even as she held her child as a baby.

The same shade of sky blue, the same damage in Maria and Elisabetta's eyes.

May 1973

Dearest Giulio,

The wedding day was a joy. Elisabetta looked so beautiful in her long white dress, Christian walking her down the aisle, to the smiles of our many friends in the church community.

When she reached John, waiting for her nervously, any last shadow of doubt on my part disappeared. He adores the ground she walks on. The way they looked at one another, theirs is a match made to last.

'I'll take good care of her, Mother,' John said to me at the reception afterwards, the brandy having loosened his normal reserve a little. I liked how he called me Mother, and I feel I've gained another son, one who knows that life isn't always straightforward or easy. He had a tough start in life too, but they both enjoy their work at the old people's home. As the caretaker, he's always having to fix things, and he seems able to turn his hand to any practical task, so I'm sure they'll make a lovely home of the flat they're renting. It certainly could do with a bit of work!

I'm sorry I didn't write sooner. Elisabetta soon fell pregnant, but she lost the baby. The doctors advised her not to try again at her age. She's had a difficult time, but John has been a great support. They've decided he's going to have the operation to spare her more heartache. She'll never know what it is to be a mother.

Maria

34

'Mamma?'

'You have news, Carlo?' My heart is beating so fast that I have to steady myself, a hand on the court cupboard beneath the Renaissance Mother and Child.

'I've managed to track down Dorothy Bianchi. We've just spoken… we were talking for a long time. She's friendly… interesting.'

The change in Carlo's tone reminds me of the young man he once was, given to romantic gestures of flowers and poetry for his first girlfriends.

'What did she say? Can she help you find Elisabetta?'

'Dorothy's confident she'll be able to find out about Elisabetta with the information I gave her and will get on to it right away. She's used to doing research, knows who to contact, how to be discreet.'

The admiration in Carlo's voice couldn't be clearer, but he pauses for a moment.

'Dorothy wanted me to tell you how sad she was to hear of Papà's death and to give you her best regards. She said something about having always been in awe of you, how clear it was that Papà adored and respected you. She asked me if you still look like Sophia Loren.'

'That's kind of her,' I reply, the compliment adding to the sense of hope building within me. *Elisabetta. Dorothy is going to find her for me.*

'Don't you want to know how I replied?' asks Carlo, a cheeky note in his voice. 'I told her my mother still looks as good as Sophia Loren!'

I laugh and Carlo continues, more thoughtful. 'Dorothy told me she wasn't completely surprised to learn about Elisabetta. She'd always suspected Papà was hiding something. Nothing more than intuition, she said.'

The chair takes my weight. *How could I have missed what Dorothy had seen?*

'Dorothy was concerned I should warn you the search for Elisabetta may not turn out as you wish... she may already have died... or she may not be quite as you imagine, shall we say... the effects of the electric shock treatment and years of medication...'

'Carlo, one thing age gives you is wisdom. Do you imagine I haven't thought of these possibilities?'

'Of course, Mamma. We just don't want you to be hurt or disappointed, not so soon after Papà's death.'

It's a bit late for that, I think, while noting the 'we' that Carlo and Dorothy have already become.

'I just want to know what's happened to Elisabetta, that's all that matters now.'

~

Flint Cottage,
Well Barnes Hospital,
St. Albans,
England

July 1978

Dearest Giulio,

She sounds like quite a character, this Dorothy Bianchi who keeps asking you about The Flower Girl of Atina. I admire her persistence. Maybe she inherited it from her grandmother. She was one of my Aunt Luisa's friends. The men liked to think they were in control of their wives and daughters, but they were a formidable group of women.

What you describe about Dorothy's look, she's a punk. I suspect it's a bit of a shock in Atina to see a young English woman return to the family village for her holidays dressed up like that!

Stick to the story about Elisabetta as it's always been told. I'm sure there's no reason to worry.

Maria

There is only one photo, black and white, of our wedding. I haven't looked at it for a long time. Because of his facial disfigurement, Giulio never liked to have his photo taken but had relented to one formal, posed shot. Never placed on display for fear of offending him, the photo was unknown even to my sons, who'd grown up simply accepting the way their Papà looked.

Giulio's head is turned to his left away from me, to show the 'good' side of his face. I stand to his right, a full head taller than him, staring straight at the camera.

Full lips painted red for the occasion, big eyes, plucked arched eyebrows, a tight-fitting suit which Signora Visconti had made, which showed off my curves.

A young Sophia Loren.

I see the gap between our bodies in the photo. What we had to slowly learn in the early days of our marriage. It hadn't always been easy. Yet we'd loved one another. Two children, the steadfast support and companionship of almost fifty years.

I bring the photo to my lips and kiss Giulio's image.

~

Flint Cottage
Well Barnes Hospital
St. Albans
England

September 1991

Dearest Giulio

How good it was to see you after so many years.

My words are clumsy, inadequate, even after all this time writing.

I can't express what it meant to see you again. You haven't changed. Still kind and caring, putting others first.

We broke our promise not to meet again, but the detour from visiting your son Carlo in London was one last little lie. Surely God will forgive us?

In those few short hours over dinner, I was able to forget about my illness and pain.

At the end of my life, I want you to know that the happiness and family I've enjoyed were only possible because of you.

It makes me proud to know that the place of my birth, Atina, my true home, has been in your capable hands all these years. Never doubt what you have achieved through your own ability and diligence.

May God continue to bless you, your family, and above all Adelina. I always knew she would be a good wife to you. She deserves the joy of marriage and family, given that I took Elisabetta from her.

We talked of so much over dinner, it was as if all the years had evaporated like the early morning mist over River Mollarino. How I wish I might've seen the river again before I die. But we have come this far, and to return to the past would only cause those we love to suffer even more.

May God forgive us our sins. We will be reunited in the afterlife, for our souls are so closely entwined.

Goodbye for now.

Maria

230

35

'We've found her, Mamma! Dorothy and I have met her. She's alive and well!' Carlo's words run away with him at the other end of the line. 'Mamma, sorry, I should have thought... I just wanted to tell you straight away... are you ok?'

'*Tutto bene*,' I lie, gripping onto the chair for support, my heart beating fast. 'I hadn't expected... not so soon. Tell me...'

Carlo is speaking fast. 'We've just got back to Dorothy's flat. I'm calling you from there. I couldn't wait to give you the news!' Would you believe it, Dorothy lives in Bushey, just a few miles from Betty in St. Albans. All these years, and they're practically neighbours. One good thing about Italians in England, they never stray far from where they landed!'

'Betty?' I stumble on the pronunciation, my heart still in my mouth as I sink into the chair. 'Elisabetta?'

'Mrs Betty Harrison, as she's now known,' Carlo announces, barely pausing for breath. 'Apparently, they first started calling her Betty at school because they couldn't get their tongues around Elisabetta. She liked it and it's how everyone knows her. She said the only person who ever called her Elisabetta was her mother. Even her brother, Christian, calls her Betty. And of course, her husband John, too.'

Betty, I repeat to myself, trying to copy Carlo's voice.

'Mamma, are you sure you're ok?'

'How is she? Is she well?'

'You'll see for yourself soon enough!'

'What do you mean?'

'Betty had John looking on the internet for tickets as we left. They're going to travel to Italy by train, take it a bit more slowly, make a couple of stopovers on the way. Because of her health...'

'Her health?' My heart thuds at the words.

'Complications of diabetes, nothing that the pills can't sort, that's what she said.'

'She's coming with her husband?'

'He's a solid sort. I think you'll like him.'

Carlo slows a little, but my mind is racing ahead.

'She told me the stories of how the two of you climbed out of the orphanage window to go to River Mollarino at first light, about how she loved Sister Beatrice and never wanted to upset her, how you used to look after her when she was ill, how you picked the flowers for the shrine…'

'She remembers?'

'Betty said that the electric shock treatment affected her memory for a while, but when she tried to talk to her mother about you and Papà and the shrine, her mother got angry with her. She felt she had no choice but to do as her mother said, to leave Italy in the past. So that's what she did. John had tried to persuade her to return over the years, but she'd always been loyal to respecting her mother's wishes.'

An image of Elisabetta comes to mind, at the shrine the final time. Speaking to Maria, the woman, not the Madonna. Elisabetta's words to Maria come rushing back. 'I knew you would come for me.'

'Please Carlo, tell Elisabetta it's been too long and that I can't wait to see her.'

36

Cristina flaps into the bedroom like a startled chicken, pricking me awake from my siesta.

'What's the matter?'

In the last snatches of my dream Giulio is on his knees begging for forgiveness, looking up at me, the girl in our wedding photo. His fuchsia cloak is one a Cardinal would wear.

The dream is already evaporating but I want to hold on to it, just a little longer. My fingertips glance my silk camisole, hoping to experience the texture of Giulio's cloak.

'Carlo's just pulled up outside in a taxi and he's with a woman with bright orange hair!'

Cristina pulls back the heavy curtains, which bear a striking resemblance to the cloak in my dream.

'That'll be Dorothy,' I reply, blinking at the light. 'Go and greet them. Tell them I was having my siesta and I'm on my way.'

'Of course!' Cristina bustles towards the door.

'Give them a coffee. And remember, some warm milk on the side for Carlo!'

I hurry to slip on a green wrap dress, and feeling light-headed, I pop one of my blood pressure tablets out of the pack, ignoring the ones I should have taken over the past few days.

A pale brown lipstick is deftly and quickly applied, the product of years of practice. Three sharp sprays of L'Air du Temps, one on either side of my neck, the other to my left wrist. A glance in the wardrobe mirror. I'm ready.

From the top of the sweeping staircase, I look down at my son. Carlo is pointing out details of the Renaissance Madonna and Child, his balding head leaning in towards Dorothy. She turns towards him with a coy smile. My hard-working daughter-in-law back in England comes to mind, a momentary pang of sorrow for her. Carlo places a tender hand just above the small of Dorothy's back to guide her towards the drawing room. Their intimacy ought to shock me, but I'm jolted back in time. Giulio, at the shrine, making way for Maria to reach Elisabetta. His hand hovering at her waist, exactly the same.

Smiling at Carlo, Dorothy catches sight of me. Her expression changes and Carlo follows the direction of her gaze.

'There you are, Mamma,' his cheeks flushing red. Soon he is beside me on the staircase, fleshy lips against my proffered cheeks.

'It's good to see you, son,' I reply, as we lace arms.

Dorothy greets me with enthusiasm and no trace of embarrassment at the bottom of the stairs.

'Adelina, I'm so pleased to see you again after all these years!' Her ample figure against my body speaks of a life full of energy and passion. 'You don't mind if I call you Adelina?'

'Of course not.' Dorothy's eccentric dress sense hasn't changed. She's wearing a long coarse tunic in a rainbow of colours, an ethnic print scarf draped round her neck, her orange hair piled up in a messy bun. Her face is a little wider, her heavily kohl-rimmed eyes slightly hooded, but everything about her screams of a confident, capable woman.

'I saw you admiring the painting. It was always Giulio's favourite.'

'There's a touch of Bellini to it, something about the gaze of the Madonna. It's exquisite.'

'Giulio was the one who liked art. I'm afraid I know so little about it. It's all lost on me.'

'Her eyes… they draw you in…'

Carlo's head tilts towards the face of the Madonna as he nods in vigorous agreement with Dorothy.

'Giulio liked her eyes too,' I reply, omitting to mention who they reminded him of. 'He said the painting was of no real value. A copy, apparently. Perhaps of a painting by the artist you mentioned?' Avvocato Locatelli may have reassured me that he has a way of dealing with the painting, but I do not want to rouse any curiosity on

Dorothy's part.

'I only wish I'd had the chance to look at it with him.' Dorothy hesitates. 'I'm so sorry for your loss, Adelina. I should have said that as soon as I arrived. Your husband was always very kind to me. I remember him fondly. And he always had good taste.' She bows her head slightly towards me.

~

Dorothy tells the story of Elisabetta and her life in England with compassion and professionalism. No mention is made of Giulio's role in covering up what happened, for which I am grateful. Carlo listens to her almost doe-eyed. In her manner, Dorothy reminds me a little of Renato, and his father before him, doctors having to deliver news people would rather not hear.

'But Elisabetta was so bright. She was the one who had the world at her feet. It doesn't seem right...' I don't need to finish the sentence for Dorothy and Carlo to understand. Me in the palazzo, Elisabetta suffering years of poor physical and mental health, still working as a cook, living in a flat on an estate.

'Betty won't want you to feel sorry for her, Adelina. I've spent a long time with her, talking about what she remembers, piecing together the story. She knew there were holes in her past, but she was so afraid to ask questions of Maria. Between them, they maintained a silence about what had happened. They had a very good relationship. Betty says how much she misses her mother, although it's now eight years since she passed away.'

'And she held this in, all these years?'

'Not quite. Betty poured her memories and her thoughts into her diaries. She told me how she's always enjoyed keeping a diary. It's been her way of making sense of her feelings.'

'Betty took quite a liking to Dorothy,' interjects Carlo as Dorothy smiles modestly. 'She said she'd be happy for Dorothy to read her diaries, in time. Maybe even tell her story.'

'That's jumping ahead,' Dorothy replies quickly. 'I'd never do anything without Betty's full agreement. And yours too, of course, Adelina.'

Her tone is sincere.

'What's important,' says Dorothy, smiling broadly, 'is that Betty can't wait to see you again. She was so pleased to learn that you and Giulio had married and were together for so many years.'

'She kept saying how much I reminded her of Papà,' says Carlo, his eyes glistening.

'There's no doubt you're your father's son, Carlo. You're both gentle, kind men,' I reply, taking his hand. 'That's what Elisabetta recognised.'

'Betty said her only sadness is that she missed meeting Giulio again,' says Dorothy, picking up the thread as Carlo blows his nose, 'But she's sure they'll meet in the next life.'

'She hasn't lost her faith?'

'She and John are very much part of their church community. Prayer groups, flowers in the church, taking communion to the sick, organising social groups for the elderly, First Holy Communion preparation groups. You name it. Betty and John are there, doing their bit.'

'But no more visions, after she arrived in England?'

Dorothy looks out of the window towards the fountain. 'No more visions.' She turns slightly towards Carlo, but he doesn't meet her eye. 'Betty wants to talk to you herself about what she saw. She said her best friend is the one she wants to tell.'

I lean back in my armchair and close my eyes.

'There's nothing that would make me happier.'

A pair of blue tits, just like the ones Elisabetta used to feed with leftover crumbs from on our orphanage windowsill, settle on the fountain in the courtyard.

~

'You're not too angry with Papà?'

Carlo has stayed with me while Dorothy freshens up after the journey. I'd asked Cristina to prepare the room next to Carlo's boyhood bedroom, at the far end of the corridor from mine.

'What's the point of being angry? Your father did what he thought was best for Maria and Elisabetta. He loved them both very much.'

'But all these years, you believed your best friend to be dead… Papà knew the pain he caused you…'

'But he did right by me too. He loved me, he gave me two fine children, a good life. In the circumstances, he did his best.'

'You never suspected anything?'

'Your father provided me with stability, security, things I craved for when I was growing up in the orphanage. I might've been young and innocent when we met, but I knew there would be no one in my life other than Giulio. Perhaps I turned a blind eye when I shouldn't have, or I could have asked more questions. But when you love someone, your heart knows how to push away inconvenient thoughts.'

Carlo sighs, fiddling with the gold band on his wedding finger.

'Life can throw up some hard choices. All that matters now is that Elisabetta and I have the chance to spend some time together again.'

37

I've never set foot in the 5-star Abruzzo Healing Retreat and Relaxation Spa. Frequented mainly by overweight, loud Americans, lured by the promise of restored health and infinite calm, our fawning little Mayor, Giulio's successor, has hailed it a grand success.

He'd been pleased to dispose of the school buildings, given the falling number of pupils and the cost of repairs. The new American owner, a shrewd businessman with a well-established worldwide chain of hotels had claimed he was delighted to be giving something back to the small town where his grandparents had originally hailed from. He built a breeze-block school on a cheap piece of land outside the town that meant that most of the kids now had to get on a bus, which he had failed to fund. In return, the school, the orphanage, Contessa Monti's home, was his for a song.

The money he didn't spend on the new school clearly hasn't been spared here. Carlo swings the car into the wide, impressive arc of the entrance driveway, the tyres crunching on the gravel. Clipped shrub balls rest among tall grasses and abstract metallic sculptures, discreetly lit.

'It doesn't look much like the place I used to drag the boys to,' sneers Cristina from the back seat. Carlo nods in agreement.

There is a large additional wing furthest from the riverside, designed to match the original style of the Contessa's home. According to the glossy brochure, the pool, hydrotherapy, and thalassotherapy facilities are housed there. The outside of the main building is unaltered, just well-repaired and repainted.

The stone entrance steps are still the same, and for a moment an image, complete with the sound of laughter, returns. Elisabetta and I, skipping down the steps, hand in hand, on our way to the river. The window overlooking the entrance has been replaced, but a shadow stands there. Could it be Sister Beatrice in her study, encouraging us with a benevolent smile?

Carlo takes an age to park the car just so in the marked space, a habit that reminds me my son is probably more English now than Italian. From our parked angle, all I can see are lights glinting from the droplets of an impressive chandelier in the study window.

The elaborate, gilded wrought-iron entrance to the garden is even more impressive than the photos in the brochure suggest. Giulio would be happy to know that the garden has been restored. I'm keen to see it again, to walk the paths where Giulio, Elisabetta and I had been happy together.

Carlo rests his hands for a moment on the steering wheel, before finally turning off the ignition. It's a hot day and sweat has gathered on his bald forehead. 'It's been so many years… you must be nervous…'

'Don't worry, it'll be fine.' Still his mother, reassuring him as if he were a child, although my heart has had fits of uncontrolled racing twice already this morning. 'Let's go. We can have a coffee before they arrive.'

My new burgundy handbag sits in my lap, and I brush it with my fingertips, feeling the grain of the leather. It matches my court shoes perfectly, complementing the predominant red shades of my floral dress. Giulio always said how much the dress suited me. Elegant, yet understated. The material hangs a little looser than I remember but moving the belt two notches inwards has done the trick.

Carlo holds the car door open for me and Cristina proffers her arm. I take a deep breath in and check my liver-spotted hands, discreetly. They aren't shaking too badly. Cristina guides me in.

As soon as we approach the steps, a lean man in his late forties, with swept back hair greying at the temples, emerges from Sister Beatrice's study. He greets us with charming deference and a broad smile.

'Signora Conti, welcome to the Abruzzo Spa,' he says, bowing ever so slightly, 'though perhaps welcome back, might be more appropriate.'

His manner has undoubtedly been well-honed over the years of dealing with demanding guests, but his tone has a genuine, sincere quality. I return his smile and my shoulders drop. The charm of the man is already having its intended effect.

'If you'd like to follow me. You're in the Venus lounge.'

He leads the way and I glance across to his office, disappointed to see that the white door is closed, and I can't get a peek into what was Sister Beatrice's study. With a gentle movement, I release myself from Cristina and indicate she should walk ahead with Carlo. She soon grasps my intention and takes Carlo in her arm, not allowing him to turn back to me.

The corridor still follows the familiar route, and I take my time, trailing behind the others. Voices of the children, chatting, shouting, taunting one another come back to me as my fingertips glance the walls. The crumbling plaster may have gone but behind the elegant textured wallpaper, every one of us orphans is still there, being admonished and chivvied by a long line of nuns. I feel my hand in Elisabetta's returning to our room after one of the lessons in Sister Beatrice's study. Elisabetta proud of her knowledge of the female saints, me just happy to be her friend, beside her.

Several identical white doors, each with an impressive silver engraved plaque, bear the names of ancient Roman goddesses. One is slightly ajar. A massage table is in the centre of the dimly lit room, birdsong and a light scent of roses emanating from within. The absolute serenity takes me back to those early snatched mornings at the river, Elisabetta and I together.

Ahead, outside what was the refectory, the manager, Carlo, and Cristina are waiting for me. 'Venus' reads the plaque on the door. With his outstretched arm and benevolent smile, the manager encourages me to enter.

As I take a step in, alone, Dorothy stands up.

'Oh, I hadn't expected you to be here first!' I stammer at Dorothy.

Dorothy helps a white-haired woman with a bun to her feet. She is tiny, like a wizened bird, but her pale blue eyes shine bright, glassy with tears.

'After all these years, I couldn't wait a moment longer.'

The voice is Elisabetta's, the words delivered in our dialect.

My heart leaps.

'Elisabetta!'

She gives me a wide smile, revealing a couple of missing teeth. She leans heavily but with determination on a worn wooden stick and takes pigeon steps towards me. An elderly man in an ill-fitting suit, clearly John, hovers behind her, ready to help, but hangs back just enough to give her a respectful space. From this small gesture, I like him straight away.

Elisabetta concentrates on her swollen feet and ankles, which puff over the top of flat, unconvincing leather-look sandals, and I walk towards her in my pinching court shoes.

We laugh, we cry, drawing closer until we are clinging to one another, just as we did in our basement room.

After a good while, Elisabetta breaks our embrace and I open my eyes down onto her. She smiles again, with her gaps and discoloured teeth, indicating that she needs to sit down. My tongue traces guiltily the gold crowns at the back of my mouth, a full set of teeth still intact.

Elisabetta keeps hold of my hand, our fingers entwined like little girls, and turns to John, who immediately comes to her aid. He helps her back into her chair while carefully ensuring we remain attached. For this, I like him even more and nod in thanks.

'My best friend, Adelina,' whispers Elisabetta to John. I may not know much English, but I understand the words 'best' and 'friend'. I hold her hand tight in mine.

'Yes, Betty,' John replies, brushing away a tear and trying to look out of the window at the same time. I wonder if that was what Carlo had tried to explain to me about the British stiff upper lip.

'Carlo,' I wave for him to step forward. He pushes a tissue hastily back into his trouser pocket and rests his hand on my shoulder.

'So pleased to see you again, Betty,' he says in English to Elisabetta.

241

He shakes John's hand in a friendly way, but neither man can look the other in the eye, for fear of welling up again. I stifle a giggle at the men embarrassed to show each other their feelings, and Elisabetta presses my hand in return.

By contrast, Cristina comes forward and gives Elisabetta a fulsome hug, kissing her on both cheeks. She cries with gusto and shows no qualms at taking her own tissue to dab at the moist tears she leaves on Elisabetta's lined face.

'Cristina is my housekeeper and friend; she knows how much seeing you again means to me,' I say by way of explanation.

Elisabetta nods kindly and looks towards Dorothy, whose eyeliner and mascara have run into sympathetic streams on her face. Carlo is beside her, a hand across her shoulders, in the manner of the couple they are undoubtedly soon to become.

A discreet tap at the door sees the manager slip back into the room and with a sign from Dorothy, he returns with a tray bearing flutes of the finest crystal, followed by a younger version of himself, equally handsome, who with a certain flourish sets an iced bucket before Elisabetta and me.

The pop of the cork sets off a flurry of applause and the manager and his assistant hand Elisabetta and me a bubbling glass each at precisely the same moment.

'To old friends!' announces Carlo.

Elisabetta hesitates for a moment, looking over at John. Her hand is shaking and I'm afraid she might drop the glass. John peers over the top of his heavy-rimmed glasses and nods slightly towards her. He pinches his thumb and forefinger together in a gesture that suggests a small amount.

'It's the medication,' she whispers as our glasses clank rather than clink. 'I'm not meant to have alcohol. It makes me more unsteady. John says it makes my head turn!'

'I'm not meant to drink with my blood pressure tablets either,' I reply, enjoying the pop of the bubbles on my tongue and the dry smoothness as the champagne slips down. 'Dottor Visconti would be sure to disapprove if he were to see me now!' I take a large second gulp and feel the hit of the alcohol. 'I wouldn't tell if you don't!'

Elisabetta giggles as she lifts her glass to her lips.

'Dottor Visconti?' She turns the words over. 'Vi-scon-ti,' she repeats, this time elongating the syllables. Her face has a puzzled, distant expression, as if trying to figure out where she might have misplaced some keys.

'Not Dottor Visconti who treated you. He's naturally long since gone.' I drain the rest of the glass and indicate towards Carlo for a refill, and he duly obliges. Out of the corner of my eye, Cristina scolds him. He shrugs and returns to making eyes at Dorothy, resplendent in a bright yellow flowing dress, which reminds me of the sun and the heat of the day outside.

'Do you remember him?' I ask.

She sighs deeply and shakes her head. 'In therapy, they said my mind, not just my treatment, may block certain memories.'

Elisabetta shrinks into her seat, swamped by the floral pattern of her dowdy dress, which reminds me of curtains long out of fashion. She looks small and vulnerable.

'I'm sorry. I didn't mean to upset you,' I reply, squeezing her hand. 'What was he like, this Dottor Visconti?'

'He was a kind, genuine man who cared for you very much.'

'That's good to hear,' says Elisabetta, nodding. 'I've seen so many doctors over the years. Not all of them have had my best interests at heart.'

'We can take our time,' I reply, enjoying the warmth from the alcohol relaxing my body and my tongue. 'I can help you, with certain memories.'

'I'd like that. Though John is worried I might find it all too much.'

She glances over to John, who is in deep conversation with Carlo and Dorothy, but he breaks off for a moment and raises his eyebrows in a question towards her. She smiles back at him. Reassured, he returns to the discussion. As I gulp down more of the fizz, a brief pang of envy creeps through me, for this couple still able to share life together.

'Anyway, if the Dottor Visconti you mentioned died a long time ago, who is this other Dottor Visconti, the one who wouldn't want you drinking?' Elisabetta smiles, taking another sip.

'It's his son, Renato. He followed in his father's footsteps and became a doctor too.'

Elisabetta grabs my hand. 'Baby Renato? We were there, together, weren't we, when he was born?'

'You remember that?'

Elisabetta sits up in her chair. A glimpse of the girl I knew, with the world at her feet.

'Afterwards, you were so upset. Your mamma and the nurse.'

I bite down on my lip. The alcohol is suddenly too much, and the room is hot and is starting to spin.

Elisabetta's words swim in the pool of alcohol playing games with my mind.

'I could do with a bit of air. Shall we go to the river?'

'Yes,' replies Elisabetta, squeezing my hand.

~

Dorothy, Carlo, and John are speaking in fast English, clearly enjoying each other's company. Cristina looks a little bored and springs to attention when I wave her over.

'We'll take it nice and slowly,' I reassure Elisabetta while Cristina helps her up and hands Elisabetta her wooden stick.

Elisabetta hooks her left arm lightly into mine. In that small action, we're children again, and the rush of warmth that fills my body and soul is one of pure joy.

'Ready?' asks Cristina.

'Yes!' we chime together, like obedient schoolgirls.

'Just going out for a breath of air,' calls Cristina to the huddle of Carlo, Dorothy and John.

'Would you like me to help you?' says Carlo, setting down his glass but I dismiss him with a gesture that he doesn't argue with.

John makes a slight movement too, but when Elisabetta shakes her head at him, he gives her an encouraging smile and returns to the conversation with Dorothy and Carlo.

~

A broad wheelchair-accessible path, punctuated with tasteful benches to rest, has been created from the spa down to the river. Part of me is relieved that we don't have to negotiate the ankle-turning pebbles and there is a smooth, safe surface under our feet, but it bears little resemblance to the route Elisabetta and I took fifty years earlier during our dawn escapades.

We pause frequently. It is hot, and I am sweating. My heart is starting to race again. Elisabetta keeps turning her head, searching for a familiar sight or object, only to look back to me, questioning. It isn't until we are about halfway, and we stop under the canopy of trees, that Elisabetta's lined face relaxes and lights up with a grin. Resting on her stick, she looks upwards. I am grateful to rest a moment and catch my breath, my heart pounding in my chest. The birdsong bounces back and forth between the branches, a flurry of excited chatter.

'Well, I never!'

'Look who it is come back after all these years!'

'The two friends reunited!'

'About time too!'

Elisabetta smiles and we draw close. She nestles in, like a baby to its mother. Her hair beneath my fingers is brittle, her beautiful chestnut mane gone. Breathing in deeply, beneath her old-fashioned lavender perfume, I find her true scent.

Sweet, like a spring morning, fifty years before. As intoxicating as the fizz we've just shared.

The last steps we take alone, Cristina discreetly taking up a spot at one of the benches a few metres back.

'I'm so pleased to be here with you,' whispers Elisabetta.

'Me too.'

The words are weak compared to the deep well that is rapidly

245

filling within me, and I hold her tight for fear of falling into the abyss and losing her again.

~

Water rushing over pebbles greets our slow approach and grows steadily louder. Elisabetta holds her breath as if about to blow out the candles on an enormous birthday cake. We look at one another and we both know what it means. *Dare you!*

With mischievous grins on our faces and a loud *whoosh*, we swing our hands together, upwards in an arc towards the sky.

We giggle like the girls we were. The layers of hurt and loss, along with wrinkled skin and ill-health disappear. Cristina joins our laughter and her smooth face glows, as if her everyday worries are no more.

Ahead lies the bathing pool, the destination of the path. The healing waters have been gathered in a smart semi-circle of stylised steel, made accessible for the spa's clientele.

The arc of the river is still the same, the clear water gurgling and bouncing downstream, alongside a broad expanse of white and grey pebbles enclosed by trees. Elisabetta gives me a broad smile of recognition. At least the spa is looking after this stretch of river and there is an absence of shredded plastic bags caught on the branches of trees and rubbish, which mars other sections of River Mollarino.

Elisabetta gasps as she glimpses the small, discreet statue of the Madonna.

'She's beautiful,' she exclaims, her hand resting across her heart. 'So simple and elegant.'

We sit at the two solid marble blocks placed at angles in front of the statue. For quiet contemplation and reflection, the caption reads beneath the photo in the spa's brochure, a nod to the multi and no faith nature of their clientele.

With a beatific smile, Elisabetta closes her eyes and clasps her hands in prayer.

I want to tell Elisabetta how the statue was the result of a small personal legacy from Sister Beatrice. She'd designed the statue herself and specified in her will that it should be carved only from the local stone, by a woman of faith, and be placed at the spot where the original broken Madonna had stood.

But Elisabetta is still praying, and I remember how when she prayed never to disturb her. I have so many questions to ask her about what she knows of her story, her father and what she has to tell me about her visions. Yet looking at her, I understand that her faith, and mine, has nothing to do with a church led by men. Sister Beatrice would be proud of us.

For a moment, my mind turns to Giulio. What would he have made of Elisabetta returning, admiring the statue whose commission he'd overseen in his time as Mayor? No fuss had ever been made of its installation. But he'd seen to a trust to ensure that the area would always be maintained, even without a plaque to commemorate what had happened there or any reference to the word *'santuario'*.

Into our silence comes birdsong again.

A sharp pain grips my chest and travels down my left arm.

My mouth is open, but no sound comes out.

I try calling out, but nothing.

Elisabetta has her eyes closed. Cristina is behind me. Frozen, I can't reach either of them.

I look towards Elisabetta one last time.

Plaits and bows in her chestnut hair, wearing the dress of white satin. At her left shoulder stands Sister Beatrice, a proud smile on her face.

Behind them, a serene, dark-haired woman with a white headdress. Her skin is pale. Just like the statue.

All three are bathed in the most magnificent golden light. Its rays brush my tired skin. A delicious, warm comfort.

Among the bird song, I hear her words.

'It's time, Adelina. Come to me.'

About Anna Lucia

Born in England to older Italian immigrant parents, Anna Lucia spent long, hot summers in the Apennine mountain village they had left behind to escape poverty and lack of opportunity. In the local dialect, she listened to the stories of elderly relatives about a time, place and way of life that was far, far removed from 1970s and 1980s suburbia.

Those voices, particularly of strong women who led tough lives, never went away, neither did the echoes of Catholicism.

Anna has been awarded support for her writing from Arts Council England, and also writes short stories, flash fiction and poetry. She is Chair of Trustees of literature development agency, New Writing South.

~

From Anna Lucia

If you enjoyed reading Broken Madonna, please do leave an online review. It's a great way for debut authors to be discovered.

I'm really happy to connect with readers - please visit my website for more about the inspiration and research behind Broken Madonna and news about my next novel.

My newsletter about all things Italy, writing, mysticism and much more is waiting for you.

www.annalucia.co.uk

Author's Note

This is a novel, rather than a travel guide.

Atina is the small town of all my ancestors, River Mollarino captivated me as a child.

How they appear in this novel is in my mind's eye.

~

Acknowledgements

Broken Madonna would not exist without the following individuals and organisations providing inspiration, sage advice, moral support and more. My heartfelt thanks to you all.

New Writing South - for recognising my potential and believing in me to become an NWS10er. Life has gone full circle.

Arts Council England - for funding to give me time to write, mentoring and research in Italy.

Italy connections - too many to list, but special mention to all the *contadini* who went before me, Villa Palazzola, Monte Giove and the Women's Fiction Festival in Matera. You gave me ideas and motivation galore.

Leaving the Waiting Room - the best writing group - Michelle Mullen, Norman Miller, Deirdre Huston & David Wilson, plus past members Samantha de Alwis, Stuart Condie and Karen Pierce. Your insight, feedback and friendship are all a writer could wish for.

Readers, fellow writers and editors who helped me think, refine and aim higher: Emma Cameron, Mariateresa Boffo, Beth Miller, Rufus Purdy, Gillian Stern, Donna Hillyer and Umi Sinha.

For the joy of learning and sharing: A Haven For Stories at Villa Pia, Curtis Brown Edit Your Novel cohort, Aki Schilz TLC, I am in Print, Society of Authors, Historical Novel Society, ALLi and Book Sisters, Rosie and Jill.

Patrick Knowles for capturing the spirit of Broken Madonna in a beautiful cover.

My parents, Pasquale and Olga Viscogliosi. May your souls rest in peace.

Last, but most important. To Keith, for always being there and supporting me to write.

Questions

For book groups or individual reflection

1. What do you believe Elisabetta experienced? Why have you come to this conclusion?

2. Adelina and Elisabetta's relationship is close but fraught with mixed emotions. What did you make of this friendship? Who did you warm to more and why?

3. Giulio is a young man left damaged by the war, physically and mentally, and his encounter with Elisabetta changes him. What did you feel towards him and what about the triangle between Giulio, Elisabetta and Adelina?

4. Maria and Sister Beatrice represent different aspects of strong women. Which of these spoke to you?

5. Whose betrayal or withholding of the truth was the greatest? Padre Bosco, Peppe (Bishop Morelli), Giulio, Elisabetta, Adelina or Maria?

6. Adelina's experience at the end – what do you believe?

7. The cult of Elisabetta quickly grows as people seek hope in the aftermath of war. What parallels are there in today's society?

8. Broken Madonna is rooted in terms of time and place to a poor corner of Italy where Catholicism held sway. What impression did you have of this Italy compared to the Italy you may have visited or imagine?

9. Maria's letters through the years touch on the Italian immigrant experience in England and the loss she experienced in not returning to Italy. What does that lead you to think about belonging and identity?

10. How much is Broken Madonna about religion? Or is it more about relationships, the impact of secrets or fate? Or other themes, such as motherhood, abandonment and corruption?